EMBERS OF SUMMER

BOOK 3 IN THE JOSEPH STONE CRIME THRILLER
SERIES

J R SINCLAIR

VOICE FROM THE CLOUDS

Published worldwide by Voice from the Clouds Ltd.

www.voicefromtheclouds.com

For my writing assistant, Jessie the cat, and his endless dedication to dancing on my keyboard.

CHAPTER ONE

For Jimmy Harper, there was one positive about being dragged out of his home at such an ungodly hour and forced to head to work—at least he got to do the journey in style.

There was no greater pleasure than driving his pride and joy, an Aston Martin DB5. Wives and mistresses might come and go, but the DB5 was a constant in his life. In Jimmy's opinion—the only one that ever mattered to him—the DB5 represented the pinnacle of design and engineering excellence from a bygone era.

The Aston Martin's four-litre inline-six engine rumbled in the background, a symphony of power and the perfect backing track to Wagner's 'The Ride of the Valkyries' playing on the car's stereo system. The music matched his pissed-off mood perfectly.

His temper wasn't being helped by the stifling heatwave that had gripped the country since the start of July. Even with both front windows wound down, it was still suffocating and made Jimmy feel like he was slowly being baked to death in an oven.

This had only added to his growing sense of irritation. The source of which, and the reason for this journey, was that, yet again, the alarm had been triggered at work.

Jimmy had already checked the security cameras for the showroom on his phone and there was absolutely no sign of anything wrong at his classic car dealership, Prestige Vintage Motors. None of the door or window sensors had been tripped, either. That meant the motion alarm had probably been triggered by a bloody spider.

Despite the cleaner's best efforts, webs kept appearing in the most inaccessible corners high in the ceiling void. The eight-legged bastards seemed to be flourishing in the hot weather, no doubt because of the increase in the fly population.

Jimmy could easily picture the arachnid doing a little tap dance on the motion sensor. It was almost like the insect population had some sort of vendetta against Jimmy getting any sleep.

This alarm callout was the third this month. Jimmy was almost ready to throw in the towel and hire a professional security firm to protect the showroom. The only problem was they wouldn't dish out the immediate form of retribution that Jimmy personally favoured—a few broken bones and, preferably, a cracked skull—if they caught someone trying to break in.

'Yes, officers, I was forced to defend myself,' he would say when they eventually turned up.

No one messed with Jimmy Harper, at least not if they had any sense. That was, apart from those bloody spiders.

Just as The Ride of the Valkyries reached its stirring crescendo, the DB5 topped a ridge to reveal a lone squat building just ahead. Its metal shutters were still pulled down over the large showroom windows.

That, at least, was a good sign.

The car's headlights picked up the raised bollards across the entrance of Prestige Vintage Motors, a dealership for the more discerning customer who had an eye for the very best in classic cars—a market Jimmy had made all his own in this part of the world.

A shrill alarm was warbling out from the siren box on the side of the building, shattering the stillness of the night. As far as Jimmy could tell, it didn't look like anyone had attempted to take an angle grinder to the door lock. Yes, he was already as certain as he could be that this was once again down to a spider doing a tap-dance on a sensor.

He pressed the button on the small black remote attached to the car's key fob. In a choreographed performance, the three electric bollards lowered automatically into the ground.

He drove through, parking in the space right next to the main door with his name on it. Of course, it was no accident the DB5 sat as close as possible to the entrance. After all, the Aston Martin was every red-blooded man's fantasy, so the deliberate parking of it in that spot was intended to encourage those same men to loosen their wallets as they headed into his kingdom of classic car nostalgia.

Jimmy turned off the Aston Martin's engine, and it burbled into silence. He reached down into the passenger footwell and picked up a long-armed wheel brace he just *happened* to leave there. It certainly had enough weight to do someone serious damage.

As he got out of the DB5, the heavy humid air wrapped around his already sticky body. Even the tarmac was still radiating heat from the daytime sun.

The alarm hammered into his ear, loud enough to wake the well-heeled in their expensive Cotswold houses scattered across the valley, all incomers from London. No doubt by now the office answer machine would be filled with their angry messages. The sooner he checked over the premises, the sooner he would quieten their wrath and could head back to the air-conditioned utopia of his penthouse flat back in Oxford.

Jimmy's gaze travelled over his business premises, looking for anything out of place. But he still couldn't see any sign that someone had tried to break in. Satisfied, he lowered the wheel brace and headed towards the main entrance, his key already extended towards the door's lock.

The alarm was even more deafening within the confines of the building. He quickly typed the security code into the control panel and hit enter. At once, the alarm turned off and a glorious silence descended. Then all he could hear was the high-pitched *yip-yip-yip* of a fox outside in the distance.

But that wasn't the only sound, he realised.

As Jimmy's hearing adjusted to the relative quiet, he noticed a loud buzzing sound coming from somewhere inside the showroom. He flicked on the banks of lights and spotted the source of the noise right away.

Dozens, no, hundreds, of flies were flying around the showroom. Some of them had even settled on the bonnet of a silver-blue Jaguar E-Type.

Where the hell did they all come from? Jimmy thought.

Then, the softest of footfalls came from behind him.

Senses going electric, adrenaline pumping through his veins, Jimmy spun around, bringing up the wheel brace to brain the idiot stupid enough to dare to break into his business.

But Jimmy was already too late. The edge of a cricket bat came crashing down onto his skull. As his head snapped back and darkness swirled through his mind, he toppled backwards, felled like a tree, and his wheel brace clattered to the ground.

Jimmy's eyes snapped open as a crackling sound came from all around him. It took him a moment to mentally process where he was. He was back inside his Aston Martin as flames licked the car's windows.

Wait, how the hell am I here?

Confusion swirled through the showroom owner as he peered through the snapping fire to see the silhouettes of other cars.

What?

Then, with a start, Jimmy realised exactly where he was— inside his own showroom. The bastard who'd snuck up behind him and knocked him out must have pushed the Aston Martin inside before torching the place.

'What the actual fuck?' he called out, but no one answered.

The flames were growing taller by the second.

Jimmy had been in his fair share of tight corners over the years and his survival instinct had already kicked in. He needed to get out of there, and fast. But it was only as he went to grab the door release, that he realised he'd been handcuffed to the steering wheel. He tried slipping the cuffs over his hands, but the steel bands bit into his wrists.

Heart racing, breaths coming in short gasps, Jimmy looked around for a way to get out of this nightmare, but there was nothing within reach that could help him. Beads of sweat dripped down his forehead as he pulled hard on the steering wheel again, bracing his feet against the dash for extra leverage, bending it the barest fraction.

'Help me!' he shouted, but there was no sound except the roar of the growing flames creeping steadily across the show-room floor towards the Aston Martin.

Bang! The nearby E-Type Jag's petrol tank detonated, and a broiling mushroom cloud of fire hit the ceiling and rolled out in a living wave of fire.

Jimmy watched the spectacle, his heart thundering in his ears, his mouth growing dry. How long would it be until the DB5 caught fire and exploded? An idea struck him and he leaned forward against the wheel, searching his jacket pocket for his mobile.

It was gone.

Despair flooded Jimmy. *I'm going to die...*

But that thought trailed away as he saw a figure in motor-bike leathers, standing just beyond the curtain of flames. The man's face was hidden behind a crash helmet, only the glint of his eyes visible through the visor in the dancing firelight.

'For God's sake, get me out of here!' Jimmy shouted.

The man stared back at him and didn't move so much as a millimetre.

'Look, if it's money you want, name it and it's yours. A million, two, make it three. I really don't bloody care. Just get me out of this fucking car.'

The figure raised a coin and showed it to Jimmy.

'What? I don't understand.'

The figure mimed throwing it in the air. Then he pointed to Jimmy.

'You want me to call a coin toss?' he asked incredulously.

The figure nodded.

'Bloody hell, you mean like Heads I get to walk out of here and Tails you let me burn to death?'

Again, the figure dipped their chin.

'You absolute psycho. I'm not going to play your sick game.'

The figure shrugged and crossed their arms like they had all the time in the world. Of course, they actually did. Jimmy, on the other hand, was the one who was about to be burned to death.

Jimmy was well used to playing the odds. If he kept quiet,

he would definitely die, but there was a fifty-fifty chance he might make the right call.

'Okay, you fucking win,' he called out.

The figure slowly uncrossed their arms and then flicked the coin up into the air, caught it neatly, placed it on the back of their hand, and looked at Jimmy again.

He glared at the figure. 'I call tails.'

The figure removed their palm from the back of their hand and peered down at the coin.

'Well, what the hell is it?' Jimmy called out.

The figure slowly raised their hand to show Jimmy the coin held between their thumb and forefinger.

Heads.

'Right, I've had enough,' Jimmy bellowed. 'If you don't want to end up in a shallow fucking grave, you'll release me right now.'

The figure ignored him. Instead, they turned and headed away into the smoke billowing throughout the showroom.

A sense of panic swept away any of Jimmy's remaining bravado as he watched them leave.

'For God's sake, don't do this!' he screamed.

But the person didn't so much as pause as they stepped outside through the rear door.

Jimmy screamed curses after them as the flames intensified and the air shimmered, as sparks danced and spiralled like tiny fireflies within the showroom. The light was flickering and pulsating, casting eerie shadows across the blazing showroom as fire licked the DB5.

The showroom owner dropped his head.

'No!' Jimmy said to himself, half sobbing as the air inside the car rapidly grew hotter.

The Aston Martin's engine started to smoulder, smoke began to billow in through the vents. It filled Jimmy's lungs, making him choke. A crack rippled across the windscreen and, with a *bang*, it shattered and the raging inferno roared into the car.

Jimmy's scream was lost in the roar of the flames, claiming his body as their own.

CHAPTER TWO

THE ENGINE of *Tús Nua* purred happily, at least in Joseph's mind, as the narrowboat chugged along the Thames past the expanse of Port Meadow. A couple of swans gave the craft a beady eye as it slowly bore down on them and, at the last moment, grudgingly glided aside.

The heat was already building rapidly despite it only being seven a.m. The DI was certainly grateful for the gentle breeze generated by the narrowboat's passage along the river.

Despite throwing every window open, the cabin felt like the inside of a sauna, rather than somewhere a human with any sense was meant to sleep. A sweat-soaked, sleepless night wasn't exactly what Joseph had envisaged when he'd invited Amy to join him on this brief holiday on the water.

Naturally, they were taking it slowly, exploring this newly formed relationship, trying to work out exactly what they had found.

Unfortunately, the previous night had not lived up to expectations.

At one point, it had become so hot Joseph grabbed a sheet and invited Amy to sleep on the roof with him. However, the local population of mosquitoes had tracked down the human *all-they-could-eat buffet* like a homing missile.

Joseph had awoken to a trail of bites across his body that bore an uncanny resemblance to the bear-shaped star constellation, Ursa Major. When Amy had discovered several on her bum, she'd been less than impressed and had taken sanctuary back inside the boat.

So much for our romantic night together, Joseph thought.

Despite the early hour, it was so hot even the ducks looked like they couldn't be arsed with the job of actually doing any paddling. They just bobbed around the edges of the river with a distinctly dozy look to them, something that Joseph could more than identify with at the moment.

In the heatwave that had descended over England, everything, including the detective, felt like it was in slow motion. Even the water looked languid as it slowly rippled past the dipping branches of the willow trees just tickling the surface of the River Thames.

As Joseph steered the narrowboat, he took a sip of the coffee, brewed from the Brazilian Yellow Bourbon coffee beans to try and sharpen his mind. Sadly, there wasn't actually any bourbon or whisky involved in the growing process. But the medium roast more than made up for that with its hints of caramel and citrus. It certainly hit the right spot on this glorious, if not somewhat stifling, summer's morning.

However, his guest had been less than enamoured when he'd attempted to use the caffeine to try to tempt her back to the land of the living. Ears still ringing from the rather inventive swearing in German that Amy had muttered when he'd offered her a cup, Joseph had come to the conclusion that she *definitely* wasn't a "morning person."

To his left, Port Meadow stretched away like the Oxford equivalent of a prairie, albeit one with very brown and parched grass. A few lone dog walkers were already out, many wearing hats, and keeping their dogs well clear of the ponies and cattle that grazed there. In the distance, at the far end of the vast meadow, the dreaming spires of Oxford rippled slowly in the growing haze.

This was definitely building to be another *scorchio* day.

Joseph passed a familiar section of the embankment and a sense of sadness filled him. This was the spot where Charlie Blackburn, a homeless guy with a heart of gold who'd never done anyone any harm, had met his end at the hands of Helen Edwards.

It often struck Joseph how random some murders could be. Sometimes, just like with poor Charlie, one was simply in the wrong place at the wrong time, the worst luck in the lottery of life.

The spot where his old friend's body had been dumped into the river slid past and the painful memory receded, slowly replaced by the sense of peace the short canal break on *Tús Nua* had created inside the detective inspector.

There was something about the slow rhythm of piloting a narrowboat along the waterways of Oxfordshire that helped decelerate the spin of Joseph's thoughts cycling around his mind. His job didn't give him much of a sense of peace, so it was important to grab these moments where he could, and *messing about on the river,* certainly did that for him.

He was just taking another sip of the excellent coffee when his mobile rang in his shorts pocket. He fished it out and looked at the screen to see Kate's name displayed on it. He pressed the call-accept button.

'Hey, stranger, how are you?' he asked.

'Yes, all good,' Kate said. 'Look, I'm really sorry to interrupt your holiday with Amy, but I thought you might want to hear the gossip and get yourself into work a bit earlier than planned.'

'Technically, I've still got another day off, so why the rush?'

'Do you remember I mentioned to you a few months ago I was investigating Jimmy Harper, who owns a vintage car showroom?'

'Yes, you thought he might have something to do with an organised crime syndicate.'

'Exactly. They're called the Night Watchmen. But this is where it gets really interesting. Derrick just told me over breakfast that Jimmy's showroom burnt down last night.'

'Okay, but surely that's a job for a fire investigator to deal with?'

'Yes, normally, but not when Jimmy himself was found burned alive inside his Aston Martin.'

'So you're saying it wasn't a suicide?'

'His hands were handcuffed to the steering wheel, so what do you think?'

'Feck, what a way to go. So foul play, then?'

'Knowing the circles Jimmy moved in, I'm sure of it. I wouldn't be surprised if this was a professional hit, and there's every chance it could be linked to the Night Watchmen crime syndicate I'm certain Jimmy was a member of. Derrick has already assigned Chris to investigate it. That's why I thought you might want to get yourself into work early. I think this has the potential to be a big case. Who knows, a skilled detective might find it a ticket to a promotion that even Derrick couldn't block.'

'So this has nothing to do with me feeding you information for your big Night Watchmen story for the Oxford Chronicle, then?'

Kate chuckled. 'That's obviously an added bonus, but I do have my husband, whose brains I can pick for that as well.'

'Yes, I suppose you do,' Joseph replied. 'Anyway, thanks for the tip-off. When I get back to my mooring, I'll head in and see if I can persuade Chris to let me join the investigation team.'

'You do that, and remember if you learn anything juicy, you'll let me have the scoop when you go public with it, alright?'

'Do you really need to ask?'

'Not really. So, work aside, how has your romantic holiday been going?'

'It hasn't exactly lived up to expectations, so far.'

'Oh, Joseph, I'm so sorry to hear that. I really thought you two would have a great time together.'

'No, not that. The heatwave has turned *Tús Nua* into a floating air fryer. Not exactly conducive to wooing a lady friend.'

Kate chuckled. 'Ah, I see. Well, maybe next time choose somewhere with air conditioning, at least in this heat.'

'Wise, wise words...'

Joseph heard the stirring of a body below deck and then the sound of bare feet padding towards him through the cabin.

'Ah, I think I hear the Kraken awaking,' he said.

'I'll tell her you said that,' Kate replied. 'Anyway, have fun, and speak soon.'

'Will try to, and I'll be in touch.' Joseph clicked the end-call button. Part of him wished the call had lasted longer, but then again, as much as he might have liked it to, conversations with his ex-wife rarely did.

Amy emerged out of the cabin, wearing nothing apart from one of his old shirts just long enough to protect her modesty.

She took hold of his face between her hands and gave him a lingering kiss. But before Joseph could pull Amy into him, she waved her mobile in his face.

'I've just had the summons from the team. Something about a fire at a classic car showroom and a victim burned to death.'

'Yes, I just got a tip-off from Kate about it as well. When we get back to my mooring, I'm going to contact Megan so she can get the all-clear from Chris for us to head over to the crime scene.'

'Hang on a moment, cowboy. There are plenty of others who can cover for us, because...' Amy ran her finger down his chest and gave him a grin, 'we really should finish off this holiday properly first.'

'Oh, right,' Joseph said, not able to suppress a grin. He patted the top of *Tús Nua's* cabin. 'You heard her, old girl, time to press the pedal to the metal so we can catch a few extra minutes together before we get sucked back into work.'

He pushed the throttle up to a blistering four mph, the speed limit on the local rivers and canals around Oxford. A few ducks responded with annoyed quacks as the massive two-centimetre-high tsunami from the boat's wake disturbed their peace.

Amy's grin widened. 'I hope it's a bit longer than a few minutes.'

'No pressure or anything,' Joseph said, raising his eyebrows at her. He pulled her to him again and kissed her on the side of the head, suddenly impatient to reach his mooring.

Amy, having made sure their holiday had been finished to her satisfaction, had headed off to the crime scene. Meanwhile, Joseph had just finished getting showered and changed.

The mini break with her had certainly done him a world of good, and he felt more relaxed than he had in a long time. Even the injury to his spleen, a memento that Joanna Keene, the Oxford boat crew murderer, had left him, had started to feel better, the pain in his side now reduced to a dull ache. It seemed his time away from work had helped to restore him in mind, body, and maybe even his spirit.

The DI was just heading out of his boat to grab his mountain bike to cycle off to St Aldates Police Station, when he spotted his neighbour, Professor Dylan Shaw, standing next to his own narrowboat, *Avalon*. His dogs, White Fang, a brown terrier, and Max, a beagle, were watching their master with the canine equivalent of a confused expression.

The professor was cursing as he bent a branch right over, which was threatening to turn him into a human trebuchet projectile and launch him skywards while he was trying to hang a bird feeder on it.

Joseph headed over and grabbed hold of the branch, pulling it down for his friend. He gestured to the bird feeder. 'What's this for then, tuppence a bag?'

Dylan gave him a blank look. 'Sorry?'

'Surely you've seen Mary Poppins? You know, that bit where she sings that song about feeding the birds?'

'Oh right! Although, sadly, the sunflower seed in this feeder cost a lot more than tuppence. Anyway, I thought it would be nice to be able to watch the birds feeding.'

'I didn't have you pegged as a twitcher.'

'I wouldn't go as far as that. I've certainly no desire to rush off to Farmoor Reservoir when some rare duck or other is spotted there. I'll leave that level of obsession for others.'

'I hope so.'

'Anyway, my ornithological hobby aside, and I don't want to be a nosy neighbour, but was that Amy I saw leaving your boat with something of a spring in her step?'

'You might have,' Joseph said, trying to keep his expression as neutral as possible.

The professor beamed at him and slapped him on the shoulder. 'About flipping time, Joseph. You deserve someone really good in your life after your long time wandering in the wilderness of bachelorhood.'

'Whoa, slow down there. These are still early days, my friend.'

'Well, I wasn't about to go and get my wedding suit dry cleaned, if that's what you mean.'

'I'm glad to hear it. I think both Amy and I could do without the weight of other people's expectations hanging over us. We've already had enough of that from my daughter and ex-wife. For now, we're just taking it slowly.'

A smile flickered across the professor's face.

Joseph narrowed his eyes at him. 'What?'

'As for taking it slowly, let's just say that maybe the walls of *Tús Nua* aren't quite as thick as you think they are. I had to cover the ears of Max and White Fang just now after you two got back from your brief holiday.'

Joseph caught both dogs looking at him and grimaced. 'Okay, we'll try to keep the volume down in future.'

'I think all the owners of the boats moored along here would appreciate that, let alone all those people who walked past, um, whilst you two were *busy*.'

'Seriously, we were that loud?'

'Well, I didn't need earplugs exactly, but...'

Joseph held up his hand. 'Bloody hell, say no more. Message very much received and understood. Anyway, before you make me feel even more embarrassed, I need to head off to the station.'

Dylan looked intrigued. 'Why, has something interesting come up?'

'You could say that. Apparently, someone was burned to death in a car showroom. Once I'm up to speed, if I need to, I'll pick your brains as usual.'

'Always happy to help,' Dylan replied.

'And you really do,' Joseph replied, as he lifted his mountain bike out of the back of the boat.

After he pulled his helmet on, with a wave to his friend, he headed off to work, hoping Megan had managed to persuade Chris to include them on the case.

His interest had everything to do with Kate telling him that the dead man might have links to the Night Watchmen. That detail alone was deeply intriguing, especially if it had anything to do with why the man lost his life.

CHAPTER THREE

In Joseph's considered opinion, Megan was having far too much fun with the Volvo V90. She was flinging the car around bends on the Cotswolds roads with a permanent smile on her face.

Meanwhile, the DI was trying to suppress a profound sense of panic coiling like a snake in his stomach. The car crash that had claimed his baby son Eoin, and still echoed in the core of his being to this very day, made it difficult to feel relaxed when travelling in a vehicle. That was especially true right now, heading along a road at such ridiculous speeds.

'Please slow down. I would really like to arrive at the crime scene in one piece,' he muttered.

'And miss the opportunity to see what this car can do? I don't think so,' Megan replied. 'The performance is so much better than the pool Peugeot. Even more importantly in this heat wave, unlike half of the police vehicles, it also has the bonus of working air con. No wonder everyone has it booked out all the time right now.'

Joseph tried to avoid looking out of the side window at the

countryside blurring past. 'So how exactly did you manage to bag it?'

'I have friends in high places.'

'In other words, you got Chris to pull some strings for you?'

'How did you guess? The DCI knows how into cars I am. I suppose it's just one petrolhead looking out for another. Ian wasn't happy though. I think he sees this vehicle as his personal motor.'

Joseph shook his head. 'You are all as bad as each other with your need for speed.'

'Just because you like to live in the slow lane,' Megan said, casting him a sideways grin and not picking up on his pale expression.

It was important for Joseph that his colleagues didn't realise he was still constantly battling his own personal demon when travelling in a car. This was his business and no one else's. Certainly, if his pain-in-the-arse superintendent, Derrick Walker, ever found out, the DSU would have him dragged in front of a psychologist faster than he could blink, hoping they would declare the DI unfit for duty. But Joseph had no intention of ever giving the bastard the satisfaction of finally being able to get rid of him.

Megan gave him another sideways look. 'Everything alright?'

So much for her not picking up on my mood... His thoughts trailed away as the DI spotted a tractor's nose beginning to appear from a gateway to their left.

'Megan!' he said, with an almost squeaky bum voice as he flapped a hand towards it.

The DC's gaze snapped back ahead, and with the barest twitch of the steering wheel, she swerved the Volvo around the tractor's nose, giving a brief blast of the siren just for good measure.

The tractor came to a shuddering stop, and Joseph tried to ignore the fist being waved at them from the cab.

'You are absolutely determined to raise my blood pressure today,' he muttered.

'I'm sure you can cope with it, especially after your relaxing holiday.' Megan's grin almost reached her ears. 'So how did it go with Amy?'

Joseph made sure he avoided any eye contact. 'Good...' he replied with absolutely no intention of elaborating further.

'Bloody hell, you men are all alike. Absolutely rubbish for gossip. Get a group of women together and we share everything, and I mean everything. That's why I'll just have to chat to Amy for all the juicy details.'

'Please don't.' Joseph was starting to feel almost as uncomfortable about his personal life being raked over by the DC as he was about her driving.

'God, you really are no fun. Anyway, I don't know why you two aren't still on your boat getting up to who knows what. After all, you do have another day of leave and I would have thought you'd want to make the most of it. Besides, Chris was going to assign Ian and Sue to the initial investigation. At least until you got me to sweet talk him round and seize this case from under their noses.'

'I needed to be involved in this one, partly as a favour to Kate.'

'Does that mean she knows something and wants the scoop?'

'Something like that.'

He caught Megan giving him another sideways look, but she said nothing more.

'Come on, say what's on your mind?' he said.

'Just, considering she's your ex-wife you two still seem to be as thick as thieves.'

'We are and always will be.'

'Right...'

'Just tell me already,' Joseph said, catching the slightly judgemental tone in her voice.

'It sounds to me like you're still carrying a candle for her. I mean, what does Amy think about the fact there are three of you in this relationship?'

Joseph felt the heat creep up his neck.

'She's fine with it, because Kate and I are only friends.'

'Okay, if you say so,' Megan replied, in a tone suggesting she was in no way convinced.

Joseph felt a flutter of exasperation with the DC, but he also knew it would be a waste of time to try to convince her his relationship with Kate was purely platonic. At least that's what he kept telling himself.

'I'm guessing that's our crime scene,' Megan said, with a welcome change of topic as she gestured with her chin towards what was ahead of them.

A column of thin smoke was rising from the top of a ridge. Wisps of grey tendrils slowly danced and swirled as they snaked their way into the sky, contributing to the hazy veil already blanketing the surrounding landscape.

They rounded a bend and spotted the source—a blackened low building with two bright red fire engines and a fire service pickup truck in front of it. A thin mist of water was being sprayed over the building from hoses held by the firemen, creating more smoke from the remains of the destroyed car dealership.

'It looks like the fire isn't quite out yet,' Megan said.

'It mostly is, but they'll be dampening it down for several more hours yet to make sure there's no chance of any further fires starting up again.'

'It doesn't sound like your first time attending the scene of a fire,' Megan said.

'Sadly, it isn't. There was one case I worked on where a former boyfriend poured petrol through the letterbox of his ex. The house burned to the ground. Neighbours only just managed to get the baby out in time, but the mother was burned to death. That sort of memory never leaves you.'

'Bloody hell,' Megan replied with a grim expression.

They approached the police car parked across the access road leading to the smouldering remains of the vintage car showroom, and Joseph recognised PC John Thorpe waving them down. For reasons best known to the young officer, he'd recently transferred across from the Cowley station to St Aldates so it was getting harder for Joseph to avoid him.

'Try not to scowl too hard at him,' Megan whispered, as she slowed their vehicle before the officer. 'I know he's dating your daughter, but you could cut the poor guy some slack.'

'What do you mean?'

'You know full well. John practically jumps out of his skin whenever he sees you these days.'

'Surely I'm not that bad?'

In answer, Megan just raised her eyebrows at him.

Joseph realised she might have a point when John visibly tensed as he spotted the DI in the passenger seat of the approaching Volvo. The PC's expression rallied into one of professionalism and he nodded towards the detectives as their vehicle stopped next to him.

Joseph tried to smile at the man, but for some reason found it had turned into a scowl.

In contrast, Megan was all sunshine and rainbows. 'Is the SOCO team already here, PC Thorpe?' she asked, with a beaming smile as she lowered the window.

'Yes, Amy and her team are just parked up beyond one of

the fire engines,' John replied, as he stepped aside to let them through.

'I don't know what you mean about giving John a hard time,' Joseph said. They headed away towards the SOCO van, a Triumph TR4 parked next to it.

'You didn't need to. Your hostility towards him was written in large letters across your face.'

'You're exaggerating.'

'Am I?' Megan replied, stepping out of the Volvo. After the air-conditioned bliss of the car, the stifling heat that wrapped around them was something of a shock.

'That's Chris's TR4 he takes racing, isn't it?' Megan asked, as they slipped their warrant cards into their lanyard holders.

'I guess so, but how do you know about it?'

'Chris and I got chatting about cars after we drove through the floods to the old sewage plant in the police Land Rover, during the Joanna Keene case. He even invited me to join him on a track day.'

'Did he now?' Joseph said, giving her an amused look.

The DC narrowed her eyes on him. 'What?'

'Oh, nothing,' he replied.

But the DI did wonder whether this might be the start of something between Megan and their boss. After all, why not? The DCI was divorced as far as Joseph knew, though maybe a bit too buttoned up for Megan. As far as he knew, the chief pathologist, Doctor Jacobs, also held something of a torch for her. Whether Megan was actually interested in either man, he had no idea, and it certainly wasn't his business. Just as his own personal life wasn't hers.

They headed towards a group of policemen, including the big man himself, DCI Chris Faulkner.

Amy was also with him, already in her white SOCO coveralls, watching the firemen hose down the last of the fire. When she spotted him, Amy gave Joseph a small lingering smile and a nod, before her professional mask slipped back into place. No hint to the others about what they'd been up to less than an hour before back on his boat. However, he could see Megan smirking at them both from the corner of his eye. He studiously ignored her, and instead turned his attention towards Chris.

'Hi boss, you seem to have beaten us to it.'

The DCI nodded. 'I don't live too far away and wanted to see this with my own eyes. Prestige Vintage Motors is something of a legend among classic car owners. I know quite a few people who bought their cars from Jimmy and they're going to be devastated when they hear the news. The man always went out of his way to organise charity fundraisers.'

Joseph filed that titbit of information away in the back of his mind. A man who was known for his charity work wasn't exactly the usual profile for someone who, at least Kate thought, was a criminal mastermind.

'So you knew Jimmy Harper well, then?' Megan asked Chris.

'Only by reputation,' the DCI replied. 'Anyway, we're only assuming it's Jimmy in there. The body was discovered inside his burned-out DB5, among the other destroyed cars in the showroom.'

Amy nodded. 'Until the fire officer comes out and gives us the all clear, we won't be able to retrieve the body for pathology, so they can run a dental comparison.'

'You're saying the fire officer is in there now whilst the showroom is still on fire?' Megan asked, wide-eyed.

'Smouldering. There is a difference,' Amy said.

'But surely it's still highly dangerous in there,' the DC said, looking at the twisted and charred metal beams of the building visible through the large shattered windows.

'It is, but that's what a fire investigator is paid to do,' Joseph replied. 'They often enter the building whilst it's still burning because there is evidence that might be lost otherwise, and that helps them assess exactly what happened.'

Amy nodded. 'After all that water and foam, it can make it difficult for me and my team to find anything by the time it's eventually extinguished. And talk of the devil.'

She pointed towards a figure wearing a fire-resistant uniform, including a full-face breathing mask and an oxygen tank strapped to his back, emerging from the smoking building.

Amy and Chris ducked under the outer perimeter tape to greet the figure, as Joseph and Megan followed their lead.

The fire investigator pulled his helmet off and unstrapped his mask to reveal a bearded man in his late-thirties to early forties with dark eyes and a greying crew cut. The deep lines etched around his eyes suggested maybe he'd witnessed one too many fatal fires in his time.

Amy reached out and shook the man's gloved hand. 'Thomas Reid, isn't it?'

'Guilty as charged,' he replied with a smile as his gaze skimmed over Amy's ID and then the rest of the detectives' lanyards. He hitched his thumb over his shoulder. 'I'm afraid it's a bad business in there.'

'So you can confirm the victim was definitely handcuffed to the steering wheel of the DB5?' Chris asked.

'Absolutely. There's obviously an outside chance this was an extreme form of suicide, where the guy wanted to make sure he couldn't change his mind. But my money is on this being murder.'

'Accelerant?' Joseph asked.

'It looks like petrol. I found some discarded cans in the corner of what's left of the showroom. Whoever torched the place made sure every single one of the vintage cars in there was burned, including the DB5 where we found the victim. They weren't messing around. When the petrol tanks detonated, there was enough of a blast wave to blow the showroom windows out. If the victim wasn't already dead, that would have definitely finished them off.'

Megan grimaced. 'What an awful way for someone to die.'

The lines around Thomas' eyes deepened. 'The very worst. It would have been a very slow and agonising death...' his gaze travelled down to her lanyard again, 'DC Anderson.'

'So when can we gain access to the crime scene, Thomas?' Joseph asked.

'Structurally, the building's sound and won't collapse on your heads. It'll be another thirty minutes or so, to make sure we have the fire totally extinguished, before we let you all in.'

'In that case, just give us a shout when you're ready for us,' Chris said.

'Don't worry, I will.' Thomas gave the detectives a nod, before heading off to join his colleagues, directing the two fire hoses onto the far corner of the showroom.

Amy turned to face the detectives. 'We're all going to need full-face respirator gas masks before any of us enter the remains of the showroom. There will be no end of poisonous vapours trapped inside the building with all those vehicles having burned up. So let me get you all suited and booted. Not that I'm counting on much forensic evidence being left.'

Joseph spotted a burned-out CCTV camera over the door. 'What about security footage?'

'I doubt any computer will have survived in there, but if we're lucky, data from that camera will be stored somewhere on the cloud,' Amy replied. 'But leave that to us and we'll hand it over to the technical forensic team to investigate.'

'Then let's hope that camera picked up something, because based on the assumption this isn't suicide, there is a truly sick bastard out there that needs to be behind bars,' Joseph replied.

Thomas led Amy and the team of detectives into the remains of the showroom.

The muffled echo of Joseph's breathing pulsed within the confines of his gas mask, providing an eerie accompaniment as they headed into the charred bowels of the building.

The walls and ceiling were blackened with smoke damage and ash rained down on them like dark snow as they picked their way carefully through the debris.

The water from the hoses had flooded the floor, covering the once-stylish polished tiles with a layer of sooty water. Joseph could feel some of the heat from the fire still radiating from the surrounding surfaces. Within a matter of moments, sweat was running down the DI's back and his mask was threatening to mist up.

The once-gleaming cars that had filled the showroom had been reduced to heaps of burnt-out scrap, their bodies twisted and deformed by the intense heat of the fire, pristine paint jobs reduced to a charred black. A wall had partly collapsed in the rear of the showroom to reveal the blackened husk of a service area. Storage racks had buckled and tipped over, spilling their tools all over the floor.

Chris gestured towards a vehicle that even Joseph recognised as an E-Type Jag. What had once been its elongated sweeping bonnet had now melted into the engine block beneath it.

'What a waste,' the DCI said, his voice muffled by his own mask. 'The collection of vehicles in here is easily worth millions.'

'*Used* to be worth millions,' Joseph corrected him. 'They're little more than scrap value now.'

'Sadly, you're probably right. I'd be tempted to think this

was some sort of insurance fraud gone wrong, apart from something I know for a fact—there are people queuing up to buy cars from Jimmy Harper.'

'*Were* lining up,' Megan corrected him.

'What are you two, the bloody past tense police today?' Chris said, shaking his head at the DC and DI.

When Megan glanced back at Joseph, despite her full face mask, her grin was still easy to make out. That expression quickly fell away as they headed towards the burnt-out remains of the Aston Martin DB5 to one side of the showroom.

Like the E-Type, its profile was instantly recognisable, as fine filaments of smoke drifted up from the remains of the car. Despite Joseph's mask, he was still able to detect a very distinct odour beneath the smell of smoke, something much worse—the smell of charred meat.

Thomas stopped by the side of the car where the driver's door was already open. Sitting in the driving seat was a person burned beyond recognition, the exposed hands and face charred to the bone and yellowed by fire.

'As you can see, the victim didn't stand a chance,' Thomas said, gesturing towards the handcuffs around both wrists looped around the steering wheel.

Amy squatted down next to the body for a closer look. 'It appears he put up a serious struggle. If you look closely, he actually managed to bend the steering wheel.'

'So you're saying he was conscious as he burned to death?' Joseph asked, his brow furrowed.

'That would be my educated guess,' Amy replied. She stood and turned to Thomas. 'I'm guessing you've already photographed everything of note in here?'

He nodded. 'I'll give you a memory card with all the files on it.'

'Good, then we can add those to any we take. Am I okay to bring my own team in now?'

'Yes, please go ahead. I've already got as much information as I can find in here,' Thomas said. 'But it doesn't take a fire investigator to state the obvious—this was a clear case of arson. Why anyone would want to do that to another human being, I've no idea.'

'Leave it to us to work out the answer to that particular riddle,' Chris said.

Megan's gaze locked onto the burned figure, who'd curled into a foetal position during their final moments of death.

Joseph gently patted her shoulder. 'Are you okay?'

She tore her eyes away from the corpse. 'As much as anyone can be, seeing something as shocking as this.'

'Isn't that the truth?' Chris replied, giving the DC a sympathetic look.

Joseph looked around. If the person before the detectives really was Jimmy Harper, then what had once been his dream had literally been burnt to the ground, and him right along with it. The question was why, and more significantly, by whom?

'I'd like you two to attend the post-mortem, whilst I set up an investigation team back at St Aldates,' Chris said, addressing Joseph and Megan.

The DI gave Megan a questioning look. 'Are you up for it?'

'As everyone keeps telling me, I suppose it would be educational,' she replied.

Amy smiled at her through the mask. 'That's the spirit, Megan.'

CHAPTER FOUR

After Joseph had given Megan a Silvermint, and taken one for himself to help combat any feelings of nausea, masked and suited, the two detectives headed into the pathology lab.

In the middle of the room, the charred remains of the victim had been placed on its side on the autopsy table, still positioned in the semi-foetal position it had been found in.

On the far side of the lab, Doctor Rob Jacobs and his assistant, Doctor Clare Reece, were both eating sushi. When it came to eating or drinking, as per usual, they seemed totally unconcerned about sharing the room with a corpse.

Spotting them enter, Rob gave them a cheery wave with the Californian roll in his chopsticks.

Joseph couldn't help but notice the beaming smile that the older man gave Megan, which was returned with an equally broad one by the DC.

The chief pathologist had struck up a firm friendship with Megan, who it turned out, was a keen archaeologist on her days off. She'd even invited Rob to join her on some digs, as he shared her passion for history.

Clare pointed to the plate of sushi. 'Fancy some? Doctor Jacobs has brought enough to feed an army.'

'I'll pass, if you don't mind. I'm not exactly hungry at the moment.' Joseph gestured towards the body.

'Ah, yes, I can see why that might put you off your food,' Rob said. 'But what about you, Megan?'

Just as it should be, the DC's attention was firmly fixed on the charred remains of the body rather than on any discussion about food.

Joseph gave her a discreet nudge.

She turned towards the pathologists. 'Sorry, no, I'm good…' Her gaze travelled back to the corpse.

The one positive for Joseph was at least there wasn't the usual awful smell of death, more the fragrance of a fatty pork belly that had been cooked over a barbecue. He found that relatively easy to deal with. It hadn't always been that way, though.

When he'd witnessed his first fire victim, a young woman who'd been trapped in her overturned vehicle after an RTA and had burned alive, he hadn't been able to touch meat for a good year afterwards. But as always, the nature of the job eventually hardened you to that sort of thing and, eventually, his self-imposed fast had been broken when he'd eaten a gourmet burger from a gastropub. Joseph wondered about himself, sometimes.

'So, it looks like you've finished the post-mortem?' he asked.

Rob finished his Californian roll and nodded. 'Just a moment ago, and the most urgent thing you're going to want to know is about the dental records. We've already been able to confirm that it is indeed Jimmy Harper.'

Joseph nodded. 'I don't think anyone was in any doubt about that, but it's good to know for sure.'

The detectives headed over for a closer inspection of the corpse.

In the stark clinical conditions of the lab, to Joseph's mind, the state of the burned body seemed more brutal than it had back inside the destroyed DB5. The skin had cracked and blistered like overdone crackling and what was left of the clawed hands had been burned down to the bone. To make sure the spectacle was as gruesome as possible, the chest cavity was still open from the post-mortem. What remained of the internal organs were little more than charred lumps.

Joseph was impressed that Megan didn't make so much as a retching sound as the two doctors joined them. Her emotional armour had definitely improved from that of the inexperienced officer he'd met six months earlier.

'To kick us off, I suppose the key question is whether the victim was alive or dead when he was burned to death?' Joseph asked.

Rob's brow knotted. 'I'm afraid it's the former. Clare, would you care to explain how we came to that conclusion?'

She nodded and took out her torch, shining it into the corpse's open mouth. 'If you look in there, what do you see?'

Joseph leant down and peered into the back of the mouth. 'It's full of soot.'

'Exactly, and you can also see soot deposits around what remains of the nostrils. What does that tell you?'

A thoughtful look filled Megan's face. 'That he was still alive when he died because he inhaled smoke?'

Rob nodded towards her. 'Spot on. Are you sure you wouldn't like to switch careers and become a pathologist?'

She arched her eyebrows at him. 'Don't tempt me.'

The doctor grinned at her. 'Anyway, to be absolutely sure, we've also sent a sample to estimate the carboxyhaemoglobin level. If it turns out to be over fifty percent, that's also pretty strong evidence the victim was alive when he started to burn, especially when looked at in conjunction with the soot found in the mouth and trachea.'

'According to Amy, the victim also managed to bend the steering wheel in his efforts to get free,' Joseph replied.

'That certainly sounds like the efforts of someone frantically trying to escape,' Clare said.

Joseph's mind was filled with a vivid mental image of the man desperately trying to break the steering wheel off as the flames consumed him.

'So what else can you tell us?' Joseph asked.

'As you can see, the victim's limbs are in the classic pugilist position,' Clare said.

'The what?' Megan asked.

'Sorry, medical speak. A classic guard position where the boxer holds up their hands near their face to protect themselves. That's caused by the heat, a contraction of the muscles that make the limbs bend. The most famous examples are the victims of the Pompeii eruption where the victims were covered with burning ash, causing them to go into similar positions as our victim here. Also, the bones have become brittle due to the fire damage, causing some of them to fracture when the victim was removed from the vehicle.'

'So, is there any evidence to support that this was a murder?' Joseph asked.

'There's evidence of an extradural haemorrhage around the back of the skull. In the absence of anything falling on the cranium, that would suggest that the victim might have been hit over the head with something. The mark could have been made by a crowbar, which is long and narrow. Apart from that, there are the marks on the wrists caused by the handcuffs.'

'That sounds like pretty compelling evidence to me,' Megan said.

Joseph nodded. 'You're certainly not alone there.'

'And we haven't actually got to maybe our most important find of all, which I think is going to be of major interest to you both,' Rob said.

He headed over to a workbench and returned with an evidence bag that he handed over to Joseph. The DI held it up and noticed a soot-covered pound coin inside.

'And the significance of this is?'

'Two things, but turn it round and you'll see something very interesting indeed.'

Joseph did as instructed and was surprised to discover both sides of the coin had a head on them.

Megan peered at it. 'A trick coin?'

'It certainly looks that way,' the DI replied.

'But why?'

Joseph shrugged as he scrutinised the coin. 'What's the second significant thing about this?'

'That's to do with where we found it—shoved into the back of the victim's throat,' Clare said.

Megan gave her a surprised look. 'To ask an obvious question, why didn't the victim spit it back out?'

'You're right, it would have triggered the pharyngeal reflex if he'd still been alive,' Rob said.

Megan frowned.

'His gag reflex,' Clare clarified.

Joseph narrowed his eyes. 'So you're saying that someone deliberately placed it in there after he'd died?'

'It certainly looks that way to us,' Rob said.

Joseph scratched the back of his neck. 'So, despite the fire the murderer hung around until they were certain Jimmy was dead, then placed this coin in his mouth.'

'What sort of sick individual would do something like that?' Megan asked.

The DI's lips pressed together in a thin line. 'Someone who really wanted Jimmy Harper dead.'

'Sadly, yet another example of the depths of depravity our species is capable of,' Rob said.

Megan's face paled, and she nodded.

CHAPTER FIVE

JOSEPH WAS HEADING to Chris'ss briefing about the arson with the team at St Aldates Police Station in Oxford.

'Can I have a quiet word?' Derrick called out, as the DI headed past his glass-walled office.

'Of course,' Joseph replied, stepping inside.

'If you wouldn't mind closing the door behind you...'

Shite, here we go again... Joseph thought.

He took the seat Derrick was gesturing towards and gave the DSU an uncertain look, not quite sure why he'd been summoned. 'Is there some sort of problem?'

'That's what I was hoping you could tell me. Kate has been incredibly withdrawn at home. I know she still confides in you, so I was wondering if she's said anything to you that I might need to know about?'

The DI felt his body relax as he settled back into his seat, because for once this wasn't about some error of judgment, imagined or otherwise, Derrick was trying to pin on him.

'Oh, right. But surely you should try talking to Kate yourself?'

'Already been there and tried that. But she just tells me

everything is fine in the way she sometimes does that tells me it really isn't.'

Joseph wrestled with his loyalty to Kate. His best guess was she'd become withdrawn because of her Night Watchmen investigation. When she got her teeth into a story, she barely surfaced for anything, including, it seemed, her husband.

'It's probably just something at the newspaper. You know what she gets like.'

'I hope that's it,' Derrick said, with a flat tone. 'Look, as one mate to another, you can tell me if there's something more to it than that.'

One mate to another, yeah right, Joseph thought. Out loud he said, 'Why, are you guys having problems?'

Derrick's gaze became flinty as he stared at the DI. 'What the hell do you mean by that?'

Joseph held up his palms. 'Absolutely nothing, it was just a question, nothing more.'

But then he remembered how Kate had told him a while back that Derrick had been drinking heavily and she'd become increasingly worried about him. Was that what this was about?

'Right... Sorry, I've been a bit on edge recently. Not sleeping well.'

The DI just nodded, partly to see if the silent approach might coax some more information out of the superintendent. When a good ten seconds had passed, he eventually tried again.

'It can all get to us sometimes. I should know. Look, I know it isn't my place, but is everything alright?'

Derrick cast him an unreadable look and just shrugged. 'Only the usual. The stresses and strains of being the guy at the top sometimes have their disadvantages.'

Says the man who backstabbed me to help propel himself to that position.

However, despite the man's hypocrisy, Joseph couldn't help

but feel a little concerned for the superintendent. This was one of those moments where if they really had been mates, he would have suggested heading over to the Scholar's Retreat for a quick pint and a chat about what was going on with him. The problem was, Derrick had burned that particular bridge years ago.

'If I can do anything to help, you only need to ask,' Joseph said, almost meaning it.

'Just keep me in the loop if Kate does eventually confide in you.'

The DI nodded, but intended to do no such thing. If his ex-wife told him something in confidence, then it would remain exactly that.

'If that's all, sir?' Joseph said as he stood.

The superintendent gave him a distracted nod, looking very much like a man who had the weight of the world on his shoulders.

———

Joseph and the others were waiting in the incident room for Chris and Amy to put in an appearance.

Every single desk had a fan on it, cranked up to the maximum and humming like a swarm of bees in an attempt to counter the stifling heat in the room. Despite the sauna-like conditions, a lively discussion was underway.

'I tell you, even today this is still the king of biscuits,' Ian said, biting down on his Jammy Dodger, the British round biscuit with a raspberry jam centre. 'Although, you're probably going to tell me that there is a different baked good of choice over in sunny Ireland, Joseph? Something exotic made from seaweed, probably.'

The DI swallowed the last of his own biscuit and shook his

head. 'There is, actually. But it's something called dulse and is eaten as a snack.'

Sue raised her eyebrows at him. 'Seriously? That's the Irish version of a biscuit?'

'God, no. As far as biscuits go, it's pretty much the same over there. Digestives, Bourbons, and maybe oatcakes at a push if you're feeling really desperate.'

'Well, a Digestive will always be the best choice for dunking,' Sue said, demonstrating by dipping her Jammy Dodger halfway into her tea. She raised it back out again and showed the almost dry biscuit to the rest of the officers in the room with a scowl. 'You see, no absorption power. Not what you need for a good dunker.'

Megan looked between them. 'The highbrow conversations we have in this station never cease to amaze me.'

'Oh, these sorts of debates are of national importance,' Ian said. 'Wars have been fought over less. Anyway, isn't that your third? Not that I'm counting or anything.'

Megan gave him a small grin. 'Who am I to look a gift horse in the mouth? I've always been partial to a Jammy Dodger.'

'If you think that, I really need to introduce you to the delights of a warm, freshly baked chocolate chip and nut from Ben's Cookies in the covered market,' Joseph said. 'Now if you want the treat of kings, you can't get much better than that.'

'I haven't tried them, are they any good?' Megan asked.

'Good? They're absolutely grand,' Joseph replied.

Sue nodded. 'Yes, you're definitely slacking on your mentoring activities, Joseph, if you haven't introduced Megan to them yet.'

'Then that's a life-changing experience we're going to need to sort out ASAP, maybe washed down with a bit of coffee from that independent place in the covered market as well, who actually grow their own coffee plants,' Joseph said.

'I sometimes wonder what the priority round here is, solving crimes or working out the best places to get food,' Amy said, overhearing the detectives' conversation as she walked into the incident room with Chris.

'I think it's pretty evenly split,' Chris said, shaking his head at the team.

Amy gave Joseph a discreet *we-really-didn't-have-sex-earlier-today* smile as she passed him. This was how it was between them at work, keeping their relationship off their colleagues' radars, apart from the notable exception of Megan. If it got out, there would be no end of friendly piss-taking.

Everyone in the room turned their attention to the DCI and the SOC officer as they set up at the front.

A few moments later, the large screen had been powered up to display the TVP's—Thames Valley Police—logo.

'Okay, let's get this briefing underway,' Chris said, clicking a remote.

An image of a grey-haired man with glasses appeared. He was wearing an expensive-looking, pale-brown suit with a red tie and perfectly matching handkerchief poking out of his top pocket. Behind him was a silver Aston Martin DB5. Below the photo was a caption that read: Jimmy Harper.

'There is absolutely no way I would have recognised Jimmy as the same man we found in that car,' Megan said.

'Nobody would have, which is why dental records are so important in a case like this,' Joseph replied.

Chris nodded. 'Unfortunately, that's very true. Anyway, to summarise what we know so far, Jimmy appears to have gone to his premises to check on an alarm that had been triggered in the middle of the night. I'll hand over to Amy to give us an update on her team's forensic findings, as it relates directly to that.'

He handed the remote over to the SOC officer.

'We were able to retrieve the footage from the cloud after

the technical forensic team negotiated access to it with the online storage company,' Amy said. 'What you're about to see is the moment Jimmy arrived at his showroom to investigate the triggered alarm.' She pressed play on the remote.

An infrared night vision video feed appeared on the screen from a camera outside Prestige Vintage Motors' parking area at the front of the premises.

Over the sound of an alarm blaring, they heard a car approaching along the road. Headlights appeared in the entrance a moment later, as three security bollards lowered into the ground.

As the car drove forward and the dazzle from the headlights reduced, Joseph could see it was the once-pristine Aston Martin DB5, pulling into a parking space next to the front door. Even on the night vision, the car looked exceptionally well cared for, not a speck of dirt to be seen anywhere on its bodywork.

'It's hard to believe that's the same burned-out wreck we found the victim inside of,' Megan whispered to Joseph.

'I know. It was obviously the man's pride and joy.'

As the video continued playing, the door opened and a man roughly in his fifties got out. He was wearing a leather bomber jacket and slacks, and also had a wheel brace gripped in his hand.

Amy paused the video. 'As you can see from the timestamp, Jimmy arrived at the premises around twelve forty-five a.m., after the alarm was triggered about forty minutes earlier.'

'Going by the pissed-off look on his face, and also based on the fact he's armed with a wheel brace, Jimmy doesn't look as though he intended on holding back,' Ian said.

'I agree,' Chris replied. 'But one strange thing that's come to light is this was the first time that Prestige Vintage Motors has ever been broken into, despite a rash of car thefts from other showrooms across the surrounding area.'

'So eventually the thieves got around to targeting Jimmy's dealership and his luck ran out,' Sue said.

'Possibly,' Amy replied, pressing the play button again.

The video started up and the officers in the room watched Jimmy head towards the showroom and disappear out of shot. A few seconds later, the alarm went silent.

'Haven't we got any footage from inside the showroom?' Joseph asked.

'No, all the footage seems to have been wiped remotely from Jimmy's phone,' Amy replied. 'It wouldn't have been hard for the intruder to use facial recognition to unlock his mobile and then access the security footage and delete it from an app. Thankfully, they didn't bother wiping the external camera feed, as they presumably thought it hadn't caught anything. Anyway, what we do have is this...' She cranked the volume up.

For a moment there was nothing, but then there was a sudden single thudding sound.

'We believe that was the moment Jimmy was hit from behind, as indicated by the injury to the rear of the cranium that Doctor Jacobs discovered during the autopsy.'

'So, that means that the intruder had already gained access to the showroom?' Megan asked.

'That would fit, as the alarm system indicates it was an internal ultrasonic detector that had been triggered. But when we double-checked that specific sensor, we actually discovered at least a dozen flies burned beneath it.'

'I may be making something of a mental leap here, but are you saying someone deliberately triggered the alarm by releasing flies into the showroom?' Joseph asked, with an incredulous tone.

'It's certainly one explanation. The intruder could then have waited until Jimmy arrived, crept up behind him, and hit him over the head.'

'In other words, they set a trap for him?' Megan said.

'Again, we can't give you a definitive answer there, but whoever it was had plenty of time to steal a car before Jimmy reached the premises, but they decided to hang around instead,' Amy said.

'That definitely doesn't sound like a break-in gone wrong to me,' one of the officers in the room said.

Joseph nodded. 'So what about the intruder? I'm assuming, based on the fact they didn't bother wiping it, there isn't any sign of them on the CCTV footage before Jimmy arrived?'

'Not directly, but we do have an event caught on the security camera just before the alarm was triggered,' Amy said. 'This next piece of video you're about to see was recorded about fifty minutes before Jimmy turned up at the showroom.' She clicked the remote's button and a new video appeared of footage from the camera outside the premises.

This time, rather than the burble of the Aston Martin, the team heard the throaty roar of a motorbike, getting louder. Then the beam of a headlight slid over the showroom entrance. There was a brief glimpse of a rider on a substantial-looking black motorbike passing by on the main road and carrying on.

'Just for a minute, I thought we were going to see that motorbike swinging into the parking area and you were about to tell us that you had a registration plate,' Ian said.

'If only our lives were ever that easy, but keep listening,' Amy said.

They all heard the bike decelerating and then coming to a stop somewhere out of view of the camera.

'There's a gate a hundred metres beyond the showroom entrance. The motorcyclist probably left their bike there and slipped round the back of the showroom and released the flies through an air vent.'

'I don't suppose you've managed to grab any frames of the motorcyclist when they passed the entrance?' Sue asked.

'Actually, we did...' Amy pressed the remote's button again.

On the grainy zoomed-in image, Joseph was just able to make out a person on a beefy motorbike in dark riding leathers and wearing a full-face black helmet.

'I'm afraid that's as much as we can do to tidy up the image. We can't even tell if the rider is a man or a woman.'

'What about the bike?' Sue asked.

'Again, too blurred to make out, apart from the fact it's some sort of high-powered sports motorbike,' Amy replied.

Chris turned to face the room. 'So, as you can all see for yourself, we don't have any obvious suspect yet, unfortunately.'

'What about a motive, then?' Ian asked.

Chris shrugged. 'By all accounts, the man was the very definition of a pillar of the community and gave a lot of money to charity.'

'I wouldn't be quite so sure about that,' Joseph said, deciding to finally speak up about the information Kate had given him.

'Why, do you know something?' the DCI asked.

'Let's just say, I have a source who's been investigating a news story about Jimmy Harper. They believe he was a member of a highly secretive crime syndicate called the Night Watchmen.'

Several people whistled in the room.

Chris stared at Joseph. 'And why is this the first time I'm hearing about it?'

'Because my source isn't in a position to provide us with any firm evidence yet, but has promised me that as soon as they have something they will give me the nod.'

The DCI narrowed his gaze at Joseph. 'And if I were to press you about who your source is?'

Joseph gave him a straight look. 'Probably best to have that conversation behind closed doors. Anyway, if Jimmy Harper really was a member of a crime syndicate, then that might explain the lack of break-ins.'

'You mean the local criminals were deliberately giving Jimmy's showroom a wide berth?'

'That would certainly make sense to me.'

Chris slowly nodded as he took the remote. 'Okay, there is one final piece of evidence that may be relevant to this being some sort of criminal vendetta.'

He pressed the button on the remote; this time a photograph of the two-headed coin was displayed.

'I realise you've all heard about this, but the coin was recovered from the victim's mouth. Right now, we have no idea what the significance of it is.' Chris looked at the team. 'Obviously, one of our key priorities right now is to learn a lot more about who Jimmy Harper really was. I think it's reasonable to assume by what happened to him, that he was a man who had enemies. That would certainly fit in with Harper being a member of this Night Watchmen syndicate.'

'Could this be a rival gangland hit?' Megan asked.

'That's an avenue of inquiry certainly worth exploring,' Joseph replied.

'We could get a forensic accountant to look over Jimmy's books and business in general,' Amy suggested.

'That's a good idea,' Chris replied. 'We should also arrange to interview people close to Jimmy, including anyone who worked at the showroom. See if they can cast any more light on his background. He also has three ex-wives who will need to be interviewed as a priority.'

Everyone nodded.

'What about searching his home to see if we can unearth anything there?' Megan asked.

'I've already got you and Joseph down to do exactly that. He lived alone in a luxury penthouse in Oxford.'

'We'd be more than happy to give it a thorough sweep, boss,' Joseph said.

'Good. Then I think that about wraps it up for now. Our immediate priority is to start digging, discover who Jimmy Harper really was and, more importantly, who had the motivation to burn him to death.'

CHAPTER SIX

OVER THE YEARS when Joseph had ridden his mountain bike along the towpath, walked along it, or taken his narrowboat along the section of canal past the former brewery converted into tasteful flats, his gaze had often been drawn upwards. The focus of his attention was always drawn to the exclusive penthouse apartments with their glass balconies that loomed over the waterway.

Many of the apartments had outdoor cooking areas festooned with pot plants. In a moment of idle curiosity, he'd once checked the prices online for one of the flats. The figure being asked had been eye-watering and certainly far beyond a detective inspector's salary. However, he'd always imagined that the view of the city from up there would be absolutely spectacular. Now he knew he'd been right.

Joseph and Megan were in Jimmy Harper's penthouse apartment in the old brewery, its decor practically dripping with money. Despite the summer heatwave, an air conditioning system was keeping the flat at the perfect temperature. Carefully chosen, large-scale pieces of abstract art, boasting bold, vibrant colours, rested against the eggshell-white walls, telling tales of trips to high-end auctions and exclusive galleries. However, what demanded the most attention was the opera music blaring out of hidden speakers, which Joseph was pretty sure was Rossini's The Barber of Seville. The DI headed over to the very expensive hi-fi system to turn it off, and a welcome silence descended.

'Thank God. That racket was doing my head in,' Megan said.

'Not a big fan of opera, then?' Joseph asked.

'Men and women screeching about something or other? I don't think so.'

'You have heard modern music, right?'

Megan shook her head at him, before turning her attention to the huge windows framing the view of the spires and church towers of Oxford, rising out of the shimmering heat haze above the city's rooflines.

'That's quite the view,' the DC said.

'Isn't it just? No wonder these flats go for well over two million.'

Megan pulled a face. 'Seriously, for a flat?'

Joseph gestured around them at the windows. 'You have to pay through the nose for that sort of view in this city.'

'That's still a lot of money.'

'It is to most of us mortals,' Joseph replied, his gaze skimming over the rest of the living room.

Designer chairs, along with one of the longest leather sofas he'd ever seen, were positioned to take maximum benefit of the pay-through-your-nose view.

Roman-style sculptures illuminated with overhead spotlights were dotted everywhere. They didn't exactly look like reproductions either, more like items that probably belonged in the Ashmolean Museum.

But the thing that caught Joseph's eye, more than anything

else, were the oil paintings of various vintage motor cars, including a particularly large one of an Aston Martin on a race-track. It had been positioned in pride of place over a modern fireplace.

Megan was looking at it as well. 'Isn't that Jimmy's Aston Martin?'

'I think it must be. I bet the other cars in the paintings are probably of his vehicles as well. We're talking a man of consider-able means here, so I wouldn't be surprised if he had these paintings all privately commissioned.'

The DI's gaze fell upon a half-drunk bottle of 1962 Château Lafite Rothschild on the coffee table, an almost full glass next to it.

'It looks as though Jimmy must have dropped everything when he received the alarm alert from the showroom.'

Megan nodded. 'That would explain why the music was left on. What exactly are we looking for here?'

'Anything that will help us build a fuller profile of the victim. Keep looking and let's see what we can find.'

Joseph led the way through the living room and the open-plan kitchen linked to it, and into a corridor. He tried the first door on the left, and they entered the room. The detectives found themselves in a wood-panelled room with a number of red leather armchairs facing a large TV screen. The heavy scent of tobacco smoke permeated the room.

Megan pointed to the glass cabinets lining one wall. They were filled with framed photos, again mainly of motor cars, but also numerous open wooden boxes of cigars.

'That explains the pong,' she observed.

Joseph nodded. 'Seems to be an old-school cigar room. Although I'm not good on my vintage years, that bottle is easily worth six hundred pounds.'

'Six hundred!' Megan replied, appalled. 'That would keep me going with alcohol for a year!'

Joseph chuckled. 'Each to their own. Jimmy was obviously a man with a taste for luxury and had a big enough wallet to indulge.'

He started perusing the contents of a cabinet lining one wall. It was filled with photos, including one of Jimmy handing over an oversized cheque for a hundred thousand pounds to a group of nurses outside a hospice. There were also several of glamorous-looking women with the vintage car dealer.

Megan was peering at one in particular. 'Isn't that Anna Millington, the actor from that BBC comedy sitcom, about those two guys she shares a flat with?'

Joseph looked at the photo of the very pretty woman with long blonde hair, wearing a silver cocktail dress. She was hanging on Jimmy's arm, who was dressed in a white dinner jacket.

He nodded. 'That was in the background files I looked at. Anna is actually one of his three ex-wives.'

'Jimmy certainly looks very James Bond in his DJ,' Megan said. 'My guess is he was a bit of a ladies' man. He certainly drove the right car to cultivate that image.'

'Is this the moment I attempt my Sean Connery impression?'

'Please don't.'

Joseph raised his eyebrows at her, then his attention was drawn to a different photo. This one was of Jimmy and two other men, their arms draped around each other, and grinning at the camera. They were all wearing one-piece racing suits. Behind them parked in a pitlane was Jimmy's Aston Martin DB5, a powder blue vintage Porsche Spyder, and a yellow Jensen Interceptor, presumably the cars belonging to the other two men in the picture. One had that permanent sooty-face look that made Joseph suspect he spent his time in a lot of garages, either in his spare time, or as his full-time job. The other man's head was clean-shaven, and he had the general physique of someone who knew how to handle themselves.

Written on a small plaque set into the frame was: *Vivere est vincere.*

'I wonder what that means?' Joseph said.

'The internet is your friend,' Megan said, pulling her phone out. A few taps later, she nodded. 'Here we go, it's Latin for *To live is to conquer.* What's that, Jimmy's motto or something?'

'Possibly.' Joseph took his phone out and started taking pictures of all the photos in the cabinets.

'You thinking those people with Jimmy might be worth tracking down and interviewing?' Megan asked.

'Absolutely. I don't remember seeing anything about them in Jimmy's file. They could possibly help give us a clearer picture about what sort of man he really was.'

With a last sweep of his gaze, satisfied they had seen everything of any use, they headed back out into the corridor and opened the door opposite. The room turned out to be an impressive office, with a curved monitor almost as wide as the glass and wooden desk it was standing on. The room was filled with trophies. When the DI took a closer look at the inscriptions, he quickly realised they were all for motor races, most of which had been for first place.

'*Vivere est vincere,* indeed,' he muttered.

'Sorry?' Megan said, as she thumbed through a bound notebook on the desk.

'Just thinking aloud.' He gestured towards the notebook. 'Anything useful in there?'

'Some names that are probably worth checking out.' She reached over and raised the lid of the laptop. The large screen connected to it turned on and a password box appeared.

Joseph headed over and started to check through the contents of the drawer.

'What are you looking for?' Megan asked.

'Something with Jimmy's password written down on it.'

'Good thinking,' Megan replied, joining in with the hunt.

After a good five minutes of fruitless searching, Joseph finally shook his head. 'It was worth a try. If you could bag the laptop for Amy, she can get one of her team to crack the password and gain access to the system.'

Megan nodded, but her gaze had been drawn to another canvas of an old Ferrari hanging slightly crooked on the wall. She headed over to it and lifted the painting a fraction so she could look behind. Her eyes widened.

'Joseph, you're going to want to see what's behind this,' she said, as she unhooked the painting. She took it down to reveal a safe, its door partially open.

'Now that's more like it...' Joseph quickly pulled on his latex gloves.

The DI carefully opened the safe to reveal large bundles of cash and a stack of gold bars.

'Bloody hell, you would think Jimmy would have been more careful about locking it with all those valuables inside,' Megan said.

Joseph was about to reply when he heard the softest footfall coming from the corridor outside.

He and Megan traded looks and headed for the door. Joseph was the first through and spotted a man creeping away along the corridor, a hood raised over his head. He also had a dispatch rider's bag slung across his back.

'Hey you, stop right there!' Joseph bellowed.

The man burst into a sprint, and the two detectives set off after him. They rushed out of the flat and charged out onto the landing just in time to see the door to the stairwell slamming shut.

'The lift?' Megan said.

'No time!' Joseph replied. He raced through the stairwell door, with Megan right behind him.

The DI leaned over the railing to see the man jumping down the stairs four at a time.

The detectives hurtled down the steps after the intruder, but by the time they'd reached the ground floor and headed out of the building, the man was already sprinting towards the road. Despite both of them being fit, the hooded man reached the wrought iron gate leading to the street a good thirty metres ahead of them. Seconds later, they heard a motorbike roar to life.

Joseph and Megan ran through the gates to see that the man was wearing a black crash helmet with a tinted visor and sitting on a powerful Yamaha motorbike. Spotting them, he revved the bike and roared away down the street before they could reach him.

Megan already had her phone out and took a photo of the fleeing motorbike as the rider turned and they lost sight of him. Joseph was already punching the number for the St Aldates Police Station into his mobile. It was picked up in two rings.

'It's DI Stone, I need a general alert for the North Oxford area for all officers to keep a lookout for a rider on a Yamaha motorbike, registration...' Megan swivelled her phone towards him with a closeup photo of the number plate. 'Bravo, Victor, two-three, Alpha, Tango, November.'

'Understood, sending out the alert now,' a man, who Joseph recognised as the desk sergeant, Jake, replied.

Megan turned to Joseph as he ended the phone call. 'The same motorcyclist who was on the CCTV outside Prestige Vintage Motors?'

'I would lay good money on it. The next question is, why did he break into Jimmy's flat and leave all those valuables behind?'

'Maybe the other thing we should be asking is what was he looking for in that safe, and did he find it?' Megan replied with a tight expression.

CHAPTER SEVEN

CHRIS PINNED Megan's photo of the motorbike and rider onto the evidence board in the incident room. It joined the other pictures Joseph had taken of the framed photographs in Jimmy's flat. To one side, the motto 'To live is to conquer' had also been written on it. On the other side of the board, Chris had also added, 'Connection to the Night Watchmen Crime Syndicate?'

The DCI stepped back to admire his handiwork and turned to Joseph. 'Any update from Amy about the photo Megan took of our mystery motorcyclist?'

The DI dragged his hand back through his hair. 'Apparently, the bike's an early Yamaha YZF-R1 model built around 2002. She told me there aren't many that old still left on the road, thousands at most. A strange choice for someone who presumably wants to try and keep a low profile.'

'Just a shame the rider was using a cloned number plate,' Megan said, as she joined the two detectives.

'That fact alone suggests we're dealing with someone highly organised,' Chris replied. 'And if he is Jimmy's murderer, this was certainly well planned, rather than something that happened on the spur of the moment.'

'I think the release of the flies into the showroom already suggested that,' Joseph said.

'True. But whoever this motorcyclist is, based on the fact that he broke into Jimmy's flat in broad daylight, he's clearly prepared to take risks,' Chris replied.

'So he's someone very cocky,' Megan said.

'Or someone desperate enough to be after something and prepared to take the risk,' Joseph replied. 'It's just a pity we didn't catch up with the toerag.'

'Such is life, sometimes,' Chris replied. 'But even if the rider used cloned plates, we should run a check for a list of owners in the area who own that specific Yamaha motorbike. You never know, we might get lucky. Having said that, I'm not holding out much hope as it was probably stolen, anyway. But the thing I really want to know is what was this man was looking for in Jimmy's flat?'

Joseph nodded. 'And once again, we find ourselves circling back to the motive. The fact the intruder left all those gold bars and money, is an interesting fact in itself.'

'How much was in the safe, anyway?' Megan asked.

'Amy's team recovered north of three million,' Chris said.

Joseph whistled. 'That's a lot of loose change to keep at home. Maybe Jimmy was one of those people who wasn't a fan of banks, or much more likely this confirms an under-world connection to the Night Watchmen, where cash is king.'

'Amy is already ahead of you there, and is running the serial numbers on the notes to check if they correspond to any recorded robberies,' Chris said.

'So does this increase the likelihood the murder is linked to the crime syndicate as well?' Megan asked.

'I'm not sure,' Joseph said. 'After all, it was fairly messy for a professional hit. Much easier for someone to take Harper out with a bullet to the head. Burning him alive feels much more personal.'

'I agree, and certainly Harper's squeaky-clean public image is starting to look pretty thin in light of what we're already digging up,' Chris replied. 'If he was a member of this Night Watchmen syndicate, it's not too much of a stretch to think he might have created a few enemies in his time.'

'Maybe if we learn what the intruder was looking for, we'll also discover the true motive here,' Megan said.

Chris rubbed the back of his neck. 'Absolutely. We need to learn who Jimmy Harper really was, rather than the image he liked to project to the world. As a matter of priority, we should track down any other business associates of his, to see if they have any ideas about who might have wanted him dead.'

He tapped the photo on the evidence board that Joseph had taken of the two other racing drivers posing with Jimmy Harper.

'Another line of enquiry is to look into his obvious passion for motorsports, starting with identifying these two fellows and interviewing them.'

Joseph pulled a face. 'I've already tried HOLMES2, but didn't find a single match.'

The DCI gave Joseph a pointed look as he took him aside, far enough to be out of Megan's hearing.

'Maybe your journalist friend who's investigating the Night Watchmen might be able to cast some light on it? See if they have any information about them, and if they're connected to this crime syndicate.'

'I'll see what I can do,' the DI replied. 'But just to be clear, you do have an idea who my source is?'

'Yes, but let's just say it's less risky for you to talk to her, rather than ask the superintendent about his dear wife's journalistic activities.'

Joseph snorted. 'That's for sure. Okay, let me give my not-so-anonymous source a call and see if I can arrange a meeting with her for some time today.'

Joseph and Kate sat at a table in the modern glass-walled restaurant on top of the Ashmolean Museum, which also boasted a spacious outdoor balcony with a view of the Randolph Hotel opposite. For those who could cope with the mind-melting heat, large white umbrellas had been set up to offer them some protection from the burning sun overhead.

However, Joseph had absolutely no desire to be outside more than was strictly necessary at the moment. Being the sensible born and bred Irishman that he was, the DI had opted to book a table in the air-conditioned interior. As always, the minor Oxford dining gem was packed, even the locals were braving it, along with the many tourists who loved to go there.

Kate tilted her head to one side as she looked across at Joseph over the three-tiered stand filled with sandwiches, cakes, and scones.

'So this is how you decided to try and persuade me to tell you everything I know about Jimmy's involvement with the Night Watchmen?'

'I know you've always been a fan of a good high tea; I thought it was worth a shot.'

Kate held his gaze and then laughed. 'You know me far too well. Anyway, before we get into that, have you seen our daughter recently?'

Joseph sat up. 'Why? Is there a problem with her?'

When Kate hesitated, Joseph's imagination started to spin into overdrive.

'Jesus, something's happened, hasn't it?'

Kate held up her hands. 'No, nothing too bad. She's just

been deliberately giving one of her parents a bit of a wide berth recently.'

A penny started to drop slowly inside the DI's skull and he pointed towards himself. 'Sorry, you mean me?'

'Says the man with the razor-sharp intellect of a detective inspector. Haven't you noticed she's been avoiding you since that meal out you had with her and John last month?'

'Ah, that...'

His ex-wife's gaze sharpened on him. 'Yes, *that*. Seriously, Joseph, did you really have to give John the full-blown frosty treatment?'

The DI recalled the meal out in the Mexican restaurant and had a vague recollection of scowling at John for most of it. Not intentionally, but just that his face seemed to have a mind of its own that evening.

Joseph shrugged. 'Look, it was after a hard day at work and I wasn't exactly in a social mood.'

Kate was already shaking her head at him. 'Whatever the reason, you ended up making John feel about as welcome as a mosquito at a barbecue.'

Joseph grimaced. 'You're exaggerating.'

'Am I? Apparently, Ellie doesn't dare bring her boyfriend within a hundred paces of—and I'm quoting here—"*the grumpy old bastard.*"'

He sucked air through his teeth. 'Ouch, and I obviously mean about the *old* part of that statement, because the rest is a fair comment.'

Kate smiled despite herself. 'Yes, our daughter has always had a knack for hitting below the belt. The question is, what are you going to do about it?'

Joseph met his ex-wife's eyes and nodded. 'Just leave it with me, and I'll try to atone for my sins. I do realise John is a decent guy, it's just...' He waved his hands helplessly in the air.

Kate's eyes narrowed. 'No one is good enough for our daughter?'

Joseph sighed. 'I know, I know. I'll have a word with myself, and I promise I'll sort this out.'

'Please do, for all our sakes, including Amy's. Ellie has also been bending her ear about this.'

He stared at her. 'She has? Amy didn't say anything to me about it.'

'That's because she's trying to keep her nose out of what she considers a family matter.'

Suddenly, Joseph sensed a female conspiracy going on. 'So you've all been talking about me behind my back?'

Kate didn't bother to grace that question with a response and instead just smiled at him.

'Okay, message received and understood. Now that's out of the way, can we move on to less embarrassing matters, if only for me?'

Kate leaned forward, her expression becoming business like. 'First and foremost, like I told you before, Jimmy Harper wasn't what he seemed. The rumour is that Prestige Vintage Motors was a legitimate business, a front to hide where Jimmy really made his money.'

'Go on...' Joseph said, intrigued.

'Do you remember, a few years ago, there was that motor museum over in Somerset that was broken into and several cars were stolen?'

'Yes, and as far as I recall, the vehicles were never tracked down. Why? Are you saying Harper was involved with that somehow?'

'I haven't got any proof, but I do have an anecdotal tale about a man who crossed paths with Jimmy. When this man—let's call him *Brad*—was having some maintenance work done on an Austin-Healey at his local garage, the mechanic discovered the chassis number didn't exist on any vehicle database. However, the car did match the description of one of the cars stolen from the museum, although its body colour had been changed.'

'And the VIN was doctored as well?' Joseph said.

'Exactly, and guess where Brad bought that particular vehicle?'

'Prestige Vintage Motors?'

'In one. Now, being a fine, upstanding citizen and obviously suspecting foul play, Brad contacted Jimmy. At first, Jimmy just fobbed him off, saying that he was obviously mistaken as he had bought the vehicle himself in good faith from a local private owner. Now, it just so happens that Brad's wife, let's call her Angelina—'

Joseph held up his hand. 'As in Brad Pitt and Angelina Jolie? Seriously, Kate? Your aliases for people need a bit more work.'

Kate laughed. 'Maybe they do. Anyway, Angelina just happens to go to the same gym I do in Oxford. And, knowing I was a journalist, she was telling me this all over a coffee after a Yoga session. I promised to do some digging to see what I could find out. I had barely started when I got a phone call from Angelina telling me not to worry, it had all been a big misunderstanding and was sorted.

'But when I pressed her, she finally admitted that Jimmy had written Brad a cheque for twice what he'd paid for the Healey. He told Brad he was going to take it up with the private collector who'd sold it to him. Believing it was an honest mistake, and that Jimmy had done the right thing, Brad decided to let the whole matter drop.'

'But that wasn't enough for you?'

Kate pulled a face at him. 'Of course not. No, my hunch was that Jimmy had got caught out in a lie. He obviously realised it was only a matter of time before Brad went to the police, so he decided to buy Brad off instead.'

'You don't think it could have been an honest mistake, then? After all, he wouldn't be the first car dealer who got caught out like that.'

'That's what I thought at first, but when I decided to do a bit of digging, Jimmy's name kept coming up again and again, often linked to some decidedly dodgy business practices. On the surface, he was a successful businessman. But the more I researched, the more I discovered he wasn't what he first seemed.

'I didn't have to scratch too deeply beneath the surface to discover there was a dark history of failed businesses owned under a shell company. And this is where it gets really interesting. Many of them suffered the same common fate, and considering how Jimmy died, it's one you're going to be particularly interested in.'

'You're not about to tell me they were all burned to the ground, are you?'

Kate nodded. 'And I believe each and every case was investigated for possible insurance fraud. However, the loss adjuster always seemed happy that no fraud had taken place and the insurance company duly paid.'

'Okay... And any thoughts about how any of this might be linked to Jimmy's murder?'

Kate shrugged. 'Maybe a disgruntled former employee who lost their job when one of the other businesses was burned down wanted some payback?'

Joseph sucked the air through his teeth. 'Taking the step from losing your job to murdering someone sounds like a bit of a leap.'

'I know it does, but it's certainly worth considering. Also, if I were you I would start by investigating that shell company I mentioned, Aura Holdings, who owned all of those businesses. I'll hand over everything I've been able to find to link between Aura to the burned-down businesses. There isn't a lot to go on, so I would try tracking down former employees to see what you can find out from them about Jimmy.'

'Chris already has the team looking at employees of Prestige Vintage Motors. I'll suggest he adds Aura Holdings' companies to that list as well.'

'Good, because from what I was able to discover, it turns out Jimmy was a ruthless businessman, who was prepared to do whatever it took to succeed.'

'Don't worry. Leave it with me and, one way or another, we'll get to the bottom of it.'

Kate's brow furrowed. 'We'll see...'

'What's that meant to mean?'

'That I suspect Aura Holdings is part of something much bigger, possibly the Night Watchmen syndicate. Make no mistake, that group has their fingers in a lot of pies. The problem is, I still haven't been able to gather any real evidence to prove it. No one I've interviewed is prepared to go on the record with what they know. But what I can tell you is some very influential people in positions of power are possibly involved.'

'Hang on, what exactly have you got yourself involved in, Kate?' Joseph asked, concern growing inside him.

Kate's expression became drawn. 'Well, I was deep enough for the Night Watchmen to send me an anonymous email threatening my life.'

Joseph stared at her. 'For feck's sake. And why is this the first I'm hearing about it?'

'Because it's the same old. They're just trying to scare me off.'

The DI gave her a sceptical look. 'Maybe. At least tell me that you've discussed this with Derrick?'

Much to his surprise, Kate shook her head.

Joseph pulled his chin into his neck. 'Why the hell not?'

'Let's just say I have my reasons and leave it there. Please, Joseph.'

The DI stared at his ex-wife, but he recognised the set of her jaw. Kate wasn't going to budge on this.

He sighed. 'Okay, but I want you to send me a copy of the email so I can have the technical forensic team look at it. Let's see if they can trace where it was sent from.'

'No need, I already had a friend who works in online security for a bank look into that. It was sent from a temporary email account that was immediately deleted after the message was sent. And before you ask, you won't be able to work out who created the account, because my friend already tried. He said whoever created it had masked their real IP address.'

'Why am I not surprised? At least let me see the message itself.'

'Okay, but keep my name out of it. Derrick can't find out anything about this. You know what he's like. He'd only panic.'

'You do realise it will be hard to keep this from the superintendent since this is an active investigation? I can't promise anything there.'

'Just do what you can.'

Joseph nodded, but he wasn't happy about it. As much as he disliked Derrick, the man still had a right to know that his wife had been threatened.

He held Kate's gaze. 'Please tell me you're going to step back from this investigation?'

'I'm too far down the rabbit hole for that to be an option.'

'Kate, you have to stop. Do you understand me? You're playing with fire here.'

She held his gaze for a moment, and then her shoulders

dropped. 'Fine, but you have to give me the scoop on the Night Watchmen case when it goes public.'

'Done.'

'For now, you can throw me any crumbs you can about Jimmy's murder, which is going to break in the press tomorrow, anyway.'

'Of course.'

Kate smiled and reached over and held Joseph's hand for a moment as an unreadable expression crossed her face. Then she let his hand go again and shook her head.

'Right, time for me to shoot. Deadlines to meet and all that.'

Joseph gestured to all the cakes and sandwiches still left on the stand. 'But we've hardly made a dent in that lot.'

'Then make sure it doesn't go to waste and grab a doggy bag for the team. That bunch of gannets will finish them in seconds.'

The DI nodded. But a sense of confusion filled him. Why was Kate being cryptic? Why was she laughing off a threat to her life like it was no big deal?

Kate pushed a large folder over the table towards Joseph. 'That's a copy of everything I have on Jimmy and the small amount of material I've been able to dig up about the Night Watchmen.'

Joseph took it. 'Thank you for this, and I will do my best to keep your name out of it with Derrick.'

Kate nodded as she grabbed her bag. 'Well, this has been nice.'

'Yes, it has,' he replied.

'Oh, just one last thing. If you want to dig up any real dirt on Jimmy, you could do worse than talking to his third ex-wife, Anna Millington. By all accounts, it was an acrimonious divorce. If anyone might know where the skeletons are buried, and is prepared to talk about them, it will be her. She lives in Great Tew, where a lot of celebrities and the well-heeled live.'

'Thanks for the tip-off, and I'll make sure I follow it up. We need to check where all of his ex-wives were at the time of his death.'

'From what I understand, Jimmy was always ruthless with his financial settlements. They would have had good reason to despise his guts, at least if you listen to the gossip columns.'

'Good to know. Anyway, leave the rest for us and I promise you will get that scoop eventually on anything we find out. But you also need to promise me you really will back off now.'

Kate crossed her heart with her finger. Then she leaned down and kissed his forehead before heading for the door.

The DI already had his phone in his hand to dial Megan before Kate had even left the room.

'Hi, can you track down the address for Anna Millington, who lives in Great Tew? We're going to pay her a little visit,' he said, the moment Megan picked up.

CHAPTER EIGHT

The late-afternoon heat was barely being held at bay by the Volvo V90's air conditioning as Megan drove Joseph through the rolling Cotswolds Hills towards the village of Great Tew. She, at least, seemed to be thoroughly enjoying herself driving the car along the winding lanes. Joseph, less so.

The DC cast him a sideways glance and, spotting the DI's drawn expression, immediately reduced the speed of the car a fraction.

'Sorry, I might have got a bit carried away there.'

'No need to apologise, but as this isn't an emergency, I'd appreciate you keeping the speed down.'

'Of course...' An unreadable look filled Megan's face.

'What?' Joseph asked, sensing there was something the DC wanted to say.

'It's just that Chris has been asking about you never driving any of the police vehicles.'

Apprehension tightened Joseph's gut. 'Shite, has someone tipped him off that I have an issue, then?'

'Maybe, or perhaps he's just picked up on the fact you never seem to take the wheel. Anyway, I covered for you, saying you always let me drive as I'm a bit of a petrolhead. But I just wanted to give you a heads-up that you've fallen into his sights.'

'Thanks...'

This was exactly what Joseph had been dreading. That one day it would come to light he was still carrying the trauma of the car crash that had killed his baby son Eoin. The DI knew it would certainly raise a question mark over his mental health and, through that, his fitness for work. He just prayed Chris wouldn't feel automatically duty-bound to take it to Derrick. If the DCI headed down that route, it would almost certainly spell the end of his career.

It was a good minute before Megan attempted to break the silence with a welcome change of topic. 'I can't believe we're actually going to get to meet Anna Millington. That woman is an absolute legend.'

'I'm sure,' Joseph replied flatly.

The detective had never been one to subscribe to the celebrity culture many people seemed to swear by these days. In his book, folk were just folk. Some were decent, some not, some had lots of money, and some needed to be locked away for a very long time indeed. Occasionally, as in the case of Jimmy Harper, they had a picture emerging of a man who might have been all of those things.

They descended a hill bounded by trees, and passing a sign for Great Tew, headed towards a very picturesque Cotswold village straight out of a tourist guidebook. In the morning sunlight, the sandstone walls of the houses glowed with a golden pink, adding to their charm.

'That's pretty then—it's little wonder celebrities flock here,' Megan said. 'Apparently, the really rich ones have built huge mansions around the edge of the village.'

'And Anna Millington lives in one of those?' Joseph said.

'As successful as she is, I don't think even a sitcom star earns enough to afford something like that. No, she lives nearer the village centre where the cottages are far less eye-wateringly priced.'

'And you know the cost of the house, because?' the DI asked, casting her a curious glance.

'Let's just say I'm a bit nosy and checked out properties on Rightmove before we set off.'

'Next, you'll be telling me you want to relocate out here.'

Megan shrugged. 'A woman can dream. I can certainly think of far worse places to live.'

They reached the bottom of the hill and turned onto a road leading past a curving green surrounded by mature trees, their leaves starting to yellow due to a month of intense drought. Most of the front gardens had also suffered thanks to the hosepipe ban the water companies had been forced to impose across the country. That seemed particularly incongruous to Joseph when, only earlier that year, Oxford had been dealing with major floods whilst they'd been investigating the Joanna Keene murders.

Groups of people were sitting at tables outside a café, come-bakery, come-tearoom, come-*you know you want to give us your money*. Based on the queue out of the door, it certainly looked like the business was doing a roaring trade.

'Oh, that's Quince and Clover,' Megan said. 'Maybe we could grab some lunch after we finish interviewing Anna?'

'So let me get this right, your homework for this interview with Anna Millington basically comprised checking on property prices and the best places to eat?'

'Among other things. Besides, knowing how much you love your grub, I thought I'd see if there was anywhere nearby we could grab a bite to eat. So I looked up Quince and Clover on Tripadvisor and their fish stew sounded like just the sort of thing you'd love.'

'I appreciate you looking out for my stomach, but I think maybe something more along the lines of a salad in this heat. Anyway, isn't it a bit soon to be thinking about lunch yet? It's only eleven o'clock.'

Megan shrugged. 'What can I say, but that I have hollow legs?'

Joseph shook his head. 'I've certainly been starting to have my suspicions about that.'

Megan slowed the Volvo to a crawl as hordes of people—presumably tourists based on the fact they had their cameras and phones out—were blocking the road and taking pictures of absolutely everything.

The DC drove slowly past a very busy pub. That was somewhat surprising as it even midday yet.

Just ahead of them, blocking the lane, was a white Land Rover with an unlit blue light bar on the roof and a fluorescent green and blue stripe along its side.

'Is that a police vehicle?' Megan asked, peering at it with a slightly confused expression.

'No, just a vehicle meant to look like one to a casual glance,' the DI replied with a scowl.

A man with a neat beard and mirrored sunglasses, a radio clipped to his belt, was already getting out of the passenger door to wave the detectives' vehicle down.

'Oh Jesus, a wannabe policeman who's watched one too many cop movies,' Joseph said.

Megan nodded. 'Ah yes, I read about the local security force here. Apparently, the rich homeowners banded together to pay for it to keep the undesirables away.'

'But here we are anyway.'

Megan snorted as she slowed the Volvo to a stop and lowered the window as the security guard approached their vehicle.

'How can I help?' she asked, with her best winning smile.

The man peered over the top of his Ray-Ban Aviator sunglasses at them. 'This is a private road and unregistered vehicles aren't allowed access without prior permission.'

Joseph resisted the urge to roll his eyes and dug out his warrant card. 'Are you sure about that?'

The security guard's gaze skimmed over the ID. 'I'm afraid there's no exceptions, even for the police, Detective Inspector Stone.'

The contrarian in Joseph had to bite his tongue to hold back his ready response, *Are you really sure you want to test me about that?* Most security guards were fine to deal with, but some were right royal pains in the arse. They often thought they could lord it over everyone, including the actual police.

He was getting ready to tell this jumped-up little fecker exactly what he thought of him, but Megan was already nodding.

'No problem, but is it okay for us to park behind you and head in on foot?' she said.

The eejit flashed her a smile. 'Absolutely no problem, and thank you for understanding.'

A few moments later the two detectives were on foot, heading up the lane. To their left was a line of stone cottages, many of which had window boxes filled with flowers, and despite the heat, bees buzzed over them, going about their business.

Joseph glanced back at the security guard, who was watching them head away. 'I have to say I admire your restraint with that arsewipe and his puffed-up sense of importance.'

'Oh, don't worry, I was just willing the guy to make an excuse for us to arrest him for intentionally obstructing an officer under Section 89 of the Police Act 1996. But then I would have missed the chance to try out that posh café and that would be a crime in itself.'

The DI laughed. 'Yes, one has to take into consideration the bigger picture in important matters, such as when to follow the letter of the law.'

Megan grinned at him as she checked her notebook and pointed to the blue door of a picturesque cottage.

'This is Anna Millington's house.' She unlatched the front gate and knocked on the door.

'Just coming,' a woman's voice called from inside.

They heard the approach of feet and the front door swung open.

Not knowing who the actress was, Joseph had been expecting to see a glamorous woman, probably wearing a designer trouser suit, along with diamond earrings and matching necklace. Maybe even sipping a cheeky early morning cocktail.

What he wasn't expecting was a woman in her forties, wearing dungarees and carrying a trowel in her hand. Her hair was loosely piled on top of her head, and she had a streak of mud across her chin.

'Anna Millington?' Joseph asked.

'Indeed, it is I,' Anna said, doing a little curtsy. 'Sorry, I was just repotting some dahlias, so you'll have to excuse my appearance.' She pulled off her gloves and extended her hand. 'You must be DI Stone and DC Anderson.'

'Yes, that's right. Would it be alright if we came in?' Megan asked.

'Where are my manners, but of course.' Anna ushered them into a small living room. 'You'll have some tea? If so, will Lady Grey suit? I always think it's a perfect mid-morning cuppa.'

'If it's not any bother?' Megan said.

'Of course not. And I have a fresh coffee and walnut cake

from Mulberry and Brambles down the road, if it's not too early to indulge?'

'It's never too early,' Megan replied with a small smile, ignoring the amused look Joseph was giving her.

A short while later, Anna was sitting with the detectives as they sipped their tea.

'First of all, we would like to extend our condolences about your ex-husband,' Joseph said.

Anna bit her lip. 'Yes, what an absolutely horrifying way to die. Have you any idea about who might have done this to him?'

'You think he was murdered, then?' Joseph asked, not wanting to give anything away.

Anna pointed to the headline 'Local car Dealer Found Dead in Suspicious Circumstances' splashed across the front page of the Oxford Gazette.

'I agree with the journalist who wrote that. Jimmy would never have committed suicide. He had far too big a zest for life. Besides, who would want to kill themselves in such an awful way?'

Joseph nodded. 'In that case, are you aware of any enemies that Jimmy might have had?'

The woman sighed. 'I'm afraid Jimmy had plenty. Although he was a darling man most of the time, there was also a ruthless streak to him, especially when it came to business. He was one of those people who wasn't afraid to do whatever it took to succeed, often at the expense of his employees. He wasn't always well-liked as a boss.'

Joseph nodded as Megan took notes. 'So do you think the way he treated people in his work could be related to what happened to him?' he asked.

'I'm not sure anyone hated Jimmy enough to burn him to death... Although...' Her eyebrows drew together.

'What is it?'

'Some of his business associates weren't always exactly savoury, if you catch my drift.'

'In what way?' Megan asked.

'Let's just say he had far too many connections with people on the wrong side of the law. And before you ask, no, I can't give you any details. Jimmy tended to keep his business dealings secret from me. He had his personal life, then his business one, and those two worlds were kept separate.'

Joseph leaned forward a fraction. 'In that case, do you have any idea why anyone might want to break into his flat in Oxford?'

Anna stared at them. 'When did this happen, exactly?'

'Yesterday, and whoever it was targeted the safe in Jimmy's office. They may have taken something from it. Do you have any idea what Jimmy might have kept in there?'

'From memory, besides money, he also kept an old business ledger in it.'

'To do with Prestige Vintage Motors?' Megan asked

'No, those were handled by his business accountants. All I know is Jimmy locked himself away in his home office to update that ledger after he'd had his meetings with those less savoury acquaintances. My guess is it was the sort of accounts he didn't want the taxman, or even the police, to know about.' She raised her eyebrows at them.

Joseph peered at her. 'Are you saying Jimmy ran a crooked business?'

Anna gave the DI a wary look. 'I suppose it can't hurt telling you as the poor man has passed. Look, I can't be certain, but I suspect Jimmy wasn't always above board. I mean, who has clandestine meetings in the middle of the night?'

'I see...' the DI replied, exchanging a look with Megan. As Anna had been speaking, he'd been formulating a mental image of a criminal who, thanks to a veneer of respectability, had managed to fly under the police radar.

'So why do you think someone might want to steal this ledger of Jimmy's, if that was indeed what was taken?' he asked.

'I honestly have no idea, but a good place to start might be to head over to one of the vintage track days they hold at Branton. Jimmy used to spend most of his time there when he wasn't at work and always updated that ledger the moment he got back. My guess is that's where a number of those business deals used to happen. On at least one occasion, I went into his home office without knocking and found him counting stacks of banknotes from a briefcase filled with cash after a race.'

'Did he now?' Joseph said, as Megan scribbled down that golden nugget of information.

'Yes, if memory serves me correctly, there was a big meet-up on the first Saturday of each month,' Anna said.

A thought occurred to Joseph, and he took out his phone to pull up the photo of Jimmy and two other race drivers. He turned the screen towards Anna.

'Do you happen to know who these two men are?'

Anna smiled. 'Of course. We had them and their wives over for dinner lots of times. That's Matthew Forbes and Ralph Richards. They both run respectable businesses. An award-winning gastropub in Ralph's case, and Matthew runs a garage specialising in vintage car restorations. Jimmy used to work with him all the time to supply the cars for the showroom. Matthew and Ralph took their own vintage cars to Branton to race with Jimmy.'

Joseph nodded as things started to slot together in his head. 'That's very useful to know.' Now to see if Anna herself could be ruled out as a suspect. 'There is one personal question I hope you don't mind me asking. But it would help us build up a picture about what Jimmy was really like in his personal life.'

Anna's gaze tightened on him. 'You want to know why we got divorced?'

'Exactly, as long as you're happy to share that information with us?'

'Of course. We had a bad falling out over the usual sort of thing that breaks up a marriage and ends up in an acrimonious divorce. Having said that, I still have feelings for Jimmy and will be attending his funeral next week.'

'Sorry, what's the *usual sort of thing* to break up a marriage, if you don't mind me asking?' Megan asked, pen poised.

'The same old story. Jimmy's eyes strayed to a younger model, and he had an affair with her. That, and the fact he tried to wriggle out of the financial settlement after our divorce, aside, I still want you to catch the bastard who did this. No one deserves to die like that.'

'Don't worry, we're going to put every effort into bringing Jimmy's killer to justice,' Joseph replied. 'Finally, I hate to ask you my next question, but I have to do so for the investigation. Where were you at the time of Jimmy's death?'

Anna stared at him. 'Seriously, you think I could have murdered him?'

'No, but I still need to know where you were and also if anyone can vouch for you?'

'Of course...' The actress' face flamed. 'I'm afraid it's a bit embarrassing. You see, I was with Tony Albright, a director on the sitcom I'm in.'

'I don't see why that's embarrassing,' Megan said.

'Let's just say he isn't single and leave it there. Anyway, we were in a London hotel. I'll give you Tony's and the hotel's numbers so you can check, but please be as discreet as you can when you talk to them.'

'You can rely on us,' Joseph said, turning to Megan. 'I think that covers everything.'

'Yes...' The DC gave Anna an embarrassed look. 'I hope this isn't too cheeky a thing to ask, but would it be possible to have an autograph? I'm a bit of a fan.'

Joseph scowled at Megan. 'You shouldn't bother Miss Millington with something like that.'

Anna made a dismissive gesture with her hands. 'Fiddlesticks. Always happy to sign an autograph.' She stood and crossed to a bureau. The actress took out a studio-taken black-and-white photo of herself and began writing on it with a flourish before handing it over to Megan, who was now beaming at the woman.

What am I going to do with you? Joseph thought, smiling at the same time.

The truth was, now that they had solid leads to follow up, thanks to Anna, he was in an excellent mood. He had no doubt her story would check out as to her whereabouts, but it was the insight into Jimmy's off-the-book business ventures that had him most intrigued.

Yes, today had turned out to be a very good one indeed. In fact, he was in such a good mood he thought he might treat Megan to lunch from that posh place down the road.

CHAPTER NINE

THE FOLLOWING MORNING, Chris called a meeting to update everyone on their progress with the investigation, specifically to highlight what Joseph and Megan had found out from Anna. Jimmy's three ex-wives, including Anna Millington, had now been eliminated as suspects as their alibis had checked out, and their pictures removed from the board.

As the detectives waited for the DCI to kick things off, Ian was doing the rounds in the room, offering officers the contents of a large Tupperware container. Joseph had already clocked other people peering inside it when it was proffered to them and quickly shaking their heads.

'Oh God,' Joseph muttered.

'What?' Megan asked, sitting next to him.

'Ian's brought some food in from home to share round.'

The DC gave him a confused look. 'That's nice of him, isn't it?'

'Trust me, it's never a good thing.'

Ian, having been rejected by three people in a row, headed towards them.

'Heads up, get your excuses ready,' Joseph whispered.

Ian arrived before them and tilted the box to reveal at least two dozen chocolate cornflake cakes inside.

'Those look great,' Megan said, despite Joseph's warning.

Ian beamed at her. 'Don't they? They're homemade. Go on, take a couple. Everyone else seems to be on a diet right now, so there's plenty left, and I know you have a sweet tooth.'

Even Joseph had to admit they didn't look too toxic.

Megan peered at the cakes, and then with a slight shrug, took one and, much to Joseph's horror, took a bite.

Her expression morphed from somebody expecting to suck on a lemon, to one of pleasant surprise.

'Not bad, not bad at all.' She reached in and helped herself to three more.

Ian turned his attention to Joseph. 'It would be rude not to.'

The DI wavered, bitter experience battling it out in his mind with the thumbs up Megan was currently giving him. Then he finally crumbled and took one. Tentatively, he took the smallest bite, like a man sampling something he wasn't sure wasn't rat poison. However, much to his surprise, it tasted like something that could have come straight from the in-store bakery at the supermarket.

He nodded. 'These are actually really good, Ian.'

'Told you. Go on, have a few more.'

Joseph, still bathing in the glow of being pleasantly surprised, took two more. 'I have to say this is your best baking effort yet.'

'Oh, it wasn't me or my wife, the kids actually made them at school yesterday.'

The DI stopped mid-bite, his mouth full of half-chewed cornflake cake, as if he'd just been told that someone had slipped ground glass into it.

'You don't say...'

Megan gave him a questioning look as she finished off her first one and set to work on the second.

Joseph was suddenly desperate to spit out the mouthful, but Ian seemed determined to hover in front of them. The DI had been in some tight corners in his time, and he knew when he had no choice. This was absolutely one of those moments.

Under Ian's watchful eye, he forced himself to chew. But as he got over the horror of the other DI's kids having made them, and God knew where their hands had been, he had to admit they still tasted alright.

At that moment, Chris entered the room and headed over to the whiteboard, a marker pen already in hand. 'Okay, let's get this briefing started.'

Thankfully, Ian took that as his cue to head back to his seat with the rest of the cornflake cakes.

Megan shot Joseph a questioning look. 'What's going on with you? You've got a face like a dog chewing a wasp.'

Before Joseph could reply, he bit down on something hard. No, not hard, but bendy, and definitely not edible. He checked to see that Ian wasn't watching, hooked his finger into his mouth and pulled out a small fingernail... *A child's fingernail.*

He wasn't sure if it was the sheer shock that triggered the physical reaction, but suddenly his body decided that the gag reflex was required in an extreme situation such as this. Somehow, with sheer force of will, he managed to override it and, with a Herculean effort, swallowed the mouthful down.

'For feck's sake,' he whispered, holding the fingernail up for Megan to inspect.

His reaction was nothing compared to Megan's, whose face paled, then went a greenish-grey colour. As Chris got ready to begin, she quickly reached over to her desk, grabbed a tissue from a box, and then, like any sane person would have done, spat the rest of the cornflake cake into it.

Ian, having missed their performances, glanced over and gave Joseph a wide smile, who only managed a weak one in response.

Never ever again, Joseph thought to himself.

'Okay, I just wanted to get everyone up to speed with the status of our investigation so far,' Chris said, totally unaware that two of his officers had almost just gagged to death. 'To begin with, the technical forensic team has cracked the password on Jimmy Harper's laptop. That's the good news. The bad news is they found absolutely nothing of any real interest. Ian, do you want to update everyone about your interviews with the employees who worked at Prestige Vintage Motors?'

'Sure,' Ian said, as he swallowed the mouthful of cornflake, presumably body detritus and all. 'Jimmy wasn't exactly a well-loved boss,' the DI continued. 'He often made his staff work overtime without pay, and always found a way to squirm out of paying performance bonuses he'd promised them.'

'Do you think one could have disliked him enough to kill him?' one of the detectives in the room asked.

'That's not out of the question, and we're going to be checking on each of their alibis, but my instinct at the moment is no. Although they all grumbled about him, they still loved their job and seemed genuinely horrified by what had happened to Jimmy. Also, none of them owns a motorbike or has a license for one, making it less likely that they're the person we're looking for.'

Chris nodded, and gestured towards the screen where the photo Megan had taken of the motorcyclist flashed up on-screen.

'As I'm sure you're aware by now, Joseph and Megan disturbed this man, who had broken into the safe in Jimmy's flat,' Chris said. 'He fled the scene and managed to escape on the sports motorbike pictured, an old Yamaha YZF-R1 fitted with false plates. We ran it through the database search and checked with the few people across Oxfordshire who own one, but there were no matches. Many of the bikes were rusting in garages and weren't rideable, or had been scrapped. That means that this particular bike is owned by someone outside the county, or possibly more likely, in the light of Jimmy's murder, was stolen. The photo of the rider has been analysed by Amy's team, and biometric measurements of his limbs and torso were taken to give us an estimated height is around five foot ten inches tall, with an average build.'

Sue pulled a face. 'So that's about a third of the men in the country, then.'

'I agree. It's not a lot to go on, but it's something. Amy also had her team compare this photo to the one captured by the CCTV camera outside Prestige Vintage Motors. I'm sure none of you will be surprised to hear the biometric data they were able to extract from that image is a match for the intruder Joseph and Megan disturbed in Jimmy's flat.'

Looking at the photo, Joseph felt an acute sense of frustration. To think that they'd almost had the bastard in their hands, but he'd still managed to get away, was beyond galling.

'At this point, I'm going to hand over to Joseph. He and Megan had a productive interview with Anna Millington, Jimmy's ex-wife, which has opened up some new lines of enquiry. But I'm going to let Joseph brief you about that himself.'

Chris nodded to the DI, who stood and headed to the front.

'Yes, our meeting with Miss Millington was very informative. The first new piece of information is that we now believe we know what the intruder was looking for in his apartment. It turns out there was a business ledger kept in the safe.'

'Hang on, why didn't he use accounting software like every

other small business owner in the twenty-first century?' Sue asked.

'Exactly. From what Anna told us, it sounds as though these particular accounts were for extracurricular business activities that occasionally required large amounts of cash,' Joseph said. 'And it's there we have a possible lead. Apparently, Jimmy Harper spent a lot of his time at Branton racetrack, where two persons of interest also attended, namely Matthew Forbes and Ralph Richards. Whether they were also involved with Harper in his more shady businesses and this mysterious Night Watchmen group, we have yet to find out.'

Chris nodded as he picked up the remote and clicked it. The photos of Jimmy, Forbes, and Richards were displayed, with their names added beneath each.

'We've already run a background check on these other two men, who both have clean records,' Chris said.

'However, it gets particularly interesting in the case of Forbes,' Joseph added. 'He runs a garage, restoring classic vehicles that he supplied to Jimmy. Evidence has emerged linking his garage to the break-in of a motor museum in Somerset. You don't have to be a rocket scientist to work out that if cars were being stolen to order, Forbes probably doctored the vehicles' VINs before selling them to Jimmy, maybe splitting the proceeds with him.'

'Okay, that I get, but how does Richards fall into any of this?' Ian asked.

'We currently have no idea, other than he runs a gastropub in the Cotswolds,' Joseph replied. 'That business could, of course, be a front for criminal activity, just as Jimmy's showroom seems to have been.'

'Right, but going back to Forbes... stealing stolen cars is one thing, but are you suggesting that he might have had a reason to murder Harper?' Ian asked. 'If so, that's a pretty big leap for your average criminal.'

'Maybe we're not dealing with our average criminals here,' Megan commented. 'Perhaps this was some feud that got out of hand.'

'Exactly my thoughts as well,' Chris said. 'That's why I'm going to authorise an undercover operation at the Branton Classic Car Track Day tomorrow. I've already entered my Triumph TR4 as part of our cover story. Thankfully, we're in luck because both Forbes and Richards have entered their vehicles into races this weekend. Joseph and Megan, you'll be joining me.'

'Wouldn't it be easier to just go and interview these men?' Sue asked.

'Normally, I would say yes, but as we're dealing with suspects here, we need to tread carefully not to tip them off that we're looking into them. Anna Millington said she saw a large amount of cash in Harper's home office after a race at Branton. That's why I think we need to start by attending the next race, this Saturday. One of the best places to find out all the gossip at any race is in the pitlane. That's why Joseph and Megan will be coming with me to poke around, and see what they can dig up about Harper, Forbes, and Richards. However, to make sure we don't draw any suspicion whilst there, I'll be out on the track racing in my own car.'

'Fancy you drawing the short straw,' Megan said, giving the DCI a pointed look.

There was a lot of chuckling in the room, including from Chris. 'As they say, it's a tough job, but somebody's got to do it.'

Ian's hand shot up into the air. 'If you want a wingman for that, I'll be happy to oblige, boss.'

It was no surprise to Joseph that Ian was volunteering, as the man had always fancied himself as an amateur racing driver.

'Thanks for the offer, but I think I've got that angle covered,' Chris replied.

Ian's hand dropped and he slumped slightly in his chair, looking like a lad who hadn't been picked for the football team.

'Right, that's it for now. I'll be updating the board with the latest evidence. Meanwhile, everyone keep digging. Somewhere buried in Jimmy's past has to be a clue as to why he was murdered. So let's do our best to discover what that is sooner rather than later.'

As the meeting broke up, Megan turned to Joseph. 'Although a track day is certainly my sort of thing, it's not what I imagine your idea of a good time is.'

Joseph shrugged. 'I don't mind being a spectator. But I have to say I'm surprised Chris didn't pick Ian to attend the race day, as the man is a real petrolhead.'

'As this is an investigation, perhaps the DCI thought Ian would get a bit distracted by all the shiny cars,' Megan replied. 'That aside, I'd take it as a vote of confidence that Chris thinks we can do a good job digging up the dirt on Jimmy and his associates.'

'You're probably right.'

Megan gestured to her three remaining cornflake cakes on her desk. 'I don't know about you, but there is no way I'm eating any more of those. The thing is, if I just put them in the bin, I'm worried Ian might spot them and I don't want to hurt his feelings.'

'In that case, I suggest we pop out to that mobile barista, The Steaming Cup, and get rid of the chocolate puke grenades in a bin outside. That is, whilst we're cleansing our palates with a cup of good, strong coffee.'

'God, yes,' Megan said, pocketing her phone as they quickly headed for the door before Ian could offer them any more of the cornflake cakes that really needed a food hygiene warning slapped on them.

They were about to leave St Aldates when Joseph almost ran headlong into John coming in through the door. The PC quickly stood aside and held the door open for the two detectives.

Joseph said the first thing that came to his mind. 'How are you doing, PC Thorpe?'

'Good, sir. You?' John replied.

'Oh, I'm grand.' Then all Joseph could think to do was nod to the PC and follow Megan out. When he chanced a look at her, she had an amused expression on her face.

'What?' the DI asked once they were safely out of earshot.

'Just that your interpersonal skills with your potential son-in-law could do with a bit of work,' Megan replied.

'Oh for feck's sake, has someone said something?'

Megan grinned and drew an imaginary zip across her mouth.

'Bloody female conspiracies,' Joseph muttered, as they headed away from the police station.

CHAPTER TEN

LATER THAT EVENING, as Joseph cycled home along the canal towpath, he was enjoying a considerable sense of lightness. He was certain they were on the right track with the case, and even the relentless heat couldn't spoil his good mood.

In response to the stifling temperature, many of the other boat owners had set up camp on the embankment to avoid being baked alive in their cabins. The DI had already passed at least six smoking barbecues, most with the inevitable sausages and burgers on them. The more adventurous culinary creators included everything from filleted legs of lamb to whole aubergines, their skin blackening, goat cheese ready to be smothered over their soft, cooked flesh when they were cracked open. He made a mental note to try that last one out sometime.

All the food smelled insanely good and if Joseph hadn't been hungry before, he certainly was now. He also needed to get something in his stomach to counteract the bacterial gut infection probably brewing thanks to Ian's kids' bloody cornflake cakes. Whisky would probably be the ticket, and maybe he'd order in a seriously strong chilli, courtesy of a Deliveroo rider, to counteract the imminent threat to his life.

Joseph reached *Tús Nua* and pulled up. He was greeted by brief barks of welcome from both White Fang and Max. Both dogs were crashed out on the roof of Dylan's narrowboat, *Avalon*. They were too hot to even bother to trot over for their customary treats Joseph kept in a tin in the cockpit of his narrowboat.

All the windows of Dylan's boat had been flung wide open, and it was from there an excellent curry smell was drifting out to put the efforts of all the barbecuers to shame. The great man himself emerged from *Avalon*, wearing an apron, his head soaked in sweat.

Dylan gave Joseph a cheery wave. 'Aha, I was keeping an eye out for your return. I hope you're hungry. I've cooked enough curry for six.'

'That sounds grand, but I'm not sure curry is quite the thing to be eating in this heatwave.'

'Trust me, it's exactly the right thing. It makes you sweat, and that helps cool your skin down. It's India's national cuisine for a good reason.'

'Fair point, but surely curry isn't your usual style?'

'You can blame the Indian Cooking school course for that. I felt it was about time to expand my culinary repertoire and branch out.'

'Knowing your already excellent skills in the kitchen, I'm all in. What's on the menu for tonight, then?'

'A spicy chicken dhansak, with a vegetable biryani, onions bhajis and also some homemade naan I'm trying to cook on my gas barbecue.'

Joseph made a show of smacking his lips. 'You really are the best neighbour a man could have. Shall I bring the beers?'

The professor shook his head. 'No, I've got that covered too with a specially selected gin off my bucket list.'

Joseph's brow creased. 'Gin with curry—seriously?'

'Prepare to be pleasantly surprised, dear friend. Gin can be a great pairing with spicy food. And I've selected none other than one from your home country. It's an Irish gin called Bertha's Revenge.'

Joseph pulled a face. 'Sounds dangerously like a recipe for Gandhi's revenge.'

Dylan laughed. 'I hope not. It's actually a small batch, Irish milk gin. It's very soft on the palate and can help defuse a curry's sting.'

The DI pulled a sceptical face, but nodded. 'Fancy, my fellow countrymen and women have managed to make gin from milk. Why am I not surprised?'

'It definitely shows a certain level of inventiveness,' Dylan replied. 'Anyway, I thought rather than eat here, we'd eat al fresco over on Christchurch Meadow where it's a bit cooler than round here.'

Joseph shot his friend a look. 'A curry picnic? Have you already made a start on that milk gin?'

Dylan chuckled. 'Not yet, but I've got a stack of brand new tin Tiffin boxes so we can do it in proper Indian style.'

The DI raised his eyebrows. 'Life is certainly never boring with you around, Professor. Give me two ticks to grab a shower and some fresh clothes, then I'll be with you.'

Joseph and Dylan sat on a park bench overlooking Christchurch Meadow. On the far side of the meadow, the college was bathed in sunlight. The deer there had sought sanctuary in the shade of a large oak tree in the middle of the meadow, as the heat of the day started to give way to evening. Everyone they had passed had the mellow look of people blessed by the long summer day's embrace.

'Okay, I think I rather approve of your choice of location,' Joseph said, enjoying the shade from the broad tree overhead.

'It's not bad, and only allows in a very exclusive clientele,' Dylan replied.

The professor opened up the stack of silver Tiffin tins he'd been carrying. Thanks to the tantalising smell of the steam curling out of them, Joseph's hunger pangs intensified. It demanded considerable willpower on his part, not to grab a tin from his friend and dive straight in. Instead, he took out the plates and cutlery from his rucksack, almost like a man who wasn't actually starving.

That job done, the DI sat back on the bench and took in the idyllic scene. The Oxford colleges, including Christchurch before them, always looked glorious in the sunlight, thanks to their Cotswold stone construction.. It was little wonder that so many tourists flocked to the city to see the sights.

'Don't stand on ceremony; help yourself,' Dylan said.

Joseph didn't need to be told twice. He quickly piled his plate high with the biryani and dhansak, along with a perfectly cooked naan, and onion bhajis.

The professor poured two milk gins, topped off with a dash of tonic, ice cubes from a cool bag, and a bay leaf.

'Go on then, let me know what you think of the curry.'

Joseph broke off a piece of the naan, used it to scoop up a generous portion of the dhansak, and popped it into his mouth.

His first impression was that it tasted absolutely delicious. Then, his mouth was on fire. He flapped his hand in front of his face as chillies tried to burn their way through the lining of his mouth, and briefly considered rushing to the nearby Isis and diving in headfirst.

The professor grinned and quickly handed Joseph one of the generous gin and tonics he'd just poured.

Thankfully for Joseph, who now had tears streaming down

his face, the relief was instantaneous. He had a vague impression of the gin's creamy flavour as it extinguished the bonfire his mouth had just turned into. He wiped the monsoon's worth of sweat that had suddenly soaked his brow and finally found the ability to talk again.

'For feck's sake, you could have warned me.'

Dylan's grin widened. 'A bit spicy for your palate, then?'

'I love a bit of chilli as much as the next man, but molten-core-of-a-planet hot, I don't think so.'

'Ah, yes, I did wonder if I overdid it a bit with those Bird's Eye chillies. I'll tone it down next time, but if you mix the biryani in, it will help defuse it.'

'Yes, and more of that gin please to help stop me spontaneously combusting.'

Dylan poured the DI a fresh glass. 'The whey they use during the distilling process certainly helps to reduce the chillies' sting.' The professor then proceeded to pop a large mouthful of dhansak into his mouth and chewed it. 'Not bad, not bad at all, if I say so myself.'

Joseph watched in disbelief when the top of his friend's head wasn't blown clean off his shoulders. 'You are certainly made of sterner stuff than me.'

The professor chuckled as they both tucked into the food.

Joseph gradually began to realise just how delicious the curry was, at least once he had the ratio of a large amount of biryani to a small amount of dhansak, worked out.

'This is absolutely cracking,' he finally said, really beginning to enjoy the curry.

The professor nodded as he watched a magnificent stag that had taken shelter under the tree stand up, its ears flicking. 'Yes, I'm rather pleased with it, but maybe I won't offer you a vindaloo when I try to make that next.'

'I think my stomach and no doubt my arse would both appreciate that.'

Dylan chuckled. 'Message received. Anyway, how are things going on the Jimmy Harper case? It sounds like a bad business, with its possible connection to that crime syndicate.'

Joseph turned to stare at him. 'And how do you know about that?'

'Ellie told me when I saw her yesterday.'

'But how did she...?' His words trailed away. 'Kate must have told her.'

'How did you guess?'

'Because it's always been the same. Even if Kate is prepared to sit on a story when it comes to Derrick, the same rules don't seem to apply when it comes to our daughter.'

'Just like you use me as your confidant during investigations, then,' the professor observed.

'Ah yes, you may have a point there. You're certainly my go-to person when I need to pick someone's brain about a case, especially when you always come up with such a unique way to look at them.'

'As always, I'm delighted to be able to help. So, why haven't I heard anything about this latest case directly from your good self, yet? I am your unpaid research assistant, after all.'

'Only because we're still at an early stage of the investigation, trying to discover all the key facts. We're also still attempting to put together a full profile of the victim, but that's trickier than usual because he kept what looks like his criminal side-business dealings well hidden. Having said that, it wouldn't hurt if you could do a bit of digging into his background for me. You've always had a knack for being able to find information we would have otherwise missed.'

'No problem. I'll see what I can discover. Any ideas about a motive yet?'

'Take your pick from a criminal business partner Harper may have crossed, to an ex-employee he may have pissed off, to something to do with this Night Watchmen crime syndicate he had possible links to.'

'So, to summarise, you're basically saying you have no idea?'

Joseph sighed. 'That's about the sum of it, and the possible involvement of this Night Watchmen has only complicated matters for our investigation. And here's the thing that's got me really worried. Kate's investigation into their activity got the syndicate's attention. She received an email threatening her life if she continued to stick her nose into their business.'

Dylan stared at him. 'You're joking?'

'I wish I were. The problem is, Kate doesn't seem to be taking it seriously.'

'Has she said anything to Derrick?'

'No, not yet. She thinks he'll go into a blind panic, which is probably the truth. But she's promised me she's going to back off until we've completed our side of the investigation. For all we know, it might have been Jimmy himself threatening her, and with him no longer around, maybe the problem has just gone away.'

'You do realise that sounds like wishful thinking?'

Joseph let out a long sigh. 'I know, but I'm hoping we'll get to the bottom of it by the end of our investigation.'

'Then I'll keep my fingers crossed that's how it works out, especially for Kate's sake. But if it doesn't, you need to be prepared to go behind Kate's back and take this directly to Derrick.'

'Kate won't like that one little bit.'

'I know, but as her husband, he deserves to know.' Dylan gave Joseph a pointed look.

The DI sighed and nodded. 'Yes, you're right, of course. But for now, let's hope that Kate just keeps her word and backs off.'

The two men fell silent as they watched a stag graze on the meadow's parched grass.

A thought popped into Joseph's mind about something Dylan had said. 'How come you saw Ellie, anyway? Kate told me she's been deliberately avoiding me for weeks over my supposedly hostile attitude towards John.'

Dylan grimaced. 'Sorry, I wasn't meant to say anything. That just sort of slipped out.'

Joseph's forehead ridged. 'Don't worry, Kate's already lectured me to death about Ellie's boyfriend.'

The professor's frown grew deeper. 'Although that was discussed, it wasn't the reason she came over to see me.'

'Go on...'

'She wanted to chat to me about whether she should drop out of the Blavatnik School of Government.'

'Bloody hell. Since when? Kate didn't mention anything about that.'

'That's because she doesn't know. To use Ellie's vernacular, she said you would both "go mental" if you found out.'

'Bloody right, I will. Ellie can't drop out. She'll be starting her final year next term. She can't throw her degree away this close to the finish line.'

'I know, I know, which is exactly what I told her. And the good news is, John didn't agree with her either. He pretty much said exactly what you just did and, with my help, managed to talk her down.'

'Then thank Christ for that. At least she's managed to choose a boyfriend with his head screwed onto his shoulders.'

The professor glanced at Joseph from the corner of his eye. 'Yes, and about that... Ellie also spoke to me about you and John.'

'Ah, right. Another lecture, is it?'

'Absolutely. It's my duty as your friend to point out when

you're getting something badly wrong. And you are in this case. Every time I've seen you with John, you've always given him the third degree as though he was a suspect in a case, rather than a police officer who has big enough testicles to dare to date your daughter.'

'Big nads, is it? You make me sound like the father from hell.'

'Have you seen your face when you're with the poor chap? Any man with a lesser backbone would have been running for the hills long before now. If nothing else, I think the fact he hasn't, means he deserves your respect.'

The DI took a sip of his gin. 'I know, I know. And like I said, Kate already read me the riot act about the way I've been behaving towards him.'

'Yes, from what I gather, Ellie has been gathering the troops to her cause.'

'Tell me about it.' His gaze tightened on the plate of curry and then on the gin. 'Is that what this impromptu curry picnic was all about then, buttering me up before giving me *the talk*?'

'Well, to be quite frank, I think you needed it. I know Ellie's your darling girl and always will be, but she is also a woman in her twenties who is free to make her own decisions. You need to respect that, especially when John is such a decent man. Let's face it, when it comes to Ellie, no man will ever be good enough for her in your book.'

Joseph stared at him. 'Okay, give it to me straight. Have I really been that big a shite to him?'

'No, but you could maybe try to go easier on him.'

The DI gazed out across the meadow and turned the thought over. 'Okay, as I told Kate, I'll try.'

'Maybe go for a drink with them and try to make John feel like part of your family.'

'Hang on, is this Ellie talking here, or you?'

Dylan smiled at him. 'Maybe a bit of both.'

Joseph rubbed the back of his neck. 'Okay, I'll do my best. So with that out of the way, is there any more of that great Irish gin before we head back? I need to try and get an early night as I'm off to the races tomorrow.'

'Horses?'

'No, vintage racing cars. It's all part of our investigation into Harper's background.'

'Then tell me more,' the professor said, pouring the DI a fresh glass of gin.

CHAPTER ELEVEN

SATURDAY HAD ARRIVED and with it, the race day at the Branton circuit. As Joseph, Megan, and Chris headed among the vehicles, the DI was struck by the sweeping lines of the cars. The sun sparkled on the glossy exteriors of the vintage motors. Every single vehicle was as immaculate as the day it had left the factory, having been polished to within an inch of its life.

Even Joseph, a man who had as much interest in cars as a cat did in baked potatoes, could almost picture himself owning one. Maybe that Morse chap had a point after all.

'I can't begin to imagine what this lot is worth,' Megan said.

'Enough money to paint the town red, blue, and white, along with every colour in between,' Chris replied.

'I'm surprised you'd risk racing your precious Triumph TR4,' Joseph said.

'Tell me about it. But a piece of motoring history like the TR4 was built for the road, not gathering dust in a private collection. I can't think of any better tribute to a fantastic piece of engineering than taking her out on a racetrack.'

'So your TR4 is a *she*, then?' Megan asked with a smile.

'Don't be daft, of course she is, just like *Tús Nua* is definitely female,' Joseph said.

Megan looked between the two men. 'And that's because?'

Chris pulled a face at her. 'Because it's an unwritten rule, that's why.'

Megan grinned at them. 'Got it.'

'I think the DC is after a slightly more detailed explanation,' Joseph said. 'It actually originated from when sailors worshipped the goddesses of the sea. That's why they named their boats after them, as a way of seeking their protection. That eventually led to boats being thought of as feminine.'

Megan stared at him. 'Where on Earth did you learn that pub quiz-winning fact?'

'From Dylan, of course, when I made the mistake of asking him and he went into a thirty-minute lecture on the subject.'

The DC shook her head. 'I should have known.'

The detectives walked through the paddock accompanied by the roar of a group of cars speeding past on the nearby track. The smell of the exhaust was almost enough to overpower the fragrance of food from the line of nearby vendors. One in particular had already caught Megan's eye, selling venison sausage baps.

'I'm rather looking forward to getting out there,' Chris said, watching the pack of cars rush away.

'Do you race a lot, then?' Megan asked.

'Probably once a month up and down the length of the country, work allowing. I'm afraid I'm something of an addict.'

'No wonder you and Megan get on famously,' Joseph said. 'I think she fancies herself as something of a Formula One driver.'

'Maybe you'd like to join me for a spin round the circuit during one of the heats?' he asked Megan. 'At least once I've taken Joseph out for the first race.'

'Sorry?' Joseph stared at the DCI, as though his senior officer had lost his mind.

'You'll love it, Joseph. I tell you now, it's intoxicating when you're out there on the tarmac. No feeling like it in all the world.'

'I'll take your word for it. Anyway, I thought you said Megan and I should concentrate on gathering what information we can from the pitlane whilst you're racing?'

'Megan can cover that,' Chris said, his expression unreadable.

Megan looked just as surprised as Joseph felt. His thoughts whirled. If someone had spilled the beans to the SIO and he knew about the DI's phobia, then why would the boss even suggest doing this, unless...

Suddenly, the DI knew exactly what was going on here. Chris was going to test him, to see how he would cope. The problem with that strategy was even the prospect of racing around a track was enough to make Joseph feel nauseous.

'Is going out there and racing strictly necessary, Chris?' Megan asked, obviously trying to help extricate Joseph from what could be a tricky situation.

'It is if we don't want to blow our cover,' Chris replied, not about to let Joseph wriggle out of it.

Chris looked past them as a Ferrari roared by. 'I'm going to nose around to see if I can find out a bit more about Matthew Forbes and Ralph Richards from the race marshals. Richards is actually due to race in the same heat as us, Joseph. So I suggest whilst I'm doing that, you and Megan ask around the paddock to see if anyone has anything to say about Jimmy Harper.'

'Isn't that going to raise suspicion?' Joseph asked, trying to distract himself by concentrating on the investigation, rather than the looming nightmare out on the racetrack.

'Not really. One of the races today is being held in his

memory as he was a patron of Branton. Trust me, his name is going to be on a lot of lips today.'

'Then leave it to us,' Megan said.

Chris glanced at his watch. 'We'll rendezvous in the pitlane garage around noon. That's ten minutes before our race is due to begin. Bring plenty of courage with you, Joseph.'

'I'll do my best,' the DI replied, not even able to raise the faintest of smiles.

With a wave, Chris headed off, rubbernecking many of the classic cars as he passed them.

'What the hell was that all about?' Megan asked the moment the SIO was out of earshot.

'Maybe he's doing exactly what I would do in his position. I'd make my own mind up rather than listen to gossip about one of my DIs. I would also make sure to keep it between ourselves rather than getting a certain DSU involved.'

'You think Chris is giving you a chance to prove yourself, then?'

'Probably. The problem is, what if I end up as a blubbering wreck by the end of it? If that happens, Chris won't exactly be able to turn a blind eye to my driving phobia. At best, I may be restricted to desk duty from now on.'

'But getting out in the field to solve crimes is in your DNA,' Megan replied.

Joseph shrugged. 'I knew this day was going to come eventually, and it seems today is that day. Maybe Chris won't notice if I keep my eyes shut through the whole nightmare. Anyway, let's focus on why we're really here and see what information we can dig up about Jimmy. Maybe it's best if we split up so we can cover more ground.'

'Good idea. I'll see you later in the pitlane, then.'

Joseph headed away, trying not to feel like a condemned man, and threw himself into the task at hand.

He didn't know a lot about car brands, other than about what his pa had driven, namely an ancient Ford Capri in canary yellow. Although his pa had loved the thing, which seemed to spend half its time in his garage being fixed, Joseph had never caught the bug from him. But now, for the first time, he found himself taking a mild interest in the vehicles around him.

A lot of that was due to the owners, who were obviously extremely proud of their motors. They exuded enthusiasm by the bucketful and happily spoke to anyone who took even the vaguest interest in their cars.

There was certainly a dazzling array of vintage motors on display, complete with information sheets stuck to their windscreens with all the key details. Everything was in the paddock, from MG Midgets to old Ferraris. There were even some Morgan 3-wheelers that looked like the love child of a car and a motorbike.

Joseph chatted casually with owner after owner about Jimmy, nearly every single one of them seeming to know something about the man, and nearly everyone inevitably bringing up how he'd died and what a tragedy it was. But not everyone. Some clammed up the moment Jimmy's name was mentioned, claiming that they barely knew him, and quickly turned their backs on the DI. Based on the sour expression on their faces, they definitely weren't fans, even if they weren't going to tell a stranger the reason why.

Joseph just hoped Megan and Chris were getting on better than he was.

The time ticked away towards midday, the race hanging over the detective like a death sentence.

An Aston Martin DB5 caught the DI's eye. Even though Joseph wasn't a car man, even he had to admit he felt something stirring in his loins when he saw it. Maybe it was that deep-buried primordial thing anyone who'd ever seen the original

James Bond films felt. The best of those for Joseph would always be the Sean Connery movies, with the big man himself at the wheel of a DB5. That had sparked the fantasy amongst countless people, imagining themselves roaring along the open road in an Aston Martin, probably while wearing a tuxedo. The same dream Jimmy had once lived for real.

Certainly, the DB5 before him was stunning, its metallic silver paint job gleaming. It must have been what Jimmy's vehicle had been like before it had been torched. Maybe that had been part of his murderer's motive—to destroy Jimmy's dream along with the man trapped inside it?

The owner had just finished chatting to an older man in a flat cap who was practically drooling over the car.

Okay, there's every chance that he may have known Jimmy as they share the same taste in cars, Joseph thought to himself.

He headed over to the owner, casting an admiring gaze over the DB5. 'She's an absolute beauty.'

The man turned and beamed at him. 'Thank you. I restored her myself when she was written off by the previous owner.'

Joseph gave the man an impressed look. 'I would honestly never have known. It must have been a labour of love, it looks like she just rolled out of the showroom.'

'That it was. It took me a year of weekends and every workday evening to restore her to this state, much to the chagrin of my long-suffering wife.'

The DI nodded as he looked over the information sheet pinned to the windscreen to see the owner's name was Bob. Now to see what, if anything, this man knew about the arson victim.

'I suppose you knew Jimmy Harper. He used to race his own DB5 here, didn't he?'

Bob's expression clouded. 'Yes, he did...'

'I imagine you two must have swapped notes all the time about your cars.'

Bob's expression hardened. 'I wouldn't bother giving that man the time of day.'

'You had some sort of problem with Jimmy?'

'Look, I'm guessing by the fact I don't recognise you that you aren't a regular at this track. I don't want to speak ill of the dead, and it is awful how he died, but let's just say, there are plenty of people here who will breathe a sigh of relief now Jimmy's gone.'

'Why's that?' Joseph asked, sensing that at last he'd found someone who was going to open up about Jimmy.

Bob gestured around them at all the classic cars. 'People here are enthusiasts who come to Branton to meet like-minded souls, have a good time, and maybe race a bit. But Jimmy and his two mates were different. For them, it was all about making money on the side.'

'I see, and his two mates were?' Joseph asked, as casually as he could.

'Matthew Forbes and Ralph Richards. All cut from the same bloody cloth and as thick as thieves.'

'Right. And what did they get up to here, exactly?'

Bob looked around to check no one else could hear him and leaned in. 'Jimmy had a knack for swooping in like a bloody vulture and making lowball offers to owners at racing meet-ups. Some actually fell for his snake-oil charm. But that wasn't the worst of it. The three of them were involved with gambling on the amateur races held here.'

'Putting some cash on the races doesn't sound too bad,' Joseph said, sensing this was heading in a significant direction.

Bob shook his head. 'You don't understand. It was much bigger than that. High rollers turned up and plenty of money exchanged hands. But that's not the problem. It's that Jimmy and his buddies fixed the races, crossing palms with silver to make sure that their chosen driver won.'

Joseph whistled. 'Bloody hell. And that's still happening?'

'I pray not. Hopefully, his two mates will just fade into the background now Jimmy is gone and leave this racetrack alone. This hobby doesn't need people like their sort, giving it a bad reputation.'

'Of course, but do you think anyone here could have hated him enough to have wanted him dead?'

Bob blew his cheeks out. 'From the things I've heard today, you're not alone in thinking that. Any of the idiots who lost big money because of a fixed race certainly wouldn't have taken it well. Whether they took it badly enough to actually murder Jimmy, I honestly don't know.'

Joseph's mind had already rushed to that conclusion. 'I see... Is there anything else you can tell me about the man?'

Bob's gaze narrowed. 'You seem to want to know a lot about Jimmy. Any particular reason for that? Please don't tell me you're one of the people I just slagged off for being stupid enough to place a bet with him?'

Joseph chuckled. 'Nothing like that, just curious, that's all.' A chirp from his phone interrupted them. When he glanced at the screen, he saw a text from Megan.

'*Shake a leg. You're up with Chris in the first heat.*'

Joseph held up a hand. 'Sorry, got to dash. The guy I'm here with today is insisting on dragging me out on the track with him in his TR4.'

Bob nodded. 'Your first time, by any chance?'

'Why, can you tell by the frightened-out-of-my-mind expression I'm obviously not hiding very well?'

The other man snorted. 'Honestly, if you're worried, don't be. It's exhilarating, but I warn you now, it will get expensive very quickly.'

'In what way?'

'I mean that by the end of the race, you'll be walking round the paddock looking for a vintage car of your own to buy.'

'Trust me, that's never going to happen.'

'Don't be so sure. Anyway, I'll pop down to the racing line to see you off when the race is about to begin. A TR4, was it?'

'Yes, a racing-green one.'

'Then, good luck, and be prepared to well and truly catch the bug.'

'We'll see,' Joseph replied, and with a wave, he headed away. If only the man realised just how badly the DI's palms were sweating at the prospect of racing.

It was then that he noticed a young guy with a thin angular face and a crew cut, wearing oily coveralls and smoking a cigarette. He was definitely watching the DI, but when the lad realised Joseph had clocked him, he quickly turned away.

What's that about? the DI thought as he headed away.

By the time he neared the pitlane, a cold sweat was building to a regular torrent, running down his back at the thought of what he was about to be dragged into. Joseph just prayed he could keep it together long enough so his boss didn't realise just how big a problem he had when it came to speed.

CHAPTER TWELVE

JOSEPH FELT sick as he sat in the passenger seat of the TR4 with its roof down. That was despite the fact that Chris'ss car hadn't moved a millimetre yet.

Mechanics and friends milled around the other vehicles, as Megan leaned on his windowsill.

'From what I've been able to find out, Jimmy seems to have been running an illegal book, along with Matthew Forbes and Ralph Richards.'

The DI nodded, grateful to have a distraction from what was about to happen. 'That matches what I discovered, too. It's certainly a possible motive for murder, especially if a punter lost a lot of money during one of their fixed races.'

Chris frowned. 'This is meant to be amateur racing for enthusiasts, where people get together for a good time. Apart from anything else, if the stewards ever heard about that, they all would have been banned from the circuit for life.'

'Maybe they slipped the stewards some money to keep quiet,' Joseph said.

Chris nodded. 'That's certainly possible. Talking of

Forbes...' He tipped his chin towards a yellow car ahead of them, near the starting line on the grid. 'That Jensen Interceptor belongs to him and he's driving. When I checked, Richards is also racing in another heat in his DeLorean. But it was Forbes's team who got very twitchy when I casually asked them about Jimmy.'

'Interesting,' Joseph replied. 'I don't think I'm being paranoid, but I'm also almost certain I had a furtive lad, a mechanic by the look of him, watching me while I was talking to the owner of another DB5. There's a danger our casual inquiries may have not gone unnoticed.'

'Maybe we should call it a day?' Megan suggested, raising her eyebrows the barest fraction at Joseph.

The DI realised what she was trying to do—give him a chance to escape the imminent race.

However, their DCI had other ideas.

'Not now we're on the track,' Chris said. 'I'm afraid that would only draw even more attention to us.'

'Okay...' Joseph replied in the resigned tone of a man whose head was already in the hangman's noose.

The speakers along the racetrack crackled into life. 'The race is about to begin. Can all crews please clear the track?' a woman's voice called out. Bonnets were lowered and fastened back into place as people returned to the pitlane.

'Okay, I think that includes me. Good luck, guys,' Megan said. She gave Joseph an encouraging look as she waved and headed back to the pitlane.

'Right, we'd better swap over now, Joseph,' Chris said.

The DI turned to stare at him. 'Sorry, what do you mean?'

'You're the one driving.'

Joseph gaped at the man as though he'd gone stark-raving mad. 'But this is your car.'

'That's why I entered your name for this race. I want you to drive it.'

'I don't understand,' Joseph said, as a raw sense of panic rose through him.

'It's time to put my cards on the table. I've heard rumours about you freezing up whenever you're at the wheel. So this is the perfect opportunity to prove to me you're on top of it, and that's all ancient history.'

Joseph's building sense of panic was now on its spin cycle. 'Why not just pull me in for a quiet chat before now?'

'Because inevitably word would have got back to our superintendent and you really don't want that to happen for obvious reasons.'

The DI struggled to get his head around what his boss was telling him. 'So you're basically giving me a chance?'

'That's about the sum of it. I know what a great officer you are and I don't want this to affect your career. We both know that Derrick would jump at the chance to use this as ammunition against you. But hopefully, by the end of this race, you will have proved to yourself that you can drive a car without breaking into a cold sweat. I'm certain that you can handle a vehicle at high speed, so prove it to yourself. You just need to overcome the mental block you have about it.'

'You're being serious about throwing me in the deep end over this?'

'Absolutely, and I didn't want to worry you beforehand, which is why I've left it to the last minute to tell you. So let's swap over quickly before this race gets started. I promise if it really proves to be too much, we can pull over. But I know you've got this, Joseph.'

The DI could barely believe he was undoing his racing safety harness as part of his brain went into autopilot. He stepped out of the TR4 and, mind numb, headed round to the driver's side as Chris jumped into the passenger seat. As Joseph strapped himself in, he saw Megan's look of shock from where she stood against the pitlane wall. Joseph raised his shoulders in response, not quite able to believe what the boss was making him do.

As the last of the people cleared the track, a klaxon sounded.

'Drivers, you may start your vehicles,' the announcer called out.

A cacophony of engines roared into life around them.

'That includes you,' Chris said with a small smile.

Joseph turned the ignition key and the TR4's burble joined the symphony of motor vehicle noise. As acid rose up his gullet, he realised he had a pack of Silvermints stuck in his pocket. He quickly popped one into his mouth and sucked furiously on it.

Then he noticed something in the sound of the engine. It was revving slightly high. There was also a smell of partially burned fuel coming from the exhaust and something of a dark haze spewing out of the back of the TR4.

'I think your engine is running a bit rich,' the DI managed to squeeze out through his clenched jaw.

Chris shot him an impressed look. 'You know about engines, Joseph?'

'Yes, I learnt a lot about them from my pa. If you want, we can head straight into the pits and I can adjust the carburettor jets for you.'

'You can do that after this race. But it's good to know you know your way round an engine. I might have to drag you over to my house to help me when I start my next car restoration project.'

'If you like...' Then Joseph realised exactly what his boss was doing—talking to him to keep him distracted from what was about to happen.

But that strategy fell apart the moment the first red light on the gantry blinked on and every driver, apart from Joseph, revved their engines loud enough to rival a wailing banshee, raising the hairs on the back of his neck.

I'm going to fecking die! the DI thought.

Four more red lights blinked on, one after another on the gantry.

Several cars ahead of them, Forbes was revving his Jensen hard.

'The moment they all go out, race, and get ready for the rush of your life!' Chris called out. 'But watch out for the clutch, it's a bit heavy.'

Joseph barely registered the other man's words as he gripped the steering wheel of the TR4. The DI's mouth went as dry as a nun's drinks cabinet during the seemingly endless wait for the lights to go out.

The moment all the lights went out, the world around them burst into a frenzied maelstrom of activity as everyone hit the throttle. Cars shot off from their standing start with the squeal of rubber. Far ahead, Forbes's Jensen was already harrying a Lotus Seven as the two cars shot away from the rest of the pack.

Joseph had pressed the accelerator only halfway as the cars raced past them.

'Give it some throttle, man!' Chris shouted.

With a prayer to the big man upstairs, the DI balled his courage and floored it.

The TR4 surged forward, and although he wasn't exactly pressed back into his seat, it still felt ridiculously rapid to Joseph. It was certainly fast enough to give him plenty to deal with when an MG Midget ahead of them shuddered to a stop as it stalled. Without even having time to think about it, Joseph swerved, narrowly missing a Jaguar MKII that had been coming up on the outside.

Although it had been years since he'd last driven any car at real speed, not counting the police Peugeot incident when he'd rushed to save his daughter held at the Pitt Rivers Museum, the instinct was still there. Joseph flicked the steering wheel to the side, before centring it again. He threaded the TR4 like a needle between the vehicles, somehow missing both. He raced away with the pack of other vintage cars, all jostling for position.

Chris clapped. 'I bloody knew you had it in you, Joseph! You just needed a bit of a push!'

The DI didn't respond. He was concentrating too hard on not losing control, or his breakfast. But as the race settled down after the drama of the start, he began to gradually find his rhythm, and his initial sense of dread was rapidly subsiding. Surprisingly, even his heart rate, which had been giving the engine revs a run for its money, slowed. The knowledge of how to handle a car was still there, buried in his brain. Joseph flicked through gears like a well-oiled machine as he got a feel for the TR4. Meanwhile, he kept catching Chris grinning at him like a right eejit.

Joseph heard the roar of another car's engine getting closer, and fast.

Chris glanced back over his shoulder. 'Watch out, you have a Rover P6 about to try to cut through on the inside line.'

The DI glanced in his mirror and spotted the blue car bearing down on them. With a slight nudge of the wheel, he took the TR4 to the edge of the racing curb, forcing the Rover to brake.

'Bloody hell, talk about slamming the barn door in someone's face,' Chris said. 'That was great racing, Joseph.'

He shrugged. 'It just seemed like the right thing to do.'

'There you go, then. You obviously have the natural instinct of a racing driver built into you, even if you didn't realise it. But the real question is, are you enjoying yourself?'

It was a good question because when Joseph thought about it, there wasn't a ball of anxiety raging in his stomach anymore, or even a hint of tension across his chest. If anything, there was a sense of exhilaration as he tuned into what this car was capable of.

'You know what, I think I'm starting to realise this is all a bit of a grand craic.'

Chris grinned at him. 'I bloody knew you'd surprise yourself. I'm sorry for the subterfuge. I just wanted to keep this between us.'

'Thank you for that, although maybe next time, try that quiet chat approach first.'

'But where would the fun in that be?' Chris said, winking at him. 'Now, show me what you can really do. If you can get us into the top three before the end of this race, then I'll buy the drinks.'

'Oh, now you're on,' Joseph said.

As they raced by the starting line for the sixth time, the DI caught Megan staring at them with her mouth hanging open, which made him grin enormously.

He dropped a gear as he sped the car into the first bend with his heart no longer feeling like it was about to burst out of his chest. If anything, with every second, he was finding himself getting calmer as he settled into the race.

'You do realise you're going to get to the end of this and want to get a classic car of your own?' Chris said.

Joseph made a scoffing sound, even though it was exactly what Bob, the owner of the Aston Martin, had said.

As lap after lap rolled past, much to his own surprise, the DI found they were advancing through the pack.

To Chris'ss obvious delight, they were slowly reeling the leaders in. Whatever else Matthew Forbes was, he was certainly one hell of a driver. He and the Lotus were battling it out through bend after bend, Forbes trying to take every opportunity to dive through the smallest gap the Lotus' driver left for him.

'If this race is fixed, they're making a bloody good performance of it out at the front,' Joseph said.

'I'm not so sure. That Lotus Seven is definitely running a bit slow. It should have pulled a long way ahead of the rest of the pack by now. But that's probably the point. If Forbes and Richards are running a book here today, most of their punters will be betting on the Lotus to win. I wouldn't be surprised if they had one of their people fiddle with its engine. You wait, any moment now Forbes will streak past it to win the race.'

'But surely if one of the men running the book ends up winning, that will look even more suspicious...' Then a thought struck him. 'But not if they have someone else running the book for them.'

'Exactly. In the heats they're directly competing in, Forbes and Richards are just regular drivers who will no doubt feign surprise when they do well in their respective races.'

'Yes, and all at the expense of their punters.'

Chris nodded. 'Exactly.'

Joseph's attention was laser-focused on the race when, just ahead of them, a plume of blue smoke suddenly erupted from the bonnet of another open-top sports car.

'Now, will you look at that? It looks like the engine on that AC Cobra has just let go,' Chris said. 'I wonder if that throws out Forbes and Richards's plans for this race. And as sad as that is, if you can just hang onto this spot for this final lap, we're going to make the bloody podium in third place!'

'Then let's make sure that happens and wipe some smug grins off a few faces,' Joseph replied, accelerating hard.

As they rounded a corner onto a straight, the DI spotted an

old Ford Cortina dead ahead of them, travelling far more slowly than any of the other cars they'd passed so far.

'You can relax,' Chris said, catching his expression. 'You're doing so well, you've actually lapped most of the field. Just get past the Cortina before the next bend to make sure no one catches up with us.'

'And lose an offer of a free drink? I don't think so,' Joseph said. He floored the accelerator and shot up to just behind the other car.

'Excellent, you have plenty of speed, just slipstream past the car on the inside,' Chris suggested.

Joseph swung out with plenty of room to spare. But as they pulled up alongside the Cortina, he spotted the male driver with a crew cut... the same lad from the paddock who'd been watching him when he'd been talking to Bob about Jimmy.

Without warning, the Cortina swerved towards them as the track tightened into another bend.

Even Joseph's lightning-like reflexes weren't enough to steer away from the imminent collision. The Cortina slammed into the side of the car hard enough to send the TR4 skidding off the track. With a bang, the front tyre exploded, and they tipped over. Suddenly, the world was gyrating past the windscreen as Joseph and Chris were jostled while held in place by their safety harnesses. The car rolled multiple times, debris flying from the TR4 as it disintegrated.

Feck! Joseph had time to think.

At last, the car came to a groaning, shuddering stop. Part of the DI's mind was already screaming that this was a sickening echo of the crash that had killed Eoin. And once again, he'd been the one at the wheel.

But although feeling battered and bruised, his attention shot to Chris. The DCI was taking in a shuddering breath as safety officials appeared from behind the barriers and ran towards their crashed vehicle.

'Bastard!' Chris finally muttered.

'Sorry, there just wasn't anything I could do,' Joseph replied. He was just relieved that his boss seemed to be pissed off at him, rather than seriously injured.

'No, not you. That prat driving the Cortina. It was obvious we were lapping him, but he deliberately rammed us to stop us getting past.'

People appeared by the car and began helping them out, as another man stuck a fire extinguisher hose under the crumpled, steaming bonnet of the TR4. Stewards were already out on the track waving red flags to warn other drivers of the crash. A few moments later, both detectives were being helped over the barrier by a medical team and escorted to a white tent.

Chris looked back to his wrecked car and shook his head. 'That isn't exactly going to buff out.'

Joseph felt an overwhelming sense of guilt for totalling what was obviously his boss' pride and joy. 'I'll pay for any damage.'

'The hell you will. That's what racing insurance is for. Although, to be honest, I'll probably do most of the work myself. Anyway, don't beat yourself up about it. If I'd been driving, I wouldn't have fared any better. The most important thing to me right now is how you're feeling, Joseph.'

'A bit battered and bruised, but otherwise fine.'

Chris narrowed his eyes. 'Are your nerves okay?'

It was a good point because, now that the DCI mentioned it, Joseph realised there was no sense of nausea inside him. If anything, there was a sense of elation that they had survived.

The DI shook his head as they were escorted into a medical tent. 'I feel great, crash and all.'

'Then, the crash aside, that's the main thing and exactly the outcome I was hoping for with your driving phobia.'

'Kill or cure, eh?' Joseph replied with a smile. 'Although, maybe don't think about taking up a new career as a psychologist just yet.'

Chris laughed. 'There, I think you may have a point,' he said, as a nurse put a pulse oximeter on his finger, and another wrapped a blood pressure strap around Joseph's arm.

CHAPTER THIRTEEN

JOSEPH AND CHRIS had barely finished getting their vitals checked when Megan came barrelling into the medical tent, face pale.

'Bloody hell, are you both alright?' she said, looking between them.

'Nothing that a good pint of beer can't sort. Although, Chris'ss TR4 was a bit less lucky, after I banjaxed it,' Joseph replied, with a rueful look.

Chris shrugged. 'If I wasn't prepared to bend a few metal panels, I wouldn't bring her out racing in the first place. That aside, I've a good mind to report that maniac driver who side-swiped us to the stewards and get him banned from the circuit.'

'Actually, about that,' Joseph said. 'I'm certain it was the same lad I saw watching me in the paddock when I was talking to the owner of that Aston Martin.'

'You're saying that bastard deliberately rammed us off the road?'

'Yes, possibly because two people in particular weren't happy about our potential podium position and how it would affect the betting.'

Megan looked between them. 'Bloody hell, that makes sense. Especially since Forbes won the race on the last bend by overtaking the Lotus he'd been trailing for most of the race.'

'Did he now?' Joseph traded a look with Chris.

A doctor appeared. 'Sorry to interrupt, gentlemen, but I need to examine you both.'

Joseph nodded, then glanced at Megan. 'Could you do me a favour and see what details you can dig up about the driver of that Cortina?'

'Leave it to me,' she said.

But as the DC headed out of the tent, she came to a sudden stop. Then Joseph saw why. A familiar motorcyclist in leathers and wearing a heavily tinted visor, who had been passing the tent, froze as he spotted the DC. There was no question in Joseph's mind—the last time he'd seen this man was when they'd disturbed him in Jimmy's flat.

'Don't move!' shouted Megan, who'd already reached the same conclusion. She burst into a run, heading straight for the motorcyclist.

Joseph and Chris were both on their feet as well, but the doctor blocked their way.

'Where exactly do you think you're going?' the man demanded.

Joseph flapped a hand towards Megan, who had just disappeared around the corner of the stands in pursuit of the suspect.

'I'm afraid you're not heading off until you've both been signed off by me.'

Chris grimaced, but nodded. 'Let's just hope Megan catches the bastard before he escapes.'

Joseph was about to ignore the doctor and push past him when Chris met his gaze and shook his head.

'We're down for now, and we need to have some faith in Megan.'

'But she's by herself and is charging after him without backup.'

'That reminds me of someone I know. But relax, the DC has a good head on her shoulders. There are also plenty of people around if she does get into any trouble.' Chris pulled his phone out. 'Control, I need urgent backup at the Branton race-track. Have we got any cars in the area that can give assistance?'

Joseph didn't hear the rest of what his boss said, because at that moment he saw Megan round the corner back towards the tent. Her gaze met his, and she shook her head. It seemed like their bloody arsonist had slipped through their fingers yet again.

But why come to the track at all? Joseph wondered. Was it a coincidence, or something else?

Megan was driving Chris's Volkswagen Passat with the battered TR4 on the trailer behind it. Neither Joseph nor Chris had been particularly keen to take the wheel after the crash. It seemed Joseph's newfound joy of driving only went so far. Thankfully, both detectives had been given a clean bill of health, despite the assortment of plasters now stuck to the minor cuts on their heads.

Megan thumped the wheel. 'I still can't believe the suspect managed to give me the slip again.'

'I certainly wouldn't beat yourself up about it,' Chris said.

'Yes, that man is as lucky as a cat with nine lives,' Joseph added.

'You're telling me. He was almost within my baton's reach when he escaped on his bloody motorbike again. Even though its plates had been changed, I'm certain it was the same bike we saw him using at the showroom and Jimmy's flat.'

'That's useful information, but in future, you mustn't charge into a situation alone without backup,' Joseph said.

Megan gave him a straight look. 'And you don't have any sense of irony telling me that?'

In the back of the car, Chris chuckled. 'I think our DC makes a very valid point.'

Joseph made a huffing sound. 'Do as I say, not as I do.'

Megan rolled her eyes. 'Right. That hypocrisy aside, it has to be significant that our suspect was there. It's almost as if he's been tailing us.'

'Or maybe it's the other way round? We're following in the footsteps of this man's investigation. First, he turns up at Jimmy's flat and steals the business ledger. Now he's here. That seems too much of a coincidence.'

'I agree, but the question is why?' Chris said.

'If this is some sort of gang dispute, maybe Matthew and Ralph are in the firing line as well because of their betting ring,' Joseph said.

'You think this is some sort of turf war, then?'

'Possibly, but whatever it is, it's rapidly complicating our murder investigation.' He glanced back over his shoulder at Chris. 'I don't suppose any more information has come to light about this Night Watchmen syndicate?'

'Apart from what Kate was able to dig up, there's not a lot. Obviously, as it falls under the category of organised crime, that's also beyond our jurisdiction, and I've had to hand everything we have over to the National Crime Agency. Derrick wasn't keen though, and felt we should sit on it until we had more solid information to give them.'

'That doesn't sound like the superintendent,' Megan said. 'I thought he normally does everything by the book and would have wanted to hand that over to the NCA as quickly as possible.'

Joseph realised the DC had a point. It wasn't like Derrick to drag his heels, especially when a major crime syndicate was such a hot potato.

Apart from anything else, even the Thames Valley Police didn't have enough resources to deal with an investigation of that size, particularly since it would almost certainly involve dealing with Interpol.

Maybe the big man had simply wanted to steal some of the glory for himself and was reluctant to let the case go.

'Well, they're assessing it now, which is the main thing,' Chris said. 'The problem is, I can see their investigation interfering with our own and stepping on our toes.'

'You're not wrong there,' Joseph replied. 'If there is any evidence confirming that Jimmy's death was a crime syndicate hit, the NCA will swoop in and take over our investigation. That'll be a bitter pill to swallow as I really want to see this through to the end, boss.'

'You're not the only one,' Chris replied with a sigh.

CHAPTER FOURTEEN

SUNDAY LUNCHTIME FOUND Joseph sitting in a camping chair set up on the towpath, nursing his minor injuries. He was with Dylan and Amy, all of them attempting to cool down with some cold beers in the relentless heat.

Along with Max and White Fang, they were also watching Dylan's bird feeder, which certainly hadn't taken the birds long to discover. Blue and great tits were currently swarming it in a feeding frenzy.

'Those sunflower seeds seem to be a huge hit with the local feathered population,' Amy observed.

'You can say that again,' Dylan replied. 'I honestly don't know why I haven't got round to setting up a feeder before. Watching them is certainly good for the soul.'

'Indeed...' Joseph said, as he felt a tickling sensation on his arm and glanced down to see a mosquito getting ready to bite him. He slapped his hand down on the beastie, but the bloody thing buzzed away as though he'd moved at the speed of a snail.

'Well, if they help to keep the bloodletting winged-assassin population down round here, I'll go halves with you on their next rations,' he said.

Dylan raised his beer. 'You're on.'

Amy took a sip of beer, her gaze lingering on the plasters on Joseph's head.

'Will you stop looking at them? Honestly, I'm okay,' the DI said.

'I'm glad to hear it. You do realise you and Chris are lucky to be alive?'

'Maybe it was the luck of the Irish,' Joseph said, his grin fading when Amy didn't smile back.

'And that luck is going to run out one day.'

'At least that day wasn't yesterday.'

She just shook her head at him, scowling.

'Look who it is,' Dylan said, trying to ignore the brewing argument between Joseph and Amy.

Joseph turned around to see Ellie heading towards them.

'Typical, she decides to pop round after it looks like I've gone several rounds in a boxing ring.'

'That's my cue to go as I have some laundry to catch up with, but we'll finish this conversation later,' Amy said.

'Grand,' Joseph replied with absolutely zero enthusiasm.

She leaned over and kissed Joseph, before waving to Dylan and heading off in the opposite direction to Ellie.

'You're in deep water there, but she's just worried about you,' Dylan commented as the SOC officer headed away.

'No need to tell me, my friend,' Joseph replied, his gaze now on Ellie approaching with a bag of provisions tucked under her arm. 'But I'll do my best to smooth things over with her when I get a chance.'

'You should; she's very good for you.'

'Yes, I know...' His words trailed away as his daughter reached them.

Ellie's eyes had already widened, seeing her dad close-up. 'Bloody hell, what happened to you?'

Joseph shrugged. 'It was nothing. Just a racing accident over at the Branton circuit. A lunatic tried to take me and Chris out on the racetrack.'

His daughter's jaw dropped open. 'Sorry, did you really just say "racetrack," and that you crashed?'

Joseph shrugged. 'Yes, but it's no biggie. There wasn't a lot I could do about it. We got sideswiped by another car.'

Ellie's mouth flapped open and closed, but no words came out.

Dylan chuckled. 'It seems your father still can surprise you. Anyway, I'll leave you two alone to catch up.' He winked at Joseph, and with a whistle to the dogs, the professor headed back into the cabin of *Avalon*.

Ellie gave her dad a hard stare. 'Next, you're going to tell me you were driving as well.'

'I was actually, and believe it or not rather enjoying myself, at least up to the point of the crash.'

'Okay, who are you and what have you done with my dad? Since when have you been able to drive again without throwing your guts up?'

'I'm as surprised as you are. Chris managed to persuade me to have a go driving his Triumph TR4 around the circuit. Well, I say "persuade", the truth was he didn't leave me much choice in the matter.'

Ellie scrutinised the plasters on his face. 'And you're really okay?'

'Much better than you might expect. Yes, a few scratches, but the headline is I think I may have finally got over my driving phobia.'

His daughter tilted her head to one side as she gazed at him and then suddenly stepped forward and hugged him hard. 'I can't tell you what it means to hear that.'

Neither of them needed to go into detail about the significance of this milestone after Eoin's death, but his daughter more than understood. When she finally pulled away, she had tears in her eyes.

'Hey, no crying or you'll set me off,' Joseph said.

She smiled at him as she smudged her tears away with the back of her hand. 'Don't worry, these are happy tears. Just as well I brought the ingredients to make you my famous spag bol as an alternative Sunday lunch.'

He peered at her bag of groceries. 'What exactly did I do to warrant this show of affection?'

His daughter just raised her shoulders, a small grin tugging at the corners of her mouth. 'Oh, nothing. I just wanted to treat you. Anyway, I hope you have plenty of gas on board, because to do this properly, it needs to be cooked for at least a couple of hours.'

'I only fitted a fresh bottle last week, so you're golden.'

'Great,' she said as she handed him a bottle of Prosecco. 'Can you put that on ice?'

'Absolutely, and just the thing for this stifling weather.'

She nodded and headed past him into the cabin.

Joseph watched as she set to work in the galley. Clutching the bottle of fizz, he wondered if he would get to eat before she gave him a lecture about John.

Joseph pushed away his empty plate. 'Well, bhí an bia blasta.'

Ellie narrowed her eyes at him. 'Okay, if you're going to go full Irish on me, you can at least tell me what that means?'

'It's Gaelic for the food was delicious, and your spag bol absolutely hits that spot dead on.'

She beamed at him. 'Then I'm pleased to have fed your soul.'

Joseph glanced over at the huge pot of the rich tomato sauce that was left over. 'I'm surprised you didn't invite Dylan over to join us.'

'No, I wanted to have you all to myself so we could have a private chat. Besides, you can give him some leftovers tomorrow. There's more than enough there to keep you both going all week.'

'A private chat, is it?' Joseph sat back. Then his very full stomach did a slow flip as two parts of the puzzle slotted into place at once. Ellie considering dropping out of university, and her keenness that he make John feel welcome in the family...

'Oh, Jesus, don't tell me you're pregnant and this spag bol is a way of softening me up when you tell me John Thorpe is the dad.'

'Would it be such a bad thing if he was?' Ellie held his gaze with hers, her chin slightly lifted.

He stared mutely back at her. Just when he was certain that his blood pressure had shot up so high it was about to burst out of his ears, Ellie finally raised her palms.

'You can stop worrying because no, I'm not pregnant. But I do want to talk to you about John.'

'Oh thank God for that, but not this conversation again.'

'Again?' His daughter gave him an innocent look.

'Do I really need to answer that when you've already sent your foot soldiers in first? I got a similar lecture from your mum. Dylan even cooked me a curry. Of course, that really was just an excuse for him to bend my ear about not acting like a grumpy old git when it came to John.'

'Then I'm glad to hear it, because it certainly needed bending. John's under the distinct impression you have a serious issue with him.'

Joseph was already shaking his head. 'Whoa there. I don't

have any problem with John, even though I realise it probably looks that way.'

'I don't think there's any *probably* about it.'

'Have I really given John that hard a time?'

His daughter held her forefinger and thumb apart a fraction. 'Maybe a tiny little bit.'

'Right...' Joseph sighed. 'I'm sorry. I know I'm probably being too overprotective of you, but you have always been my lass, and I don't want to see you get hurt.'

Ellie sucked a big lungful of air in, getting ready to hit him with a serious comeback, but Joseph was already holding his hands up.

'Before you say it, yes, I realise you're not twelve anymore and don't need me to protect you. Besides, as boyfriends go, John is certainly a good guy, and believe it or not I actually do approve.'

'You do?'

Joseph nodded. 'As I told your foot soldiers, I will try to do better, making sure I make time to get to know him properly. So if you want to set something up, I promise I will be there with a smile on my face this time.'

Ellie leaned across the table and kissed him on the cheek. 'That's so good to hear, Dad.'

He smiled at her. 'I'm glad that's out of the way. Anyway, what's this I hear about you considering pulling out of your MA course at the Blavatnik School of Government? I thought you were loving it?'

His daughter pulled a face. 'Dylan's been talking, then?'

'He has indeed, although I believe John has also given you something of a talking to, which is a definite plus for the man in my book.'

Ellie sighed and nodded. 'Okay, before you waste your

breath laying into me, you should know I've already decided to stay.'

'I'm glad to hear it, but what led to this wobble in the first place?'

'There are just a few students who make life difficult for me sometimes.'

Joseph sat up straighter. 'Anything I can help with? A night in a cell, perhaps?'

Ellie laughed. 'Honestly, don't worry. I can fight my own battles. Besides, pursuing a future in politics was never going to be an easy ride. Just look at Westminster—that's full of plenty of dodgy characters.'

That brought a smile to Joseph's face. 'You can say that again. But you're sure you're going to be okay?'

'I've got this, Dad. Really.'

'Then I'll relax. I bet mum has been bending your ear over this too.'

Ellie shook her head. 'No. I've barely seen her. She's still working on that big story of hers.'

An immediate sense of frustration filled Joseph. 'Still? She said she would let it drop.'

'Well, that may have been a bit of a fib on her part. You know she finds it near impossible to back away from a story she's really sunk her teeth into.'

Joseph briefly toyed with the idea of telling his daughter about the note warning Kate off investigating the Night Watchmen. However, he didn't want to worry her either. No, he would need to follow this up with Kate in person. So instead, he just picked up the prosecco from the ice bucket and poured them both a glass.

Ellie's gaze fell upon a vase of flowers on a shelf, and she smiled. 'I see Amy has been brightening up the place, then?'

'Yes, she's left her mark here and there,' Joseph replied.

'Does that include leaving a spare toothbrush round here?' Ellie asked with a grin.

'That's for me to know and you forever to wonder about. A gentleman never speaks of such things.'

'You old romantic. But things are going well between you two then?'

'If you mean, are we still enjoying each other's company? Then yes. She brightens my days when we're together, and I hope I do hers. The only problem is, it's rare for us to be off at the same time, so we don't exactly get a lot of time together. But to be honest, that probably suits us well. We both enjoy our independence.'

'As long as you're happy.'

'It would seem so.'

'So does that mean I can take your profile down off Tinder now?'

Joseph stared at her. 'Please tell me you never actually put me up on there?'

Ellie's grin almost reached her ears. 'You really are so gullible sometimes.'

Joseph dragged his hand through his hair. 'Yes, it would seem that I am.'

They heard Dylan shouting from outside. 'Bloody thing, clear off!'

When they looked out through the cabin window, they saw the professor chasing a squirrel off his bird feeder which had been helping itself to its contents.

'Ah, so much for Dylan's new hobby,' Joseph said. 'What do you say we invite the professor over to share some of this food, especially now we've got our chat out of the way?'

'Great idea, especially as he's bringing the Eton Mess for pudding.'

He narrowed his eyes at her. 'So you're telling me, Dylan already knew about your *impromptu* visit?'

'Of course, consider it a pincer movement to make sure you saw sense.'

'And there he was, pretending to look surprised when you turned up. Jesus, you two really are as thick as thieves.'

'You better believe it; he's pretty much an honorary uncle anyway,' Ellie said, beaming at him.

CHAPTER FIFTEEN

'BLOODY IRRESPONSIBLE, that's what it was!' Derrick bellowed at Chris and Joseph the following Monday morning as they stood in his office like two naughty schoolboys summoned by the headmaster. 'What the hell were you thinking, taking part in an actual bloody race?'

'It was a necessary part of keeping our cover story intact,' Chris replied, not a hint in his expression that his other reason had been to help Joseph overcome his phobia about driving.

Derrick growled at the DCI. 'I'm not buying it. Apart from anything else, you neglected to tell me you were going to attempt to gather intelligence from people associated with Jimmy Harper. Of more immediate concern is you showed a considerable lack of judgement in actually heading out to a race-track at all. What would have happened if you'd both ended up killed because of this foolhardy stunt?'

Well, we wouldn't be bloody having this conversation for a start, Joseph thought to himself.

'With all due respect, Derrick, I've raced on tracks hundreds of times without any problem,' Chris said, without batting an eyelid. 'This was simply me using my hobby as an opportunity to see what we could find out about the world Jimmy Harper moved in.'

The veins on Derrick's forehead bulged. 'But you weren't the one driving, Joseph bloody was. No wonder you ended up crashing.'

'None of this was Joseph's fault. We were deliberately side-swiped by a driver we've now discovered is called Daryl Manning.'

Joseph nodded. 'And there wasn't exactly a lot I could do about it. On the plus side, Manning is now firmly in our sights. He obviously had a vested interest in making sure that we didn't affect the final podium position. That alone impli-cates him in the race rigging and illegal betting ring. There is also the fact that the motorcyclist turned up at the track as well.'

'Who managed to escape you yet again.' Derrick sat back in his chair. 'You ended up putting your lives on the line, and for what? Yes, we now know that Harper was colluding with Forbes and Richards, who were running an illegal betting ring. But isn't that something you could have just found out by taking a more measured approach?'

If Joseph's ears weren't deceiving him, the DSU almost sounded sincere. He could easily imagine the man caring about Chris, but himself? The ball-ache Derrick was currently giving them aside, what had happened to the usual open hostility the man reserved especially for the DI? Maybe the guy had got out of bed on the right side or something.

'Don't worry, I'll make sure I run anything like this past you first in the future,' Chris said.

'Bloody right, you will, or I'll have you and anyone involved in one of your botched operations on a disciplinary,' Derrick said. 'Do I make myself clear?'

Chris nodded. 'Absolutely.'

Derrick sighed. 'So, are you planning to pull this Daryl Manning in for questioning?'

Joseph shook his head. 'We don't want to tip off whoever is pulling the strings. We've been looking into Manning's background. He worked as a backstreet mechanic in Abingdon before he disappeared off the map.'

'When we checked out the address he gave the race organisers, it turned out to be an empty flat,' Chris added.

'Okay, that sounds suspicious,' Derrick said. 'So what's the next step, gentlemen?'

'I'm about to gather the team together to discuss exactly that,' Chris replied.

'In that case, keep me posted. And please, no more reckless stunts in the future. Do we understand each other?'

Both Chris and Joseph nodded.

Derrick waved a dismissive hand towards them.

The moment the two detectives were safely clear of the superintendent's office, Chris turned to Joseph. 'So no more reckless stunts, then?'

'What can I say, but I'll do my best?' Joseph replied with a grin.

Chris snorted. 'Okay, let's gather the troops to brainstorm those next steps.'

The moment they entered the incident room, Ian clocked Joseph and sprang to his feet.

'So the gossip going round the office is true. You went all Fast and Furious and managed to total the boss's car?'

A voice from behind Joseph responded before he could.

'Not totalled, more an unintended disassembly event, which sadly means my TR4 will be in my garage for months,' Chris said.

'And unbelievably, the DI still has a job here after doing that?' Sue asked, only half joking.

'It was just a racing accident and in no way was Joseph responsible,' Chris continued.

'Sorry, we're talking about the same person whose idea of speed is something akin to a hot pursuit of someone on one of those mobility scooters?' Ian asked.

Once again, before the DI could reply, another voice had piped up, this time Megan's, as her head appeared above her computer screen. 'You had to be there to believe it. Joseph was like a regular speed demon out there on the track. He could certainly show you a few tricks, Ian.'

Every set of eyes in the room turned towards Joseph, who just shrugged. 'What can I say, other than I've been hiding my light under a bushel all these years so as not to blind you all?'

There was a universal chorus of laughter as he headed over to his desk.

Chris retrieved a photo Megan had managed to take of Manning before he'd had a chance to get away. The DCI stuck it to the evidence board, just beneath the photo of Matthew Forbes, and drew a line linking the two.

He clapped his hands together. 'Okay, everyone, let's have a quick update about where things currently stand with our investigation. As you can see, we have a new suspect on the board after our little visit to the Branton circuit at the weekend. Thanks to the sterling work of Megan, who got his details from the stewards, we now know this is Daryl Manning. He's the little bastard who deliberately rammed our car as Joseph was trying to get past him. And before you suggest it, no, this wasn't just a typical racing accident. Joseph, can you tell the team what you discovered?'

The DI nodded and turned to face the room. 'I was chatting to the owner of an Aston Martin who was attending the race. He didn't have anything positive to say about Jimmy Harper. But more significantly, he confirmed what Megan found out independently. Harper was part of a group that included Thomas Reid and Ralph Richards. Together, they ran an illegal book on the outcome of the races. The rumour, one that's certainly supported by the fact we were deliberately driven off the track, is that they attempted to fix the outcome of the races and were prepared to do whatever it took.'

'So I'm guessing we're not talking about just betting a few quid here?' one of the detectives asked.

'No, apparently some high rollers were invited to the races,' Megan said.

'That means there could be someone who lost enough money to have wanted Jimmy dead,' Joseph added. 'There is also something else of significance that happened. Our motor-bike suspect was also at the racetrack.'

Several people in the room whistled.

'Yes, but I managed to let him get away,' Megan said, ashen-faced.

Joseph was already shaking his head at her. 'That isn't on you. But obviously, this is a significant development as it might suggest a link to Richards and Forbes.'

'Supporting the idea there was a feud between them and he was their hitman?' Sue asked.

'Right now, we have no idea,' Chris said. 'To try and find out the answer to that, we need to continue our efforts to dig into Jimmy's background, along with Richards and Forbes. That's why we're going to start by visiting Forbes's car restoration business out at Didcot, and Richards's gastropub in the Cotswolds. Let's also see what else we can dig up about how deep this business partnership with Harper ran, and whether there might have been a motivation for them to have had Jimmy killed.'

'So you're saying'—Ian paused for dramatic effect—'let's go and kick the tyres on this one?' He grinned.

A chorus of groans filled the room.

Chris just raised his eyebrows at him. 'I really am going to have to bring in a bad pun jar. If you had to put a pound in for every bad one of yours, Ian, we'd all be able to split the proceeds and head off on exotic holidays.'

'What can I say? It's my calling,' Ian said.

'Unfortunately, that would seem to be the case,' Chris replied, before turning his attention to Joseph and Megan. 'I'd like you two to head over to Forbes's garage to see what you can find out. Ian, Sue, you go and have a similar chat with Ralph Richards at his gastropub. These two gentlemen could be the key to the puzzle of who Jimmy Harper really was, and more importantly, who his enemies were, and also specifically, who this mystery motorcyclist is.'

'Leave that to us,' Joseph replied, nodding to Megan, who was already grabbing her things, as Ian and Sue did the same.

───────

Joseph felt surprisingly relaxed as he drove the Peugeot through the gates of the old business park, its sign over the entrance long since vanished. He'd actually volunteered to take the wheel and had even impressed himself, as he'd barely sweated during the journey over to Didcot. That was particularly noteworthy considering it had been less than two days since the crash. Yes, it seemed Chris's kill-or-cure approach had actually worked.

Most of the units in the derelict business park were empty, with the inevitable graffiti of the local "*intelligentsia*" scrawled across the shuttered entrances. Weeds had broken through the concrete floor and many of the windows were cracked. All it needed was a few burning oil drums to complete its post-apocalyptic look.

'Not exactly a lot of thriving businesses around here, then,' Megan said, eyeing the decaying buildings.

'Yes, it does have a bit of a whiff of where dreams of running your own business come to die.'

Megan gestured forward. 'Apart from the one ahead of us.'

Ahead, a red sign hung, spanning the width of at least three units, with *Classic AutoWorks UK* written on it in a flowing gold script.

At least twelve cars were parked up outside, but what caught Joseph's eye was the yellow Jensen Interceptor belonging to Forbes, parked among them.

The roller door was raised in the middle unit, revealing what looked like an ancient two-door Mercedes, its bodywork completely rusted away. The detectives parked up and got out of the Peugeot, to be greeted by the growl of a sandblaster. Then they spotted the man in coveralls with a mop of brown hair who was responsible for the racket. He was directing a nozzle towards a Mercedes, blasting off the rust to reveal the dull grey steel beneath.

'Going by the state of that old wreck, they do serious restoration work here,' Megan said, as they headed towards the entrance.

'Yes, that car definitely looks like it belongs in a scrapyard to me,' Joseph replied.

When the detectives stepped into the garage area, the noise from the sandblaster was even more deafening in the confined space. Apart from the Mercedes, they could now see two more cars in a similar state of repair, being worked on by at least six other people.

Spotting them, a lad put down the torque wheel brace he'd just been using to try and remove a rusted-on wheel from an old Alfa Romeo sports car and headed over.

'Can I help you?' he shouted, over the din echoing through the garage.

'Yes, we're looking for Matthew Forbes,' Joseph called back.

'Sorry, can't hear you. Who?'

The DI raised his voice to a bellow. 'Forbes!'

The lad nodded, and headed over to the man sandblasting the car. He tapped on his arm and gestured towards Joseph and Megan. The man switched off the sandblaster and a welcome silence descended. As Forbes walked towards them, Joseph took in his oil-stained skin, suggesting a lifetime of working in garages.

'Hi, I'm Matthew—you're looking for me?' he asked.

'Yes, that's right. I was wondering if we could ask you a few questions about Jimmy Harper,' Joseph said. 'I believe you worked on some of his cars.'

Forbes's eyes narrowed. 'And you are?'

Joseph and Megan both showed him their warrant cards.

His face relaxed. 'Right. I've sort of been expecting you to show up at some point to ask me about Jimmy. It was a bad business the way he died.'

Megan nodded. 'It certainly was. I'm sure you've seen all the speculation in the press by now that he was murdered. We were wondering if you could help us with why someone would want him dead?'

'I'm not sure I can tell you a lot, but follow me.'

Joseph couldn't help noticing there was a certain wariness in the eyes of the other employees as they watched them follow Matthew into a small corner office.

The detectives entered the room to see paperwork piled up everywhere and a yellowing computer on the desk that looked like it belonged to the last century.

As they all sat, Matthew leant his elbows on his desk, hands clasped together. 'So what would you like to know?'

'First of all, how did you know Jimmy?' Joseph asked.

'We actually went to the same secondary school here in Didcot. Jimmy was the first of our gang to get a car, a beaten-up

Mini Cooper, and that lit the spark in the rest of us. His passion eventually turned into running his own vintage car dealership. As for me, I had an old Saab I was forever having to fix to keep running. Eventually, that led to me setting up my own garage.'

'And you did work for Jimmy as well?' Megan asked, writing his answers in her notepad.

'Yes, quite a few motors over the years. You see, we specialise in restoring old wrecks like the ones out there in the garage area. That old Merc 300SL you saw me working on just now, is a 1959 model. We found her in an old barn, rusting away under some hay bales. But when fully restored, she will be worth up to two million.'

Joseph blew his cheeks out. 'Bloody hell, now there's a business model.'

'Yes, and it's a good one. Plus, there's the satisfaction of saving a classic vehicle from the breaker's yard. Like I said, quite a few of our projects ended up with Jimmy, who sold them on for a good profit. That was apart from the Aston Martin DB5 he kept for himself. He couldn't bring himself to part with it. It's an absolute crying shame it was destroyed in that fire.'

Joseph nodded. 'Since you were at school together, I imagine you were friends as well as business colleagues?'

Matthew pulled a face. 'I suppose so, but we weren't exactly close. Obviously, it was awful to hear about what happened to him. But between us, that man was a right royal pain in the arse to work with.'

'Enough for someone to want to murder him?' Megan asked.

Forbes scowled at them. 'Hang on, if you think I had anything to do with that, you can think again. Sure, he wasn't exactly someone I would want to share a pint with on a Friday night, but that's as far as it went.'

Joseph made a mental note. That didn't quite tally with

what Anna Millington had said about Forbes and Richards coming around regularly for dinner. Could that be significant?

'So if I were to ask if you could supply an alibi for the night of Jimmy's death, you'd be able to give us one?' Joseph asked.

'Bloody hell, so I am a suspect?'

'No, we're just trying to build an accurate picture of the whereabouts of anyone who knew Jimmy around the time of his death.'

'Right. Well, for your information, I was with the missus at home. You can ring her right now if you like.'

'If you could give us her contact details, so one of our officers can follow up, that would be a great help,' Megan said.

Matthew shrugged, grabbed a notepad, scribbled down a number, and handed it to the DC.

He looked between the detectives. 'Is that it? I've lots of work I need to get on with, if it's all the same to you.'

'There's just a couple more things we'd like to ask you about, and the first is regarding your motor racing hobby,' Joseph said.

He looked at them warily. 'What about it?'

'You raced with Jimmy and another man called Ralph Richards, didn't you?'

'Yes, I often take one of the cars we've restored here. Last weekend I was racing on the Branton circuit in the Jensen Interceptor parked outside that me and the lads fixed.'

If Forbes knew Joseph had been in the same race, he wasn't giving anything away.

'I see... And how is it you know Ralph Richards?'

'The same way that I know Jimmy, the three of us were at school together.'

'And Ralph is a business associate as well?' Megan asked.

'Hell no. The man runs one of those gastropubs. Too fancy for my tastes. I'm more of a burger and chips man. And before you ask, other than sharing an interest in classic motors, that's as far as our friendship goes.'

Once again, the denial of any real friendship between them made Joseph even more suspicious.

'Right...' Joseph replied. 'Okay, one last question, and we'll be out of your hair. Can you think of anyone with a motive to murder Jimmy?'

'God knows, he wasn't everyone's cup of tea, but to burn him to death?' Matthew shook his head. 'What sort of psychopath would do that to someone?'

'Okay, then I think we can leave it there for now.' Joseph handed Forbes a card with his contact details. 'If you think of anything that would be useful to our investigation, just give me a call.'

Matthew's gaze skimmed over the card. 'Of course, Detective Inspector Stone. Let me show you out.' As they left the garage, Forbes added, 'If you ever want a car restored, you know who to call.'

'I'll certainly keep that in mind.'

Once Megan and Joseph were out of earshot, the DC turned to him. 'I think it's fair to say that Matthew wasn't exactly a fan of Jimmy's.'

'Don't be so sure about that. He may be deliberately trying to underplay it, especially as we know they ran a crooked betting ring together at Branton. Also, don't forget that photo of Jimmy, Matthew, and Ralph. They certainly looked like the best of chums in that to me.'

'Hopefully, Ian and Sue will have managed to get some information to corroborate that when they interviewed Ralph.'

Joseph nodded as they got into the Peugeot. It was at that moment that a set of double doors to one of the adjacent businesses opened and a weasel-faced man emerged, a beanie hat pulled down over his head, despite the heat of the day.

The air caught in the DI's throat. It was none other than Daryl Manning, the toerag who'd deliberately rammed him off the racetrack. But of even more significance was what he caught a brief glimpse of before the door was closed again.

Even though he wasn't a car man, even Joseph recognised the purple vehicle as a very expensive Lamborghini, and a new one at that. But then, any sight of it was lost as the door was closed again and Manning disappeared into the main garage.

Megan, who'd been concentrating on putting her seatbelt on and had missed the entire show, caught Joseph's expression. 'You look like a man who's just been told they've won the National Lottery.'

'Oh, this is a much better feeling than that. I've just spotted Manning, which suggests a direct connection between Forbes and what had happened at the race. We need to get back to St Aldates and persuade Chris to mount a surveillance mission on this place ASAP. I think it might also be worth doing the same over at Richards's gastropub. I think if we scratch the paintwork, we'll quickly discover a whole other criminal business, just beneath the not-so-glossy exterior of this establishment.'

CHAPTER SIXTEEN

UNDER THE COVER OF DARKNESS, Joseph and Megan sat in the Peugeot parked at the end of a lane in a wood next to the business park. The trees gave them the perfect cover to watch Forbes's garage from the comfort of their vehicle without the danger of being spotted. The only problem was the night was almost as hot as the day. Even with the windows cranked down, Joseph's shirt was already sticking to his back.

'Another day, another surveillance operation that's bad for my waistline,' Megan said, tucking into her third almond croissant of the night. The crumbs from it were only adding to the fine dusting of icing sugar she'd already dropped on her clothes.

'You really don't need to eat them all in one sitting,' Joseph replied, watching the garage doors of Classic AutoWorks through the telephoto lens of a Nikon camera.

'What can I say? I have no willpower when it comes to tasty pastries.'

'Or any other food, for that matter. Not that you need to worry, you're still as thin as a whippet.'

'Oh, you sweet talker, you.' Megan licked the icing sugar from her fingertips and then set to work trying to shake the crumbs from the creases in her top. 'Any sign of activity in the garage yet?'

'Going by all the lights showing through the skylights, they're definitely in there. The only problem is whatever they're up to is hidden away behind those doors. Considering the lateness of the hour, my instinct is this has everything to do with Matthew Forbes's criminal sideline.'

Megan nodded. 'Chris wouldn't have been able to get Derrick to sign off on our operation, including a tactical support team running video surveillance across all the access roads, unless the DSU felt there was sufficient evidence. He even managed to get his authorisation for a stakeout of Richards's gastropub, The Feasting Fox, to play things on the safe side. Although word on the street is that he still wasn't exactly keen. Anyway, that brand new Lamborghini hidden away in the other garage only adds to the suspicious nature of the businesses being run in there.'

'It does seem Matthew may have his fingers in a lot of pies, especially as there's no record of any Lambo registered to him. Rather significantly, it also matches the description of a car stolen from a research lab in Oxford only a week ago. That's the fourth supercar to have disappeared in as many weeks. In my experience, if you can manage to trace one stolen car, that often leads to uncovering a whole series of connected thefts.'

Megan nodded. 'Apart from pointing us in the direction of Jimmy's murderer, hopefully, we're also on the verge of cracking open a major car-theft operation. Maybe when we eventually haul Forbes in for questioning, we might even unearth links to this Night Watchmen crime syndicate. Talking of which, any word back yet from the NCA about the files Chris handed over to them?'

'Nothing yet, but that's not unusual if it's become an active investigation, especially if they're working with Interpol. The boys and girls at the NCA tend to keep things to themselves, especially as they may be inserting an undercover officer to infiltrate the organisation, and want to avoid any leaks. The first we'll probably know about it is when any arrests are announced in the papers.'

'But surely there has to be some crossover with our own investigation into Jimmy's murder?'

'Almost certainly, and to be honest, I'm surprised the NCA didn't want us to hold off with this surveillance operation on Forbes's garage. Which is why you can bet Derrick had to secure their blessing first. That tells me the NCA may have bigger fish to fry, probably based on what they've already learned from Kate's research. Alternatively, maybe we're the equivalent of a sharp stick being poked into a hornet's nest. They may just want to see what we stir up here.'

'Oh, how I'd love to be a fly on the wall of the NCA investigation.'

'You and me both,' Joseph said.

The DI's phone vibrated, and he took it out of his pocket to see Martin Seven's name on the screen. He was one of the TSU officers who was currently camped outside the business park in a converted Ford Transit van filled with surveillance equipment.

'Hi, Martin,' Joseph said, taking the call. 'Anything interesting turn up yet?'

'Indeed. A lorry just turned off the main road, and is on its way into the business park.'

Joseph glanced at the Peugeot's dash clock to see it had just edged past one a.m. 'Not exactly the time you'd expect deliveries to arrive.'

'I know. We've already run the plates which, surprise, surprise, seem to be cloned.'

'Okay, that sounds promising. Keep us updated if you see anything else.'

'Will do,' Martin replied before ringing off.

At that moment, a nondescript grey lorry came into view on the access road. Both detectives hunkered down in their seats as the vehicle's headlights skimmed over their hiding spot in the trees. The vehicle swung around and began reversing rapidly up towards the same unit where Joseph had briefly caught sight of the Lamborghini.

As the lorry came to a stop, Joseph already had his finger on the shutter release of the camera and started taking photos.

'Come to papa,' he whispered to himself.

A driver and two other guys leapt out of the lorry. They headed around to the back, pulling the rear doors open and quickly hauling two metal ramps down. One of the men disappeared inside the lorry and, seconds later the rumble of a high-powered performance engine started up. A red Ferrari came into view, reversing down the ramp as the roller door to the garage was raised. That was the moment both detectives spotted what had been previously hidden from them.

A collection of high-end exotic supercars glinted under the garage's fluorescent lighting. The detectives could also see Forbes inside talking to his men as they watched the Ferrari being reversed into the unit to take up its position among the other vehicles.

'Bloody hell, we've hit the jackpot,' Joseph said, continuing to take photos.

'You're telling me,' Megan replied, peering through her binoculars. 'I can see a Porsche 918 Spyder, a McLaren Senna, and even a Pagani Huayra among them. Based on a quick mental calculation, collectively those ten vehicles are easily worth over five million.'

Joseph sucked air through his teeth. 'And if I'm not

mistaken, despite the colour being wrong, four of those cars, including the Lambo we already know about, match the description of cars stolen in the area recently.'

'Forbes's team certainly has all the gear in there to respray them.'

'Along with the ability to alter their VINs, and no doubt, creating fake documentation. That's one hell of a side hustle for someone who already makes a lot of money from restoring vintage cars.'

'Why bother doing it at all?' Megan asked.

'Greed? Some people are just addicted to making money and don't know when to stop. Or maybe this is all about funnelling cash into the Night Watchmen to pay for things like drug shipments. These sorts of crimes are never as straightforward as they first appear. The most relevant question for our investigation is, how, if at all, does this link to Harper's murder?'

'We've still a way to go working out that riddle,' Megan said, as the driver got out of the Ferrari.

Moments later, the Porsche had been started up and driven up into the lorry. By the time the garage door was rolled down again, the lorry was already heading off into the night.

'I wonder where they're taking that Porsche?' Megan asked.

'Wherever it is, Martin and the TSU team will be all over it like a rash on a baby's bum and setting up an alert on any ANPR cameras to keep track of it. Hopefully, that will help lead us to another link in the chain of this crime gang.'

'But surely, cars worth that much have some sort of tracking device installed on them?' Megan asked.

'No doubt. That's why you can guarantee the lorry and the garage both have jammers installed to kill any hidden trackers. Then Forbes's team can take their time locating and neutralising them. One thing is for sure, we're dealing with a very slick and organised criminal gang here. And for all we know, they're also part of a much bigger operation working for the Night Watchmen.'

'Talk about winning the lottery with this stakeout,' Megan replied with a smile. 'So, do you think we've got enough evidence to persuade Chris to organise that raid yet, at least if the NCA don't want to swoop in and steal all the glory from us?'

'Damned right we have. When we show these photos to the DCI, I don't think he'll have any problem getting Derrick to sign off on a raid, and hopefully as soon as tomorrow. Meanwhile, let's see what other goodies we can dig up tonight. I'm feeling lucky.'

As the detectives' surveillance shift crept towards the early hours of dawn, Megan ended the call she'd been on. 'Good news. The ANPR cameras tracked the lorry with the Porsche 918 Spyder inside it to Dover, and TSU has alerted the NCA. They're going to be liaising with Interpol to see where it ends up on the other side of the channel.

'Excellent news. This is looking like it's going to be the start of a very bad week for Forbes and his business associates. We'll keep this place under constant surveillance until Chris presses the button on the raid. Hopefully, by the end of this little episode we'll have a clear lead on why Jimmy was killed and by whom.'

'Here's hoping.' Megan gestured at the garage. 'I wonder why Forbes is still in there. All his guys left over an hour ago. You don't think we missed him slipping away, do you?'

'Based on the fact that his Jensen Interceptor is still parked outside, and as we haven't heard anything from the team who has his house under surveillance, I think we can be as sure as we can be that he's still in there.'

The DI looked through the zoom lens at the light glowing from a skylight. Forbes had no idea how his whole world was about to come crashing down around him, especially if he had a hand in Harper's murder.

Then he spotted a flickering orange glow reflected in the glass.

What?

Suddenly, a smoke alarm shrilled out into the night as smoke curled out from beneath the garage door.

'Feck!' Joseph said. 'Call the fire brigade and ask for backup.'

'Already on it,' she said, punching the number into her mobile.

Joseph leapt out of the Peugeot and sprinted towards the garage as the veil of smoke pouring out beneath the door grew thicker. The DI reached a door next to the unit's garage entrance and yanked it open, charging into the small office where they'd spoken with Forbes earlier.

On the other side of the office window, flames and smoke were billowing out of a vehicle inspection pit inside the garage. The fire was already reaching up towards the ceiling and spreading outwards. Even through the glass, Joseph could feel the temperature was already intense as the fire started to consume the cars in a flowing circle of expanding flames.

Then he saw a man staring at him from the far side of the garage beyond the wall of flames, wearing a crash helmet and dressed in motorbike leathers. Spotting the DI, the figure darted through a door at the rear of the property.

Joseph's mind whirled. Was Forbes actually their mystery motorcyclist, and attempting to torch the evidence before he escaped?

The DI rushed back outside, almost running headlong into Megan, coming to help him. Then they both heard a motorbike being revved and the next moment, the detectives caught a brief glimpse of a rider on a trail bike emerge from the side of the garage. But rather than head away on the road out of the business park, the motorcyclist turned left through a gate at the far end of the business units and raced away over a grassy field. Joseph just had a chance to snap a photo of the motorbike's number plate before it disappeared from view.

'Get Uniform to set roadblocks up around the immediate area as fast as possible to try and intercept that bloody motorcyclist,' Joseph ordered.

Megan nodded as a sickening scream came from inside the garage.

'Bollocks!' Joseph said, turning around to head back inside.

The DC grabbed his arm. 'You can't go back in there; you'll be killed.'

'I can't just stand here and let someone burn to death,' the DI shouted. He shook her off and raced back into the office.

Beyond the glass window of the office, the fire was expanding rapidly, already far beyond the capabilities of the lone extinguisher hanging on the office wall. Searching desperately for the source of the cry they'd just heard from outside, he spotted movement in the inspection pit.

Two burning hands were clawing at the edge of it as someone inside tried to pull themselves out.

Shite! The DI looked around for anything that would help protect him from the growing inferno. He spotted a towel dumped in a sink in the corner. He rushed over and stuck it under the tap, before draping it over his head and grabbing the fire extinguisher.

Joseph took a deep breath a split second before reaching for the door handle to the garage. Searing pain burned through his palm, and he yanked his hand away.

'For feck's sake!' he growled, wrapping the towel around his hand and trying again.

He pulled the door open. A wall of heat and smoke rushed into the small office. His animal instinct was already screaming at him to get out of there, but he was too hard-wired and far too stubborn not to help someone in trouble, whatever the danger to himself. That drove him forward towards the figure still desperately hanging onto the edge of the blazing inspection pit.

The smoke billowed through the room, stinging Joseph's eyes and making it almost impossible to see anything. He dropped to the floor, where there was a space beneath the swirling fumes. The DI crawled across the floor on his belly towards the hands of the figure.

An anguished man's cry came from the pit. 'Help me!'

Joseph recognised Forbes's voice. The DI quickly unhooked the hose from the extinguisher and squeezed the trigger. He directed the white foam from the nozzle into the pit, dampening some of the flames around the garage owner. He knew in that moment this was his one and only chance to save the man. Joseph reached in and grabbed hold of one of Forbes's wrists and hauled the man, his coveralls blazing, out onto the floor.

Forbes's blackened and blistered skin made bile fill the back of Joseph's throat. But he fought through it, directing the last of the foam in the extinguisher over the burning figure, just as the inferno roared up again in the pit.

Joseph heaved Forbes with him under the thickening cloud of smoke, back towards the office. Every centimetre of movement felt like a marathon, the smoke pressing ever lower and stealing the last of the oxygen away. The DI dug in with everything he had, hauling the injured man towards the open office door and their only means of escape. A massive boom rocked the garage as a petrol tank exploded, the shockwave pushing the smoke downwards to envelop them.

The DI choked as the impossible heat wrapped tighter around them, and he knew that neither of them was going to make it.

Suddenly, hands grabbed the DI and began dragging him outside into the sweetest, freshest air. They helped him up into a sitting position. Megan crouched next to him, and Martin Seven squatted by Forbes, as the burnt man's charred lips opened and closed.

'Are you okay, Joseph?' Megan asked.

He nodded. 'Just get me over to Forbes.'

With Megan's help, he crawled over to Forbes, who lay in a foetal position. He was almost burned beyond recognition, a long gash down the back of his head like he'd been struck with something.

The injured man's eyes locked onto the DI's as he neared. Joseph lowered his ear to the man's lips and heard the barest whisper.

'Revenge...' Forbes said, his voice barely audible.

With a loud groan from behind them, a section of the garage roof fell in an explosion of sparks.

Forbes's gaze turned towards his business as it burned to the ground. Then, with a rattling sigh, the man's eyes glazed and his mouth stilled as the last of his life fled.

Joseph dropped his head and began coughing violently, trying to clear the sting of smoke from his lungs. Megan gently rubbed his back as blue lights appeared around the edge of the business unit and raced towards them.

CHAPTER SEVENTEEN

After Joseph had been signed off by the paramedics for what thankfully turned out to be only mild smoke inhalation and a slight burn to his palm, he'd made a point to ring Amy before word got back to her about what had happened.

After he'd reassured her that he really was fine and there was no need to rush straight over, he'd finally grabbed some much-needed sleep.

However, from the moment he'd woken up, a feeling of foreboding had filled the DI about the implications of this latest fire. If the arsonist had already murdered two people, there was no reason he wouldn't strike again, and if so, where?

Ignoring Chris, who said he should at least take the day off, Joseph was determined to go in. Although he had no reason to like the man, witnessing Matthew Forbes burn to death had sickened the DI to the core of his being. No one deserved to die like that. That was why he and Megan had just arrived back at the garage to find two fire engine crews rolling up their hoses. They looked as exhausted as the DI felt.

The DC grimaced as she took in the scene of devastation before them. The three garage units had been reduced to nothing more than a pile of rubble and twisted girders. The burnt-out remains of a dozen cars poked out of the wreckage like the carcasses of metal animals.

Amy's forensic van was already parked up nearby, as was a fire service pickup truck.

'Are you doing okay there, Megan?' Joseph asked her as they got out of the Peugeot.

'Okay, although I'm not sure I'm going to get the image of Matthew Forbes's burned and blistered face out of my mind in a hurry.'

'You and me both. It was an awful way to go.'

'It's also one hell of a way to be ruled out as a suspect. At least it's already confirmed in his post-mortem, that Rob came in especially early to do, that Forbes was assaulted with the same weapon that was used on Harper, directly linking both murders.'

'Not that we needed it confirming, we saw the motorcyclist fleeing the scene of the crime,' Joseph replied.

Amy, standing in front of the wrecked garage doors, spotted them and waved the detectives over. They ducked under the inner perimeter tape and headed towards the SOCO.

Amy's eyes narrowed on Joseph as they neared. 'What are you doing here? You should at least be taking the day off.'

'I'd just end up pestering you all about the case anyway. Besides...' The DI held up his bandaged right hand from where he'd grasped the door handle. 'Apart from this, I'm as right as rain.'

'Then you were extremely lucky. I know you can't help yourself, but running into a burning building? What the hell were you thinking?'

Joseph shrugged. 'It seemed a good idea at the time.'

Amy shook her head. 'Make no mistake, we're going to have words about this later.'

'Good luck with that,' Megan said. 'Joseph's pig-headiness aside, how are things going with the crime scene?'

'Slowly,' Amy replied. 'We're still waiting for the fire investigator to make his initial assessment before my team and I are allowed onsite.'

'Not that there's going to be a lot of forensic material left for you to discover after this blaze,' Joseph said.

'Don't I know it, but there's always a chance we'll get lucky and find something.'

'So what about our mystery motorbike rider, any leads from your team there?' Megan asked.

The SOCO pulled a face. 'Apart from some wheel tracks one of my team managed to get a cast from, we haven't unearthed any other evidence yet. But we've already been analysing the photos you snapped last night. The bike was an off-road Yamaha YZ250, built around 2002. Also, in case you were in any doubt, we ran biometric measurements of the rider and guess what?'

'They match the rider caught by the CCTV outside Jimmy Harper's showroom, as well as the man we chased from his penthouse flat?' Joseph asked.

'You nailed it.'

The DI thought of the last word Forbes had said. 'The last thing Matthew uttered was the word revenge. That suggests this really is some sort of vendetta. So whoever this person is, it turns out their sights obviously weren't just set on Jimmy.'

'So what about the rival gang theory?' Megan commented.

'That's certainly still a possibility,' Joseph replied. 'But if this is something like a turf war between gangs, there's a real danger that it could escalate quickly. If that's the case, we'll need to call in the big guns and have the NCA take over.'

'But we're not there yet, either,' Amy said.

'I agree. Once Chris and the team have rounded up

everyone who worked here, hopefully we'll find out some answers when we interview them.'

Amy nodded as a firefighter wearing breathing equipment and a full face mask emerged from the burned-out shell of the garage.

'So what's the news, Thomas?' Amy asked, as the firefighter pulled off his breathing mask when he reached them.

It was only then that Joseph recognised the guy as the same man he'd met at the showroom fire.

'As you probably guessed, it was definitely arson,' Thomas replied. 'The fire was deliberately started in the inspection pit, with petrol from some fuel cans which were thrown in there, too. I also found the remains of a shattered bottle in there, suggesting a Molotov cocktail was used to ignite it. Whoever did that was almost certainly responsible for pushing Forbes into the inspection pit as well.'

'But surely Forbes would have put up a stiff fight?' Megan asked.

'Maybe, but not if the arsonist crept in and knocked him over the head so he couldn't resist,' Amy said.

'However he ended up in there, once the fire was lit, Forbes didn't stand a chance,' Thomas added. 'The fire quickly spread from the inspection pit into the adjacent garages through the roof void. Unfortunately, a sprinkler fire suppression system that the garage had used wasn't working as it doesn't seem to have been maintained.'

'That doesn't exactly surprise me, considering the amount of illegal activity going on here,' Joseph said. 'The fewer people who knew about what was really happening inside these garages, probably the better as far as Forbes was concerned.'

'The value of the cars in the other garage that also burned is enough to make anyone's eyes water.'

Megan raised her eyebrows. 'My heart bleeds for the gang.'

Amy gave her a wry look. 'Is there anything else to report, Thomas?'

'No, that's about it from my side. You're free to send your people in whenever you're ready to, Amy.' With another nod, Thomas headed off towards the pickup truck.

'Okay, time for me and my people to see what, if anything, we can find in there,' Amy said. With a wave, she headed off to her team, who'd gathered around the forensic van, waiting for her.

An unmarked Volvo V90 with Chris at the wheel parked up, and the DCI climbed out. He took in the burnt-out garages as he reached them. 'Christ, someone wasn't messing around.'

'They followed a similar MO to Harper's murder,' Joseph replied.

'Then we need to get to the bottom of this investigation as quickly as possible, and there, I come bearing some good news. We've rounded up all of Matthew's employees including, Daryl Manning.'

Joseph raised an eyebrow. 'And what about our mystery motorcyclist?'

'I'm afraid I've got bad news there.' Chris scowled. 'Despite flooding the area with officers, he managed to evade all our road-blocks, and there's been no further sightings of him. We suspect he kept to an off-road route. Unfortunately, it was too late to get a helicopter out to start an air search.'

Joseph picked up on his boss's tense body language. 'In other words, a certain senior officer, who will remain nameless, wouldn't sign off on it?'

Chris gave him a wary look. 'I never said that.'

Joseph shrugged. 'You didn't need to.'

The DCI grimaced. 'Then, quickly moving on... We do have another piece of key evidence. Doctor Jacobs just rang from the post-mortem to say they found the murderer's calling card stuck in the victim's larynx.'

'A two-headed coin with heads on both sides, by any chance?' Megan asked.

'Two-headed, but it was actually tails this time,' Chris said.

Megan frowned. 'So why tails in this instance and heads for Jimmy's murder?'

Joseph scratched his chin. 'There has to be some significance to it. And, of course, there's another thing that links Forbes and Harper.'

'They were both involved in running a crooked gambling ring at the racetrack?' Megan said.

'Bingo.'

Megan looked at the other detectives. 'What if this double-sided coin business was all about a fixed toss? The victim calls heads or tails, but they lose either way. That would certainly fit with the theory that this is a disgruntled punter who lost money on one of their fixed races.'

'Bloody hell, you could be onto something there,' Joseph said.

Chris nodded. 'If there is a punter who's hell-bent on vengeance, maybe one of Forbes's employees will be able to cast some more light on it when we interview them. Talking of which, if you fancy catching a lift back to the station, you can join me in that interview with Manning, Joseph.'

'Oh, I'd be bloody delighted to,' the DI replied. He turned to Megan. 'You could do worse than stay here to watch Amy and her team at work, which is never an opportunity to miss.'

'Will do. I'll catch you both later. Just take it easy on Manning and remember to punch him somewhere the bruises won't show.'

Both Chris and Joseph stared at her.

'Got you,' she said, grinning at them, and then heading over to the forensic van to help herself to a suit and mask.

'She really is a quick study,' Chris said as they watched the DC walk away.

'You better believe it,' Joseph said with a smile.

'Just tell us what you know and it will go far easier for you,' Chris said, sitting back in his chair in interview room one.

Daryl Manning sat across the table from them with his solicitor, who seemed as disinterested as his client.

'I'd listen to the man, Daryl,' Joseph said. 'We already have a long list of things to prosecute you for.'

Manning sneered at them. 'Such as?'

The DI started counting on his fingers. 'One, being involved in an illegal gambling ring working out of Branton and God knows where else. Two, not only helping to fix the outcome of races held there, but also making sure that any challengers on the track were driven off it. Just to refresh your memory, in case there is any danger of forgetting, that included deliberately ramming a car on the track last Saturday with two Thames Valley Police detectives inside it, namely us. Three, being involved in stealing highly valuable supercars to-order. So, DCI Faulkner, how many years inside do you think that all adds up to?'

Chris moved his palms further apart. 'A very long stretch indeed. Daryl here will probably get out when he's ready to draw his state pension.'

Manning raised his eyebrows at the detectives and crossed his arms. 'No comment.' He smirked at his solicitor sitting next to him, who gave him a small nod.

'Are you sure about that?' Joseph replied. 'Especially since whoever killed Matthew Forbes may want to come after you next?'

Of course, the DI knew nothing of the sort, but this was a calculated fishing expedition to see if they could prompt the gobshite to open his mouth.

Surprisingly, that seemed to suck some of the arrogant confidence out of the lad.

His expression became wary. 'What do you mean?'

'We mean that unless someone starts talking, we will have no idea of who may have murdered your boss. And until we find out more, that may mean that the individual responsible for dousing Matthew in petrol will come after his employees next.'

The solicitor held up a hand. 'That is pure speculation on your part.'

Joseph nodded. 'Maybe it is.' He narrowed his eyes at Manning. 'The question is, are you prepared to gamble your life on it, Daryl?'

The lad scratched his neck. 'You're offering me police protection, then?'

'Oh, we can do better than that. We can lock the psychopath away,' Chris said. 'Also, if a certain someone were cooperative, the CPS might be open to negotiating a reduced sentence, especially if any information given helped lead us to a breakthrough with Jimmy Harper's murder as well.'

This time, the look that Daryl exchanged with his solicitor was a lot less cocky. The man frowned back at Daryl.

Daryl closed his eyes for a moment, then opened them again. 'Okay, what do you want to know?'

Joseph resisted the urge to punch the air. They'd hooked the gobshite. Now to reel him in.

Chris leaned across the interview table. 'To start with, do you know anyone who might have wanted to murder Forbes?'

Manning laughed. 'How long a list do you want? Probably

about half the punters who lost money on the races we fixed, and some of them were big rollers too.'

So that supports that theory, Joseph thought.

'What about a rival gang wanting to take him out?' Chris asked.

'They wouldn't dare. Matthew was untouchable because of who he knew. There was this one local group of car thieves who made the mistake of trying to lift a motor from one of our garages. Not only was Matthew tipped off long before it was going to happen, but let's just say his connections organised a little reception committee.' Manning held up his hand and spread his fingers wide. 'Then, puff, they were gone.'

Chris leaned forward on his elbows. 'You mean they were taken out?'

'Who am I to say? But one moment the other gang were crowing about how they were going to steal a car from Matthew and the next they simply vanished off the face of the planet.'

Joseph made a mental note to check any disappearances of local gang members around the Didcot area.

'Can you give us the names of Forbes's associates?' Chris asked.

'Well, you get one for free, as he's dead now anyway, Jimmy Harper. Now that man was as big a bastard as they come. We used to supply his showroom with stolen-to-order vintage motors. A lot of the time, they were cars he hadn't been able to persuade the owner to sell at a knockdown price. Then, after enough time had passed to avoid raising suspicions, we stole the vehicle, resprayed it in the shop, changed the chassis number, and Jimmy would sell them on to an unsuspecting buyer.'

Chris nodded. 'We guessed as much. So what about the modern supercars? Who were they for?'

'Again, stolen-to-order, and we shipped them off overseas, mainly for parts. But that's as much as I'm prepared to say about that, at least without a written plea bargain in the hands of my solicitor. Even then, I may think twice about it. We're talking seriously dangerous people here.'

To Joseph, it certainly sounded like the Night Watchmen crime syndicate that Kate had been busy investigating.

'Okay, let's put that aside for a moment, while we see what can be sorted out with witness protection, especially if you can supply names,' Chris said. 'But for now, let's just concentrate on Forbes. Is it possible that one of these powerful contacts decided to take him and Jimmy out for some reason?'

Manning shrugged. 'It's certainly possible, but that wouldn't make sense. Look, it sounds like you know about some of the motors that were torched. Why would the people we supply cars like that to, want to burn them along with everything else? Besides, we made them so much money, your idea doesn't hold water. No, my bet is some pissed-off punter ordering a hit job, without realising exactly who they were taking on.'

Joseph thought of the motorcyclist. Is that who he was, a hitman? If so, where did the missing business ledger fit into all of this?

'So what about Ralph Richards?' Chris asked. 'What connection did he have to Matthew and Jimmy?'

Daryl shook his head. 'Sorry, I'm keeping schtum about him until I have that deal on the table.'

'Okay, but do you think Richards might have a motive to have the other two men burnt to death?'

'Nah, those three went way back. Also, apart from being in business together, I think they had so much blackmail material on each other, none of them would have dared to make a move on the others without some serious blowback.' Manning slouched in his chair, his sneer back in residence. 'Anyway, I think that's as far as our chat is going to go for now until we have that written plea bargain agreement.'

Joseph glanced at Chris, who nodded.

'Okay, when you've finished talking to your solicitor, we'll have you escorted back to your cell and we'll see what we can do.'

'Then it's been a pleasure, gentlemen,' Manning said with a smug expression, as though he thought he had just won a get-out-of-jail-free card.

Joseph resisted the urge to slap the eejit across the face as he got up and followed Chris out of the interview room.

CHAPTER EIGHTEEN

It had been a long day at work for Joseph and the rest of the team, interviewing Forbes's employees from Classic AutoWorks. All of them had been much more tight-lipped than Manning had been, but the team hadn't contradicted anything they'd learned from the lad, either.

Now, at last, the DI had made it home to *Tús Nua* after grabbing one of the more upmarket burgers from the Five Guys on St Giles. He'd managed to cram it with all the toppings it was physically possible for them to put on a bun.

The DI had just thrown the windows open to try and dissipate some of the heat trapped in the cabin, and was getting ready to tuck into his feast, when a knock came upon his cabin door.

'Hi there,' Joseph called out.

'It's only me,' Dylan said as he came in with Wild Fang and Max at his heels, both sniffing the air. Then, like laser-guided missiles, the dogs were sitting before Joseph, looking up at him and his burger, expectantly licking their lips.

'Talk about cupboard love,' Joseph said. When he held out a curly fry to each of them, the dogs' licking grew more frantic, bodies quivering with anticipation, eyes locked onto his. 'As my ma would say, dig in, guys.' The dogs didn't need to be told twice. Both chips vanished from his hand in a blink of an eye.

Joseph gave Dylan an impressed look. 'That obedience training is going well then.'

'When it comes to food, they are the perfect pupils. But try calling them back when they're chasing a pigeon and it's another matter.'

Joseph ruffled both dogs' heads. 'Creatures after my own heart.'

'You like to chase pigeons as well?' the professor said with a small smile.

'Metaphorical ones, if you think of them as criminals.'

'Ah, of course, talking of which, how is your latest investigation into the two murders going?'

'How do you know it's two now?'

In answer, Dylan held up the newspaper he'd been carrying, along with a folder.

It was one of the tabloids, with the headline, *Burning Man Arsonist Strikes Again.*' Scanning the article, he wasn't surprised to see it had been written by the festering armpit of a journalist, Ricky Holt.

Joseph shrugged. 'I suppose it was only a matter of time before the news broke in the press about the second murder. Chris isn't going to be happy, though. But on the upside, we now have something to call the arsonist.'

'Yes indeed, and almost erudite for a tabloid, no doubt based on the Burning Man Festival held in the Nevada Desert.'

'Tabloid reporters have never been shy about borrowing and then twisting a name. Anyway, to answer your question about the investigation, we appear to be on the right track now. We have one of Matthew Forbes's employees giving evidence in exchange for a plea bargain with the NCA. Thanks to that, it looks like we're on the verge of cracking open a car-stealing gang who specialises in some very expensive motors.'

'It sounds like you've had a very productive time of it. But how is the first murder investigation coming along?'

Joseph sighed. 'It's sort of a case of not being able to see the wood for the trees. Apparently, there are a lot of punters who placed bets via an illegal gambling ring to fix vintage car races. The ring was run by Jimmy, Matthew Forbes, and Ralph Richards. Needless to say, two of those people are now dead and from what we've learned, it sounds like there are plenty of scammed punters out there with a motive to want them dead. The problem is we have no way of identifying who they are, as there are no records of who gambled with them...' Joseph snapped his fingers. 'Of course, the missing business ledger. I bet there was a list of punters in there who have been scalped.'

'You're saying the reason for breaking into Jimmy's flat and stealing the ledger was to make sure anything linking the person behind these murders to a badly judged bet was removed?'

'It would certainly fit the facts we know. Thanks for this chat, Dylan, it's really helped clarify my thinking.'

'You do realise that I actually didn't come up with anything on this occasion and it was all you?'

'Sometimes it just helps to think things through out loud. First thing in the morning, this idea about the ledger is going to go up on the board as a working theory.'

Dylan smiled. 'Then I'm pleased to have been your sounding board.'

Joseph's phone warbled, and he saw Chris's name on the screen. 'What is it, boss?' he said, as he took the call.

'I thought you'd want to know that a plea bargain has just been agreed between the CPS and the NCA about Daryl Manning. According to Derrick, all the paperwork has been done and we're going to be transferring him tomorrow to a high-security unit.'

'As much as it irritates the hell out of me that Manning might be about to walk free, if it helps prove a connection between the Night Watchmen, Harper, and Forbes, then I can live with it.'

'That's good, because Derrick wanted two detectives for babysitting duty for the prisoner transfer.'

'Seriously? Can't Uniform deal with it? Manning isn't exactly a kingpin.'

'Oh, don't you worry, Uniform will be there, as well. Derrick just thought it would help with the formal handover to the NCA officers so we can brief them in person.'

'Great, but what a waste of time. All of that could have been done with a phone call.'

'I agree, but Derrick insisted. However, Megan was picking my brains about what the NCA do, so I thought it might be a good opportunity for her to meet them. Besides, I could do with having two officers there who know the case inside out. That's why I've nominated you two to escort the prisoner transfer.'

Joseph kept the groan in. 'Okay, if we must. But boss, I think I may have just come up with a possible motive for why that business ledger was stolen.'

'Go on.'

With a thread of an idea that was rapidly starting to take shape in his mind, the DI proceeded to brief his senior officer.

The following day, Joseph had taken the wheel of the unmarked Volvo with Megan riding shotgun. Ahead of them was the police van, driven by none other than PC John Thorpe, along with PC Paul Burford, with Daryl Manning held securely inside the prisoner compartment in the back.

Realising that fate had provided Joseph with an opportunity to mend some broken fences with John, the DI had been good to his word. He'd been positively pleasant to the young officer before they set off, not a scowl to be seen. Hopefully, that would mean when Ellie's boyfriend reported back to her, Joseph's good behaviour would spare him from another ear-bending.

The DI glanced at the satnav again, wishing the journey could go more quickly. 'I still think having us on security escort detail is serious overkill,' he muttered.

Megan shrugged. 'Look, it's only going to take a few hours out of our day, then we can get back to the murder investigation.'

'Which we may not have for much longer if the NCA manages to dig up anything to link Harper and Forbes's murders directly to the Night Watchmen. If so, you can guarantee they'll take over our murder investigation as well.'

'We're not there yet, especially when everyone has warmed to your theory about the ledger being stolen by some disgruntled punter who hired a hitman.'

'We'll see, but it wouldn't be the first time the NCA has swooped in to take over all aspects of a case,' Joseph replied.

'You do realise we're all on the same side and this isn't some sort of competition?'

'Even so, I would like to see this one through to the end.'

Megan nodded. 'You're not the only one. But I'm still looking forward to meeting the NCA team. It must be really interesting dealing with the big picture stuff they handle, like drug trafficking, money laundering, and the rest.'

'Oh, are you now?' Joseph said, casting her a sideways glance.

'What's that look meant to mean?'

'Just that it sounds like the sort of thing someone who fancies working there one day might say.'

Megan shrugged. 'Who knows, but it never hurts to be ambitious.'

'Don't you enjoy my company?'

'It's nothing like that. It's just the idea has intrigued me of one day, in the far future, working at the NCA.'

Joseph nodded. 'Fair enough, as long as you don't mind through-the-roof stress and long hours.'

'Hang on, that sounds just like our current job.'

The DI grinned. 'Yes, now you mention it, it does a bit.'

Their convoy was now heading out of Oxford on the A420 along a single-carriageway section. Joseph checked his mirrors again but couldn't see a single vehicle in sight.

The DC spotted what he was doing. 'That must be the hundredth time I've seen you do that since we started this journey. You can't seriously be worried we're going to pick up a tail?'

'In my experience, it's always good to maintain situational awareness and not get complacent. Just because Manning is a low-hanging fruit as regards the Night Watchmen, that doesn't mean someone won't do their best to stop him talking to the NCA.'

'You mean you think they'd try to snatch him during the transfer?'

'I know it's highly unlikely, especially as there's no way they could know he's negotiated a plea bargain. Besides, only a handful of people are in the loop about Manning being transferred today, let alone the route we're taking, so I'm not expecting any problems. But that doesn't mean we should get complacent.'

'You do realise that sounds a bit like paranoia?' Megan said.

'Maybe, but it's also based on many years on the job.

Besides, you'll need that in spades yourself if you're seriously thinking about joining the NCA one day.'

The DC made a show of looking in her own wing mirror. 'Better?'

He gave her a slow smile. 'Much.'

But then a frown filled Megan's face as she took a second glance. 'Looks like we have an emergency vehicle rapidly approaching.'

Joseph glanced in his own rear-view mirror to see strobing lights in the distance. Then he made out the ambulance, closing rapidly as the sirens grew louder.

He picked up the radio mic and pressed the transmit button. 'We should let the ambulance pass, as it's obviously on an emergency call. Over.'

'Roger that, out,' John's voice replied.

The DI tucked the Volvo in as close as he could to the kerb as the police van in front did the same, leaving plenty of room for the ambulance to get past.

Sure enough, with a blaze of light and sound, the emergency vehicle streaked past them and was soon heading away into the distance.

'Maybe we should do the same and use the lights,' Megan said. 'At least we would get there faster.'

'Once a speed freak, always a speed freak,' Joseph replied.

'Says the man who was tearing around a racetrack only last weekend. Talking of which, are you really okay to drive?'

Joseph held out one hand flat above the steering wheel. 'See, steady as a rock. I'm doing absolutely fine.'

'I sort of guessed that since you haven't given me a chance to drive since then.'

'What can I say other than my car phobia seems to be behind me, and in no small part, thanks to our boss.'

'Chris is certainly one of the good ones. Anyway, at this rate, you'll be buying yourself a new vehicle and selling off your mountain bike.'

Joseph made a scoffing sound. 'As if.'

Joseph frowned when he noticed the ambulance had come to a stop about half a mile up the road. A black BMW 5 series had partly skidded off the road. The emergency vehicle had parked in the opposite carriageway, effectively blocking the road, and traffic was already starting to build up in the opposite direction.

As the detectives neared the crash site, they could see the BMW's door was open, and the driver was lying on the ground.

'For feck's sake, an RTA is all we need,' Joseph said.

'We can always get the ambulance driver to move so we can go round,' Megan suggested.

Joseph shook his head. 'No, we can't drive past a road accident. They may need our help.'

The car's radio bleeped and Joseph picked up the mic again.

'Hi, what do you want us to do?' John's voice asked from the speaker.

'You and Paul sit tight with your prisoner. Megan and I will see if there's anything we can do to help.'

'Understood—out,' John replied, as he slowed the police van to a stop just before the crash scene.

Joseph pulled the Volvo up behind it. As he and Megan got out, the DI was already scanning the devastation beyond the police van. There wasn't a sign of so much as a broken bumper or bent panels on the BMW. In fact, the more the DI looked at it, the more it looked like it had just been parked. The only sign that anything was wrong was the paramedic bending over the driver, lying on the ground.

'Do you think the driver had a heart attack at the wheel?' Megan asked, obviously also confused.

Too slowly, Joseph's instinct kicked in. Something was off

here. But before he could say anything to Megan, the paramedic spun round to reveal he was wearing a black balaclava. More significant was the Heckler and Koch MP5 submachine gun in his hand.

Everything went into slow motion in Joseph's mind.

Without even pausing to shout out a warning, the man pulled the trigger, spraying the police van with bullets. Then the BMW driver, who'd been lying on the ground, jumped to his feet. He was also wearing a balaclava and brought up a Glock to point straight at the detectives.

Without thinking, Joseph grabbed Megan. He hurled her and himself to the ground as the man fired three rounds that whistled over their heads.

'Stay down!' a man with an East End London accent shouted.

Adrenaline thrummed through Joseph's body as time sped up again.

Two drivers from the vehicles at the front of the tailback on the other side had got out to see what was going on. Thankfully, they jumped back into their vehicles as the gunman waved his Glock towards them.

'What the hell are we going to do?' Megan asked as she looked up.

'Call for backup; they're armed and we're not,' Joseph replied.

The blood pounded in his ears as he pulled his mobile out and punched the call button. 'Emergency, emergency, emergency, this is DI Stone. Location is on the A420 just south of Oxford. Police convoy intercepted by two suspects armed with firearms...' His voice trailed away as the other gunman ran up alongside the police van, slipping a fresh magazine into the MP5.

'Shite, they are going to spring Manning—' The words died

in Joseph's mouth as the man aimed at the rear doors of the van and opened fire.

Bullets punctured the metal panels, sending sparks flying. The pungent smell of cordite filled the air as the gunman emptied the MP5's entire magazine into the prisoner compartment of the van.

As the submachine gun rattled to silence, anger roared through Joseph. Without thinking, he was pushing himself up onto his hands, intending to charge the fecker, when the other gunman aimed his Glock straight at him and Megan again. The gunman raised his other gloved hand, and shook his finger slowly from left to right.

Joseph checked himself. No, any foolhardy heroics would get them both killed.

'Don't move a muscle, Megan,' he hissed.

Megan managed the smallest of nods, her back rising and falling as she stared at the ground.

Joseph's heart crowded his mouth as those terrible seconds extended. Was the gunman weighing up whether he needed to end their lives?

'Don't be so bloody stupid,' he called out, glowering at the man, trying to ignore the churning fear in his gut.

The gunman held the DI's gaze a moment longer, then turned to his accomplice and nodded. Without a word, both men raced back to the BMW and leapt into it. Within a handful of seconds, their vehicle was racing away down the road past the queue of stationary traffic on the other side of the road, into the distance.

Joseph and Megan jumped to their feet and raced to the cab of the Transit, its windscreen crazed where the bullets had smashed through it.

The DI yanked the driver's door open, his heart hammering hard.

John was slumped in his seat over the steering wheel, blood bubbling up between his fingers as he pressed them into the wound in his shoulder. Paul Burford was slouched over as well, but hanging against his seatbelt like a marionette.

'Paul's in a bad way,' John said through gritted teeth.

Megan was already yanking the passenger door open. When she pulled Paul forwards, Joseph saw the bullet wound to his left temple. The DC placed her fingertips against his neck.

'He's got a pulse, but it's weak,' Megan said, her hand trembling.

'Right, you stay here and call for the air ambulance. I'm going to check on Manning.' Joseph reached down and unhooked the keys from John's belt. 'Don't move. Understand, John?'

'Don't you worry about that,' the PC replied, almost managing a smile.

Joseph gently patted his arm, then ducked back out of the transit to see a woman running towards him from the line of parked cars.

'Please get back in your car,' the DI called out.

'No, you don't understand. I'm a doctor,' the woman said as she reached him, raising her medical bag in her hand to illustrate the point.

'Then please do what you can for the two injured officers.'

She nodded and headed for the open driver's door.

Joseph steeled himself as he headed to the back of the van.

His sense of foreboding was confirmed as soon as he unlocked the rear door and opened it. Daryl was lying on the floor of the prisoner compartment, his body riddled with bullet holes, his eyes staring lifelessly up at the ceiling.

Joseph put his hands on his head. 'Shite!'

CHAPTER NINETEEN

Joseph held Ellie's hand as they sat in the hospital waiting room. She rested her head against his shoulder, both of them sitting in silence. They were waiting for the doctor to make an appearance to let them know about the surgery John was undergoing to remove the bullet from his shoulder. Ellie had been the first to arrive at the hospital and John's other family members were already on their way.

Amy had gone uncharacteristically quiet at the other end of the line when Joseph had told her what had happened. Kate, on the other hand, had taken the news badly and was heading over as soon as she could to support him and their daughter. But for now, at least, his instinct told him the fewer people pacing the hallway as they waited for news, the easier it would be on Ellie.

Opposite them sat Paul's wife, Sarah, who had a young girl with her. The mother clutched the child's hand, gently murmuring to her as she attempted to read a picture book to her daughter through her tears.

But Joseph was barely able to comprehend any of this.

His head was filled with a roar of noise, hardly able to process what had happened. But the overriding emotion already making it through the throng to the front of his mind was a terrible feeling of guilt. Somehow, he'd made it through the ambush unscathed.

He would give anything to be able to trade places with either of the two officers who'd taken a bullet. Worst of all, he'd been the senior officer at the scene and couldn't escape the feeling that the responsibility for this shite show rested on his shoulders. His mind had already come up with a dozen *what-if* ways he could have done things differently.

Megan and Chris entered the waiting room with cups of tea in their hands. The DCI peeled away to talk to Sarah, as Megan headed over to Joseph and Ellie.

'Any news?' Megan asked as she sat down next to them, offering each of them a cup.

Ellie lifted her head and wiped away her tears as she took one. 'They haven't told us a thing about John, other than to tell us to try not to worry.'

Megan reached out and squeezed her hand. 'That sounds like good advice to me.' She looked at Joseph. 'What about Paul, any update there?'

Joseph's gaze travelled to Sarah, who was listening to Chris and nodding. His heart went out to his boss, who was doing his best to comfort the wife of an officer who'd been badly hurt in the line of duty. That responsibility was one of the hardest when you were the one in charge.

'Not looking great,' the DI said, returning his attention to Megan. 'He'd lost a lot of blood, but they're doing what they can...' He balled his hands into fists. 'If I ever get my hands on the arsewipes that did this...'

Megan reached out and took his hands in hers to squeeze them. 'That's for another time.'

The DI sighed and nodded. 'Is there any news about those scumbags yet?'

Megan pulled a face. 'Not a sign, despite Derrick authorising two police helicopters for the search. It was certainly a well-planned operation. It turns out that the ambulance they used had been stolen from the vehicle bay at the John Radcliffe Hospital. It only came to light that it was missing when its crew turned up at the start of their shift. They reported it missing after the ambush had already happened.'

Joseph blew his cheeks out. 'The thing I can't get my head around is how they knew that Manning had made a plea bargain, which is presumably the reason they took him out.'

'Yes, that's what Chris has been asking too. The suspicion is currently about the solicitor, who may have been leaned on by somebody, not that he's admitting it if he was. But there is a more worrying idea that's been floating around, too.'

Joseph nodded. 'It's already occurred to me as well. We may have someone on the inside who leaked the information to the Night Watchmen syndicate.'

Ellie, who'd been listening, stared at both of them. 'You're saying there's a bent copper at St Aldates who could have tipped them off?'

'I hope not with all my heart, but we also have to consider all possibilities,' Joseph replied.

'That's why the NCA has taken a very active interest in what happened, and is going to be interviewing everybody involved in the case,' Megan said.

'If we've got a leak, let's hope they find the gobshite sooner rather than later and make them pay.'

Megan nodded. 'Apparently, Chief Superintendent Kennan has given Derrick a roasting about not carrying out an adequate threat analysis for the prisoner transfer beforehand and arranging an armed guard.'

'Damned right,' Ellie said. 'If Derrick had done his job properly, John and Paul wouldn't be lying in surgery now.'

Joseph looked at his hands as he grimaced. 'I just wish I could have done more.'

Megan's eyes narrowed on him. 'Please tell me you're not blaming yourself for any of this?'

'It's hard not to...'

'Oh, give me strength,' Megan said. 'It wouldn't have worked out any differently if it had been Chris or anyone else there. And before you say anything, there wasn't any time to even try to negotiate. They opened fire without giving anyone a chance. Besides, if you hadn't thrown me to the ground, I would probably have ended up in surgery as well, if not killed outright. I owe you everything, Joseph.'

'But John and Paul...' the DI gave them both a hopeless look.

Ellie took a shaky breath and put an arm around his shoulders. 'You can't protect everyone, Dad. You know that deep down, right?'

He met her gaze and then cupped her face with his hand. 'Since when did you become so wise?'

'It's one of the entry criteria to get into Oxford, so I had to get my act together.' She gave him a small smile, which elicited one in return.

A female doctor in a white coat appeared and headed towards Sarah and the child. Chris watched with a wary gaze as the woman approached. The doctor squatted down before Sarah, saying something they couldn't hear. Sarah burst into tears, and then, nodding, with her child in tow, followed the doctor as she led them away.

Chris headed straight over, meeting their worried looks. 'They've had to induce a coma. It turns out the bullet literally scraped the side of his brain. But the doctor is hopeful Paul should survive, although they won't know the extent of his brain injury until they eventually bring him out of the coma.'

'Oh, Jesus,' Joseph said. 'Chris, I just wish—'

The DCI cut him off with a shake of his head. 'No, before you say anything, this isn't on you.'

'That's what we've been trying to tell him,' Ellie said.

'It's the natural response to second guess oneself in a situation like this, and that includes Derrick and myself,' Chris said. 'Our DSU is currently beating himself up over it, and I certainly am too. The thing we all need to remember is that even the NCA didn't have any intelligence that someone would seriously consider targeting Daryl. At most, he was a minor player.'

Joseph sighed. 'I think we were all blindsided by this, boss. Not that it's any comfort to Paul and John right now.'

Before Chris could respond, Ellie suddenly gripped her dad's arm as a male doctor headed towards them.

'Ellie Stone?' the man asked when he reached them.

'Yes...' She reached out and squeezed Joseph's hand hard.

'John is now out of surgery. The bullet shattered his left clavicle and we've put a plate in. But with physio, I'm pleased to say he's going to make a full recovery. We would be having a very different conversation if the bullet had been just a few centimetres down. Your boyfriend is a very lucky man indeed.'

Ellie nodded and then burst into full-blown sobs.

Joseph scooped her into his arms, as some of the tension that he'd been carrying loosened its stranglehold on him a fraction. He kissed the side of his daughter's head as she shook.

'You did hear the part where the doctor said he was going to be alright?' he said, gently.

She hiccupped a laugh as she pulled away from him. 'Why do you think I'm crying so hard, Dad?'

Joseph rubbed her shoulder, before turning to the doctor. 'Can we go and see him?'

'He's only just come out of surgery and is still a bit woozy. So it's best if it's just one visitor for now.'

'Then you'd better get going, love,' Joseph said to Ellie.

She smeared her tears away, nodded, and followed the doctor, the three detectives watching them go.

Chris turned to Megan and Joseph. 'Okay, this is the first proper opportunity to ask how you both are after the shit hit the fan?'

'I can't lie, I've had better days,' Megan replied.

The DCI nodded. 'And you, Joseph?'

'Looking down the barrel of a gun never gets easier. But I personally want to get hold of the scrote, and get up close and personal with him in a cell.'

Chris grimaced. 'You do know that even if they're caught, that may never happen as the NCA will definitely take over the reins of the murder investigation as well, especially after what happened.'

Joseph sighed. 'I know, but as long as those feckers get to face the music, I can live with it, even if we're not the ones making the arrests.'

'Good, but for what it's worth, I actually feel the same. But talking of handing it over, the NCA team has already launched a full investigation into a possible leak at our end.' He held up his hands. 'And yes, I know, this has nothing to do with either of you, but at best someone has slipped up. At worst, something more worrying is going on here and we need to get to the bottom of it as quickly as possible.'

'Well, I'm happy to do whatever that takes,' Joseph replied.

'And me,' Megan added.

'Good, then when you can, head back to St Aldates for your formal interviews with the Internal Affairs Department, that way you can both be eliminated from the NCA's investigations. Then, after everything you've been through, I don't want to see hide nor hair of you in the station until Monday. Take a moment to catch your breath, that's an order.'

'Understood, boss,' Joseph said.

'In that case, how do you fancy doing something to take your mind off things?' Megan said.

'Such as?' Joseph said.

'If you fancy joining us, I'm heading off with Rob to an archaeological dig on Saturday.'

Joseph caught Chris's surprised look. 'Apparently, the DC's idea of a good time is to spend time digging holes in the ground.'

'I see, each to their own, and all that,' the DCI said.

'Don't knock it until you try it,' Megan said. 'Anyway, I was also thinking of asking Dylan because I thought it might be his sort of thing.'

'He's a huge fan of anything to do with history, so you might be right,' Joseph said.

'And yourself?'

The DI considered the alternative of ruminating about the case all weekend, then shrugged. 'Why the hell not? So now I appear to have caved in, is this Rob character a certain pathologist I know?'

'In one—it's Doctor Jacobs.'

Chris's eyebrows arched. 'You're going out with him, Megan?'

'God no, but we are friends. Rob shares my passion for archaeology and we recently started going to digs together in our spare time. Anyway, what about you, Chris? Fancy joining us as well?'

'I'm afraid I'm going to be up to my eyeballs with the aftermath of what happened today, but thanks for the offer anyway.'

'There will always be other occasions.'

'No doubt,' Chris replied in a tone that left Joseph in no doubt he wouldn't be taking Megan up on that particular offer anytime soon.

Joseph had just finished his interview with the Internal Affairs Department, going over every detail of the ambush that had led to Manning being executed, John being seriously injured, and Paul fighting for his life. An Investigative Officer had picked over Joseph's statement with a fine-tooth comb. But when the DI hadn't been able to add anything, the woman seemed satisfied and had finished the interview.

He was just heading out of the room when he ran into Megan, waiting for her turn to go in.

'How did it go?' she asked.

'Absolutely fine.'

'Good...' the DC said, wringing her hands.

'Please relax. This is just a formality.'

'Then why do I feel like a criminal getting ready to face the music?'

Joseph chuckled. 'Oh, that's completely normal when you're on the wrong side of the interview table. The important thing is that neither of us has anything to hide. But it's Internal Affairs's job to try and work out how those hitmen knew that Manning was being transferred at that particular time and location.'

'Of course...' Megan said, setting to work on nibbling the quick of her right thumb.

Joseph gently took hold of her hand and lowered it from her mouth. 'Don't take your nervousness out on your fingers.'

'Sorry, a bad habit of mine.'

'It will be a breeze, trust me. Anyway, do you want me to wait until you're finished?'

'No, you get yourself home and try to put today behind you.'

'Well, if you need me...' Joseph made a phone with his hand and held it to his ear.

'Oh, don't you worry, I will.'

The interview room door opened and the Investigative

Officer appeared in it. 'DC Megan Anderson, I'm ready for you now.'

Megan nodded, and Joseph gave her a thumbs-up as she headed into the room.

A short while later, having changed into his cycling gear, the DI was just unchaining his mountain bike from the stand in the car park at the rear of the station when he heard someone approaching. He looked around to see Derrick heading towards him with an expression he wasn't used to seeing on the man's face—a look of concern.

'I'm glad I caught you before you headed off,' Derrick said. 'I just wanted to check you're okay, Joseph.'

The DI looked at the superintendent. 'Well, it's certainly been a bit of a day of it. All we can do now is pray that Paul makes it.'

'I'm going straight to the hospital after this to check in on him and John. But first I just wanted to see that you and Megan were really alright?'

Joseph was taken aback by the slight quaver in the man's voice. 'We're both okay, although I wish Megan hadn't been subjected to something like this so early in her career.'

'Absolutely,' Derrick replied, nodding vigorously. 'I also just wanted to say you should take as much time off as you need.'

'Chris has already beaten you to it, and told us to take the weekend off.'

'That was generous of him,' the DSU replied with a small smile.

Joseph snorted. 'No, it's not like that. We're fine, Derrick. We both just need to take a moment to catch our breath and then we'll be back at the coalface. Besides, in my experience, the best way to cope is to get straight back on the horse after it's thrown you.'

'Of course. But if you need longer, just ask.' Derrick took a deep breath. 'Look, I just wanted to say that although we haven't always seen eye to eye, you're a good copper.'

Joseph had to fight hard to stop his jaw from hitting the floor. 'Thank you for saying that.'

'I mean it,' Derrick said. Then, of all things, he patted Joseph on the shoulder before turning and heading back into the station.

Well, colour me fecking surprised, Joseph thought as he got onto his mountain bike and got ready to set off for home.

CHAPTER TWENTY

JOSEPH HAD ENDURED a listless night on *Tús Nua*. Apart from the extreme heat, whenever he closed his eyes, the first thing his mind returned to was the ambush. Then, reliving the moment they'd opened the door to the police van to see John and Paul shot. That was quickly followed by the guilt that Manning, a prisoner under their protection, had been executed.

The DI kept trying to rack his brains about what he could have done differently, but kept coming up blank. Intellectually, Joseph understood there was nothing else he could have done to prevent what had happened, but his subconscious still hadn't got the memo.

Everything pointed to the Night Watchmen having Daryl assassinated before he could talk. Biometric data based on the security footage from the van's dashcam had shown the builds of the two hitmen didn't match those of the Burning Man arsonist. So everything pointed towards a crime syndicate, determined to do whatever it took to keep its secrets. If nothing else, the attack on a police convoy in broad daylight showed just how confident the Night Watchmen felt that they could reach out and act with impunity. That line of thinking had led to him becoming even more worried about Kate's safety.

Would a hitman eventually turn up on her doorstep to silence the journalist who'd been poking her nose into their business?

But one question kept bothering him about that anonymous email she'd received. Why bother to issue a warning at all? Why not have Kate experience an unfortunate accident and be done with it?

That riddle aside, Derrick's lack of judgement about not including an armed escort was the icing on the cake. It seemed everywhere the DI looked, all he could see were problems, and now he felt worn down to his bones by the weight of it.

However, of all things, it was a quote his pa once called out during an eight-hundred-metre school race when Joseph had been a lad, that rose to the surface of his mind in those early hours of the morning: *'Don't break when you're worn out. Break when you've crossed the finish line.'*

That had focused his mind. He might not ever have access to the big-picture answers about the Night Watchmen, but he could certainly throw himself into solving the murders of Harper and Forbes. Solve those, and it might at least give him some peace.

The unending spiral of questions swirling inside his head was the reason Joseph was on his way into the incident room, having finally decided to put his insomnia to good use.

His plan was to pick over the statements of all of Forbes's employees to see if he could spot anything. As he opened the door, the DI was surprised to see Megan in a t-shirt and shorts, sitting at her desk, sipping from her water bottle and staring at her screen.

'What brings you in at this Godforsaken hour?' Joseph asked.

'I couldn't sleep. Anyway, look who's talking.' Megan couldn't hide the grimace behind her forced smile.

That notched Joseph's worry up. 'Are you okay?'

'To be honest, I've been better. I know we haven't really had a chance to talk about it, but that ambush really shook me up.'

Joseph met her gaze and nodded. 'You're not the only one.'

'Yeah, I imagine that seeing fellow officers get shot never gets any easier,' Megan replied.

Joseph was impressed the DC's first concern was about her colleagues, rather than the fact she herself could just as easily have been killed. Which was exactly the same attitude he had about what had happened. Worry about them first, before getting around to yourself.

'Something like this weighs on everyone,' Joseph said. 'The best way I know to help deal with it has always been to throw myself into work. In an ideal world, we would get the opportunity to arrest the bastards who did this. But we've been deprived of that opportunity because the NCA is dealing with the Night Watchmen case. However, we can still throw ourselves into our murder investigation, before the NCA has any ideas about taking that from us as well.'

Megan nodded. 'If we can bring the arsonist to justice, it will certainly help me sleep a lot better at night.'

'You're not the only one.' Joseph's gaze travelled to the evidence board. Jimmy Harper and Matthew Forbes's photos were at the top of it. Next to that, Chris had written, '*Connection to Night Watchmen?*'

Megan followed his gaze. 'I keep thinking we're missing something key in this case. Maybe some time away from it at the archaeological dig will help me gather my thoughts.'

'Shite, that completely slipped my mind.'

'You're still coming, though?'

'A promise is a promise, but I'm afraid I forgot to tell Dylan about it.'

'Don't worry, I gave him a ring because I thought you might be a bit preoccupied. He sounded very enthusiastic about the whole idea, and promised to make some epic sandwiches.'

'Now you're talking. Dylan's BLTs are some of the best.'

'Then it sounds like you're still in?'

'It does, doesn't it?' Joseph replied, raking his hand through his hair.

The sun was beating down over the corner of the farmer's field where Joseph, Megan, Dylan, and Doctor Jacobs were digging with the trowels they'd been given by the dig organisers, along with their Hi-Viz vests. They were working alongside a team of at least ten other amateur archaeologists, who'd been painstakingly helping to excavate the site of what was once a Roman villa.

As a last-minute thought, Joseph had even tried to persuade Amy to join them for the dig, but she'd responded over the phone with, *'And why would I do that?'*

He was beginning to think she had the right idea.

The DI's back was aching after working crouched down for so long, carefully scraping away the dry earth from the side of one of the outer walls of the building with his trowel. Every inch of him was dripping with sweat, his mouth as dry as the fine dust blowing over the excavation site in the scorching heat. He stood up, rubbing the small of his back, and grabbed his water bottle from his bag.

Megan looked across at him from one of the internal walls she was helping to excavate with Dylan and Rob.

'Fun, isn't it?' she asked him.

'Up to my knees in dirt has always been my definition of a good time,' he replied, giving her a straight look.

Dylan put down his trowel and looked across at him. 'You mean it's not firing your imagination? Just try to picture the original villa that stood here somewhere around the fourth century. Personally, I find that rather inspiring.'

Joseph looked around them at the parched field on the edge of the Cotswolds, with not a lot going on anywhere. 'If you say so.'

'What's happened to the Irish poetic spirit inside you?' Dylan asked.

'I think I must have missed the handout on that one when I was born.'

Megan shook her head at him. 'At least tell me it's helped to take your mind off things a bit. Goodness knows we both need some time away from our jobs after the week we've had.'

Rob sat back on his haunches. 'Yes, such a bad business. You and Megan must be traumatised about nearly getting shot.'

Megan pulled a face. 'That's the thing. All things considered, I feel fine. What I am cut up about, though, is what happened to John and Paul. Those gunmen didn't even give them a chance.'

Joseph nodded. 'It's clear their lives meant nothing to those hitmen.'

'That's actually what bothers me about this whole thing,' Megan replied. 'Why were they both shot, but we were spared, Joseph? It doesn't make any sense.'

'That's often the random nature of these things,' Rob said with a shrug.

Joseph remembered how one of the gunmen had wagged his finger at him. 'Actually, now you mention it, Megan, I think you may have a point there. They could've easily finished us off.'

'Exactly. Not that I'm complaining.'

'I'm just relieved that you're both okay,' Dylan said. 'However, Ellie must be incredibly stressed about what happened to John.'

'She's a lot more relieved now she knows that he's going to be okay, albeit with enough hardware inside him to set off the scanners at the airport,' Joseph replied. 'But it's also shaken her. I don't think she quite thought through the flip side of dating a police officer. Although she hasn't said anything, I know what's happened to Paul has really got to her, especially as she realises it could just as easily have been her boyfriend in that coma.'

Joseph noticed a frown flicker across Rob's face, who was gazing off into the middle distance. He caught the DI looking at him and nodded. 'Such a bad business. Anyway, coffee anyone? I've got a thermos back in the car.'

The two detectives and the professor shook their heads.

'As big a coffee lover as I am, even I'm going to pass in this heat. Thanks all the same,' Joseph said.

'Lightweight,' Rob said, winking at him.

'What about some fresh homemade lemonade with plenty of ice in it?' Dylan asked.

'Now you're talking my language,' Joseph said.

'God, yes please,' Megan added.

'Then I'll head back to the cars with you, Rob, to get our supplies.'

As the two men walked away, Megan turned to Joseph. 'Although I'm pleased you decided to come, I'm also surprised. I would have thought you would have wanted to be with Ellie, giving her a bit of moral support.'

'Don't worry, Kate has that more than covered. Besides...'

Megan tilted her head. 'Besides what?'

'I can't be in the same room as John without feeling a massive guilt trip right now.'

'Bloody hell. Don't be daft, this isn't on you. If you want to lay any blame on anyone, it's Derrick. The rumour is that the DSU, being the DSU, thought an armed protection unit was totally over the top for such a low-level criminal transfer.'

Joseph sucked air through his teeth. 'For once, I can see his point. However, I expect the NCA will take a dim view of that. The thing I keep wondering is how the leak happened.'

'That's exactly what everyone else is wondering, as well. Hopefully, Internal Affairs will get to the bottom of it with their investigation.'

'Here's hoping. Anyway, as regards the murder investigation, I'm interested to hear what you think the next step should be for our investigation?' Megan asked.

'The disgruntled punter is definitely one avenue we shouldn't give up on just yet. However, if I were Chris, I'd be increasing the number of bodies on the ground for the surveillance operation on Ralph Richards. Right now, we can't rule him out as a suspect. He could have hired this Burning Man arsonist. Of course, this could all be linked to the Night Watchmen syndicate somehow, too.'

'So many questions, so few answers. Just as well I don't have a personal life as I wouldn't have the headspace for it right now. Talking of which, how are things going between you and Amy?'

'Why do you ask?' Joseph asked, giving her a questioning look.

'It's just that you two barely seem to spend any time together.'

'Yes, two ships passing in the night and all that, because of our work.'

'But surely, even if you are both flat-out busy, I thought you would have still made sure you carved out some time for each other.'

Joseph sighed. 'You're not wrong.'

That was the thing. If he was entirely honest with himself,

there was one thing holding him back from really throwing himself into his new relationship with Amy. In a word, Kate. They might be divorced, but he still carried a candle for her, and it made trying to navigate a new relationship extremely tricky.

'Maybe I've been a bachelor too long and just need to get over myself,' he eventually said.

Megan gave him a small smile and nodded. 'If you say so.'

Rob and Dylan were headed towards them with a flask and several bottles of lemonade.

'Here we go, everyone,' Dylan said as he handed them each a cold bottle.

As the DI took his first sip, he gave the professor an impressed look. 'That is absolute nectar in this heat.'

'Isn't it just?' Megan said, wiping her mouth with the back of her hand.

Dylan smiled. 'Are you sure I can't persuade you to try some, Rob?'

'Maybe after I've finished my coffee,' he said, brandishing his thermos.

Joseph returned his attention to the digging and quickly became lost in his own thoughts. Now that he thought about it, he realised he'd hardly given any real thought to Amy. Normally he would have simply put it down to being intensely busy with the investigation. But maybe he'd also been keeping her at arm's length.

Kate, however, was well and truly at the forefront of his mind, despite hearing next to nothing from her since she'd said she was going to back off the Night Watchmen case. Derrick's increasingly erratic behaviour was also a cause for concern. Was his ex-wife simply keeping her head down because she had a lot going on in her personal life?

He put down his trowel for a moment and took out his phone, quickly composing a text to Kate.

'*Are you free for a quick catch-up this evening?*' he wrote, then hit send.

Her reply came back in a handful of seconds. '*To be honest, I'm a bit snarled up with work.*'

Are you now?' Joseph thought. '*Then maybe I can swing by the newspaper and bring you some takeout from that Lebanese place you love,*' he texted.

'*You sweet talker, you always know your way to my heart! See you later then. X.*'

Joseph pocketed the phone again and got back to work. He scraped his trowel through the dirt to reveal something silver hidden there.

He gestured towards it. 'I think I may have found something.'

Megan's eyes widened as she spotted the object he'd uncovered. She quickly slipped on some latex gloves, hooked her fingertips and carefully lifted it to reveal a silver coin.

'Is that Roman?' Rob asked, peering at it.

'Yes, and on Joseph's first bloody dig too, talk about beginner's luck,' Megan said.

She picked up the coin and carefully began dusting the remaining dirt away with a brush that had been hanging from her belt. She turned the coin over to reveal the same image of a two-headed man, the faces looking out to the left and right of the coin.

Dylan leaned in to look at it. 'Will you look at that? This coin has the god Janus on both sides.'

'And who was Janus when he was at home?' Joseph asked.

'He was the Roman god of beginnings, endings, and transitions,' Dylan said. 'Janus was often depicted with two faces looking in opposite directions, symbolising his ability to see both the past and the future.'

Joseph felt a prickle running up his spine. 'Feck, and it's also a two-headed coin. That almost feels like a sign that we need to keep pushing with our investigation; we may be getting somewhere.'

Rob smiled at the DI. 'You're not telling me that you've suddenly become superstitious, are you?'

'Who knows, maybe a teeny tiny bit.'

Dylan gave him an amused look. 'If you're going to subscribe to signs from the gods, maybe you should consider taking this archaeology gig up full-time.'

'Well, if it helps encourage me at moments like this during an investigation, I just might,' Joseph replied, smiling.

CHAPTER TWENTY-ONE

AFTER HAVING BEEN BUZZED in by the security guard who knew Joseph, the DI walked up the stairs of the Oxford Chronicle, making his way towards Kate's office. He headed along the glass-walled corridor and spotted her in the corner of the open-plan office at her desk, the only person in the room.

All the windows had been flung open, and she'd positioned a floor-standing fan to blow cool air directly at her face. The moment the DI opened the door, he understood why, as a wall of sauna-level heat hit him square in the face.

'Bloody hell, and I thought our office was hot,' he said.

'Not compared to ours, it isn't,' Kate said. 'With the wafer-thin budget we run this paper on, there's not exactly a lot of money left for air conditioning.'

'The people in charge might want to rethink that strategy if we keep getting heat waves like this. Anyway, I come bearing gifts,' Joseph said, waving the Lebanese takeout bag at his ex-wife.

'And your gifts are very welcome, good sir,' Kate replied, smiling at him as she cleared a space on her desk so there was somewhere for Joseph to actually place the food among all the chaos.

He started to unload the containers of salad, hummus, koftas, and flatbreads out of the bag, and glanced at Kate. 'So, why are you burning the candle at both ends yet again this evening?'

Her gaze quickly slid away from his, and she shrugged. 'Oh, just the usual.'

'Right. So this has absolutely nothing to do with the Night Watchmen story you promised me you'd back away from?'

Kate winced. 'I know what I said, but...'

Frustration boiled up through Joseph. 'Kate, what in the hell are you thinking? If you keep down this road, poking your nose into that crime syndicates business, it could end badly for you.'

Kate shrugged. 'And what sort of journalist would I be if I allowed them to scare me off by just going *boo* at me in an email?'

'For feck's sake, it's a lot more than *boo*! We're talking dangerous people here, who, to be honest, I'm amazed gave you a warning.'

She gave him a thin smile. 'Maybe they like my face?'

Joseph had to force himself not to grind his teeth. 'Give me strength. Please, Kate, you've got to stop your investigation. Just think of how Ellie would feel if something happened to you?'

'I hope she'd feel proud that I'd been dedicated enough to root out a criminal organisation by putting my life on the line.'

Joseph stared at her in disbelief. 'You can't be serious?'

'Actually, I am. When you discover how, among other things, teenage girls have been trafficked for prostitution... Well, it's not exactly the sort of thing I can just walk away from.'

'But you've already done your bit. Let others take over from here, specifically the NCA, who know how to deal with these organised crime groups. This doesn't need to be your battle anymore. Besides, didn't the NCA tell you to back off as well?'

'They did, but I work for this paper, not them. I'm following my instinct, which is telling me to keep digging.'

'You really are the most stubborn woman on the planet.'

Her gaze tightened on him. 'Joseph, as a detective, I thought of all people you would understand why I need to pursue this. In only the last few days, you could have died on the racetrack and again when your police convoy was ambushed. But I don't see you backing off.'

'That's different.'

'Is it really, though? You do know how hypocritical that sounds, right? You sound just as bad as Derrick, who keeps telling me to back off; pleading, actually.'

Joseph at least felt some relief at hearing that. 'So you've finally told him about the threatening email?'

The hardness that had started to appear in Kate's eyes evaporated. 'Yes, not long after you said I had to. Needless to say, he took it badly.'

'I'm not surprised. Anyway, that explains a few things. The guy is obviously worried sick about you. His mind certainly isn't on the job like it should be.'

Kate frowned. 'In what way?'

'For example—and this needs to stay strictly between us—he didn't authorise an armed guard protection for the prisoner transfer.'

His ex-wife's expression grew pale. 'What on earth was he thinking? If Ellie ever hears of this, she'll go ballistic.'

'Don't I know it, and it was Derrick's lapse in judgement that caused all this fallout.'

Kate closed her eyes. 'I had no idea it had become this bad.' She opened her eyes again to look at Joseph. 'Something's been wrong with Derrick for a while now. He's been drinking too much, and has major mood swings. And it's been getting worse. I've started to really worry about him, Joseph.'

Much to his own surprise, the DI felt the stirrings of real concern for the DSU. 'What do you think is at the bottom of it?'

'Maybe he's just burning out on the job. He certainly hasn't seemed happy at work for a while now.'

That was news to Joseph. He was often under the impression that the superintendent had been put on Earth just to give him permanent ball ache, a job he seemed to relish. But it was getting hard to ignore there was something increasingly erratic about Derrick's behaviour.

'I can't quite believe I'm going to suggest this, but would you like me to have a quiet word with him?' Joseph asked.

'I wouldn't waste your breath. I've tried dozens of times. I'm just hoping whatever it is, the man I know and loved will eventually surface again.'

The past tense of the word *love* made Joseph's ears prick up. But then he immediately felt cross at himself, not least because he was meant to be in a relationship with Amy. But that aside, his deepest wish was to see Kate happy. If there were problems in her marriage, all he hoped was that they could work it out, if only for her sake.

'Right...' he said. 'But Derrick aside, after everything that's happened this week, I'm increasingly worried about your safety. I know how important this story is to you, Kate, but there's every chance the NCA will stop you publishing anything in the press until they've finished their investigation, and even then, they may never want all the details to come out in public.'

'Oh, this is far bigger than just a story to me now, Joseph. I need to keep going on this until I know the whole stinking edifice supporting that crime syndicate has been destroyed.'

A small smile tugged the corners of Joseph's mouth. 'A woman on a mission, huh?'

'Bloody right, you know me so well.'

'Okay, in that case, I won't waste any more breath trying to change your mind, but please be vigilant. The moment it starts to feel like you're getting in over your head, you talk to me. Do we have an understanding?'

Kate gave him a salute. 'Yes, sir.' Then she smiled at him. 'So now you've given me the lecture, what do you say we tuck into this food? I'm starving.'

Joseph nodded and began helping her plate up the food.

'So, I want to hear all the latest gossip about you and Amy,' Kate said, steering their conversation into safer waters.

'It's all grand,' Joseph said, avoiding her gaze as he took out the hummus.

'Oh, you man of few words. Anyway, I expect you're at that stage of not being able to keep your hands off each other.'

'Wouldn't you like to know...'

'Well, she's a lucky lady to have snagged you. I'm just so pleased for you, Joseph. You two are perfect for each other.'

He gave a small smile. But he could tell by the look on her face that Kate wanted him to find happiness, as much as he wanted that for her. Whether she would with everything that was currently going on in her life, he wasn't sure anymore.

When Joseph arrived back at *Tús Nua* on his mountain bike, he found Dylan sitting like a guard on duty in a deck chair next to his boat, *Avalon,* a water pistol on his lap, scowling at his bird feeder.

'What's with the face?'

'A squirrel, that's flipping what. One of the blighters discovered the bird food and keeps driving the birds away.'

Joseph gave him an amused look. 'Let me get this right. You've been sitting here, ready to squirt if it tries its luck again?'

'Damned right I will.'

'I can see a slight flaw in this plan of yours. Doesn't that mean you have to sit here each and every day to guard your feeder?'

'Oh, don't you worry about that. I have a plan. A passerby suggested I should get myself a squirrel-proof feeder. So if you could order one for me from Amazon, I'll pay you back.'

'Consider it done and my shout. After the number of things you've helped me with, it's the least I can do.'

'Then, thank you, you're a gentleman and a scholar.'

'I'm not so sure about the scholar part; that's more your area of expertise.'

Dylan chuckled, then his expression grew serious. 'Actually, I may be able to pay you back in kind, sooner rather than later.'

Joseph gave him a curious look. 'How so?'

'I've dug up something about someone with an even bigger motive to murder Harper and Forbes than a disgruntled punter. I discovered something very interesting indeed that you're going to want to hear.'

Joseph knew that look in his friend's eyes. It meant he'd come across something really significant.

'Go on...'

'I was looking back through the news archives at the library, and came across an article from eighteen years ago with a photo of Jimmy Harper and Matthew Forbes.'

'Something dodgy?' Joseph said.

'Possibly. You see, when the Gambling Act was first intro-duced, they launched a licensed casino called Excalibur up in Birmingham.'

The DI arched an eyebrow. 'That's news to me.'

'I wouldn't go beating yourself or anyone else up over this.

Excalibur was actually owned by a group called Aura Holdings. However, when I checked the listing of the business at Companies House, Jimmy and Matthew weren't even down as the men who ran the casino. Both men had listed their mothers as the directors.'

'That hasn't got a decidedly dodgy whiff to it at all,' Joseph said. 'A casino would have been an ideal venue for money laundering, perhaps even for this mysterious Night Watchmen crime syndicate.'

'I certainly wouldn't be surprised if there's a connection,' Dylan said. 'Also, and more relevant to your murder investigation, three years after it was opened, the casino was burned to the ground. Two employees were killed in the blaze, and it was reported as a tragic accident.'

Joseph gawped at Dylan. 'So you're telling me that Harper and Forbes, both victims of arson themselves, also happened to run a casino, which also burned down? Surely, that's no coincidence.'

'That's exactly what I was thinking. However, the only fly in the ointment is that the investigation came to the conclusion it wasn't arson. Instead, the fire investigator tracked it down to a gas leak in the casino's kitchen, so foul play was ruled out. I'm afraid that's where the trail goes cold, and there was nothing more reported about it in the papers. Of course, you'll be able to access the police records from the original investigation, so I was wondering...'

Joseph nodded as excitement pulsed through him. 'Leave it with me. This is going right to the top of my list of things I need to look into urgently. You, Dylan, like always, are a bloody marvel.'

'I'm just glad to be of assistance,' his friend replied with a broad smile.

The DI nodded. Once Joseph had grabbed some much-needed sleep, despite Chris's order to stay away from work for the weekend, he was going to sneak back into St Aldates first thing tomorrow so he could dig through the files about the original investigation. He could already sense in his bones that he was on the right track.

CHAPTER TWENTY-TWO

JOSEPH's large Single Estate coffee was almost empty by the time Megan showed up to work, after he'd called and asked her to come in. She also noticed two other empty coffee cups as she headed past him to dump her things on her desk.

'We must stop meeting like this,' Megan said, raising her eyebrows at him.

Joseph shrugged. 'Yes, so much for having the weekend off.'

'Just how long have you been here to get through that much caffeine?' she asked.

'Since five. I was anxious to look up some information on HOLMES2 that Dylan unearthed about Forbes and Harper.'

'Which was?' Megan asked.

'They co-ran a casino over in Birmingham called Excalibur, which just happened to burn down sixteen years ago.'

Megan stared at him, her coffee paused halfway on its journey to her lips. 'A fire you say?'

'Yes, I can tell you're already thinking along the same lines I am. And this is where it gets really juicy. The lead detective on the investigation was an officer called DCI Lewis Sanders. And although it wasn't reported in the press, according to the files, he was convinced it was a case of insurance fraud, but they couldn't prove it.'

'So you're saying it was arson?'

'In the case notes I've read, even though DCI Sanders wasn't able to dig up the evidence to prove it, all the indicators pointed to that. Also, there was more than a passing suspicion that money may have been laundered there.'

'Just like the illegal gambling ring at the racetrack, in other words?'

'Exactly. We're onto something here, Megan. I can feel it in my bones. Thank God for Dylan and his ability to dig up information that everyone else misses.'

Megan raised her eyebrows at him. 'Someone who is still a civilian.'

'I know, I know, but you and I both understand the professor can be absolutely trusted not to say anything.'

'Oh, I do,' she admitted. 'So, what motive did Forbes and Harper have to burn down their own casino?'

'Apart from claiming the insurance money, maybe the fire was a way to get rid of any evidence of money laundering. However, there is another grimmer aspect of this case. A married couple who worked there were killed during the blaze.'

The DC stared at him. 'Hang on a moment, if it really was arson for insurance fraud purposes, why would Forbes or Harper have wanted anyone killed inside the casino?'

Joseph raised his shoulders. 'It might have been an accident, and they were simply in the wrong place at the wrong time. Of course, I suppose there's still a chance it could have just been an accidental fire that led to a tragic outcome.'

'You really believe that?'

'Not if we're talking about Forbes and Harper being involved. Now we may never know, as they've taken their secrets to the grave with them.'

'But this sounds far too promising a lead to just give up on,' Megan said.

'Who said I was going to give up? Remember, the last thing Forbes said to me was *revenge*. That's why I looked up DCI Sanders to see if we could talk to him about the original investigation. He's long been retired from the force and now lives in Stow-on-the-Wold. So I was thinking, if you're up for it, we should pay him a visit today.'

'Leave it with me; I'll give him a ring now.'

Joseph gestured to the clock. 'Maybe give the poor man a moment to wake up first, rather than drag him out of his bed.'

'Ah, good point,' Megan replied.

Joseph turned his attention to the evidence board. On it, Chris had already written under possible motives: *A hit authorised by the Night Watchmen?* Maybe Forbes and Harper had got greedy and kept more money than they should have from their illegal sideline. But the more he thought about it, the more he realised this was far more personal than that. Yes, this definitely felt like a vendetta, and instinct was telling him it had everything to do with the casino fire.

Megan and Joseph were heading along a country road over the rolling Cotswolds towards Stow-on-the-Wold. The DI was humming along to the track *Experience* by Einaudi that he'd managed to persuade Megan to let him play on the Volvo V90's sound system as he drove.

'You sound like you're enjoying yourself,' Megan said.

'I have to admit, I've missed driving, especially through a landscape this beautiful.'

'It seems your crash on the racetrack hasn't put you off your newfound love of driving, then?'

'Ironically, I think that experience finally helped to exorcise the last few demons I'd been hanging onto, especially as Chris and I walked away from the crash relatively unscathed.'

'Which is great, but just one small plea. Do let me have the occasional chance to drive. You're not the only one who likes to sit behind the wheel.'

Joseph chuckled. 'Sorry, I'll try not to hog it all to myself in future.'

'Good to hear.'

They drove past a sign for Stow-on-the-Wold and were soon heading through what, in Joseph's opinion, was one of the prettiest market towns in the Cotswolds. Picture-perfect honey-coloured stone buildings were everywhere, and tourists crowded the pavements.

'As somewhere to live, this town is rather nice, if not a little bit hilly,' Megan said.

'It would certainly keep you fit. Also, if there's time, there's a tearoom here that does the best cheese scones, made from a secret family recipe.'

'Is there anywhere you don't know about all the best places to eat?'

'In a word, no, although you're giving me a run for my money with your Tripadvisor research.'

Megan laughed. 'Then I look forward to trying some of these famous cheese scones.'

'I promise you'll love them, and I'll have to make sure that I pick up a couple for Dylan as well, who's something of a fan. Anyway, here we go. According to the satnav, this is the road that DCI Lewis Sanders and his wife live on.'

As the Einaudi track soared, the detectives drove up a hill with a view back over the town, nestled in the landscape beneath them. Yes, Joseph could certainly see the attraction of

living somewhere so charming and quintessentially English—
even if he was an Irishman.

The destination marker led them towards a house at the end
of a cul-de-sac, set back from the road on a short gravel driveway.
They pulled up in front of a house, the very definition of an idyllic
stone cottage. A tumble of roses was growing up one side of the
house and well-tended flower beds edged the immaculate lawn,
which was green despite the drought. Butterflies flitted around
the bushes and at least a dozen small birds fed on several feeders
hanging from a tree that would have seriously impressed Dylan.

'So this is what retirement looks like,' Joseph said, turning
off the engine.

'You said that with an almost wistful tone,' Megan observed.

'Maybe I did,' the DI replied.

They got out of the vehicle to be met by the heady scent of
honeysuckle growing over a trellis.

'Hello there,' a cheery voice called out.

A man in his late sixties, with an impressive mane of silver
hair, emerged from the shadow of a tree with a pair of secateurs,
waving at the detectives as he headed towards them.

'DI Stone and DC Anderson, I assume?' the man said,
shaking each of their hands.

'Yes indeed, DCI Sanders?'

'In the flesh, although please call me Lewis.'

'Will do, if you'll call me Joseph.'

'Of course, Joseph,' Lewis replied, smiling. 'So I believe you
want to pick my brains about the Excalibur casino fire all those
years ago?'

'Indeed, we do, and thank you so much for taking the time
to talk to us,' Megan said.

'To be honest, I'm delighted to. You know what some old
cases are like when they didn't turn out how you would have

liked—a constant itch at the back of your brain you've never been able to scratch. I've certainly never been happy that we didn't get to the bottom of what really happened. Anyway, if you'd like to follow me...' He cupped his hand to his mouth. 'Janette, our guests have arrived.'

A woman, her grey hair tied back in a bun, hands covered with flour, stuck her head out of the top half of an open stable door in the cottage. 'Wonderful to meet you, Detectives. I'm just baking, but I won't be two ticks and then I'll bring some tea and sandwiches out.'

'That's incredibly kind, but only if it's no bother,' Joseph said.

'Of course it's not. Besides, Lewis loves any opportunity to talk shop, even if he's been retired from the force for twelve years.'

'You know me, my love, any excuse,' Lewis said, as he directed Megan and Joseph to some garden seating under an awning.

The DI sat and took in the sweeping views of the Cotswolds.

Lewis followed his gaze and nodded. 'It's quite the view, isn't it? It certainly makes a difference after working in Birmingham for thirty-five years.'

'I bet it does,' Megan said. 'You do appear to be living the dream life up here.'

'I suppose we are,' Lewis replied with a smile. 'But you didn't come all this way to talk about my retirement. I dug out my old notes on the casino case to refresh my memory. What would you like to know exactly?'

'Megan filled you in on our current investigation over the phone?' Joseph asked.

Lewis nodded.

'Then anything you think that could be relevant,' Joseph

said. 'As you're probably aware from the news, Jimmy Harper and Matthew Forbes, who ran the Excalibur casino, were both murdered in recent arson.'

Lewis's face became drawn. 'Indeed, I am. And I take it by your presence here, you think there might be a link to the casino fire?'

'It certainly struck me as a potentially strong line of enquiry, particularly as I believe a husband and wife team used to work there and were also killed in the blaze.'

'Norman and Clare Robinson, you mean.' Lewis's gaze tightened on the two detectives. 'Does that mean you think revenge might be the motive connecting these latest murders to my old case?'

'That's what we're trying to work out,' Megan said. 'First of all, what can you tell us about the Robinsons?'

'They were a married couple working as entertainers at the casino...'

His words trailed away as Janette emerged from the house, carrying a tray of sandwiches and cakes, along with a large pot of tea and a Victoria sponge cake. There was also a box file on it.

Joseph jumped up. 'Please, let me take that for you. It looks rather heavy.'

'Do I look that frail, then?' Janette said, giving him a straight look as she refused his help and set it down on the table by herself.

'Sorry, I didn't mean—'

Janette cut him off with a wave of her hand. 'I'm only teasing you.'

Lewis raised his eyebrows at his wife. 'As you can see, my wife has rather a dry sense of humour.'

'Somebody has to keep you on your toes, my dear,' Janette said, pouring tea for everyone.

Joseph was already warming to this couple. Once, this had

been his dream of retirement for Kate and himself. But sadly, that happily ever after was never going to happen now.

A black and white cat emerged from beneath a hedge and sauntered over. He barely paused before choosing Joseph's lap to leap onto.

'Goodness, Tux doesn't normally take to strangers,' Janette said. 'You must be a cat person.'

'I've never thought of myself as one, although my grandma had a big tabby called Loki. He had half an ear missing and used to beat up the rest of the cats in the village. Now, there was a cat you really didn't want on your lap, as he was likely to suddenly decide to take a chunk of flesh out of you just for fun.'

'Well, Tux is nothing like that,' Janette said. 'He's a British Shorthair cross, as gentle as they come, and also an excellent judge of people.'

'There you go, Joseph, you're a cat person after all,' Megan said, barely able to suppress her grin.

Joseph scowled slightly at her. Then he took a bite of the Victoria sponge cake. 'This is excellent.'

'It's certainly one of my better ones,' Janette replied with a pleased look.

Joseph returned his attention to Lewis. 'You were just saying that Norman and Clare Robinson were entertainers at the casino. I was just wondering what sort of thing they did?'

'They were a magic act, with Clare performing as Norman's stage assistant. They did the usual sort of thing—card tricks, rabbits out of hats, even the good old sawing a woman in half.'

Megan exchanged a look with Joseph as his pulse quickened, sensing they were on the right track here.

He leaned forward in his seat. 'Did they happen to use coins as part of their magic act?'

'Actually, now you come to mention it, I think they did,' Janette said. 'Why, is that of importance to your investigation?'

If there had been any lingering doubt in Joseph's mind, it was swept away in that moment.

'Sorry, you know about the Excalibur case, as well?' Megan asked.

Lewis smiled at his wife. 'Yes, indeed she does. I confided in Janette many a time over the years. She was my unofficial police partner on plenty of investigations. My dear wife often spotted things that everyone else missed.'

Janette smiled. 'I tried to help where I could. A fresh pair of eyes and all that.'

'That sounds a bit like me with my neighbour, who's a retired Oxford professor,' Joseph said. 'Of course, Megan doesn't approve of me talking to a *civilian* about a case.'

'Actually, I'm starting to warm to the idea after all the help he's given us,' Megan replied. 'But back to the coin tricks. What sort of thing did the Robinsons do with them on stage?'

'Norman usually borrowed a coin from the audience,' Lewis replied. 'Then he would make it disappear, then reappear inside a sealed glass bottle. They also did the classic, plucking a coin out from behind a person's ear. Norman used to carry a lucky double-headed coin in his pocket for that specific trick, which was found on his burned body in the Casino.'

Joseph sat up straighter, and looked at Megan. 'That can't be a coincidence.'

'I agree,' Megan replied.

'What, you mean the double-headed coin?' Janette asked.

The DI nodded. 'This detail never made it into the papers, and I know I can rely on your discretion to keep it to yourselves.'

'Don't worry about it, once a police officer, always a police officer,' Lewis said.

Janette made a zipping motion with her hand across her mouth, making both detectives smile.

Joseph clasped his hands together as he looked at the

couple. 'What you've just told us is very significant to our investigation. Both Jimmy Harper and Matthew Forbes were found with a double-sided coin in their mouths. Harper's coin had two heads, and Forbes's had two tails.'

Janette stopped sipping her tea, mid-sip. 'A coin palm; it has to be.'

'Sorry, I'm not sure I follow,' Joseph said.

'It's literally the oldest trick in the book. You tell someone to choose heads or tails in a coin flip and then palm the coin to make sure they always lose.'

Megan quickly nodded. 'So someone must have asked Jimmy and Matthew to choose the coin toss, heads or tails, and they lost either way.'

'And then they were burned to death,' Joseph replied with a grim face. He looked at the retired couple. 'Do you have any idea who might have known the Robinsons were killed in the casino fire, and would have a motive to kill Matthew and Jimmy?'

Janette and Lewis exchanged a long look.

'What?' Megan asked.

'Well, I hate to think it could be anything to do with him,' Lewis said, 'but Norman and Clare Robinson had a son who was thirteen at the time. He was obviously traumatised, blaming Jimmy and Matthew for what happened to his parents.'

'What did happen?' Megan asked.

'Late one night, they were packing up after a show, when the fire started in the kitchen and quickly spread throughout the casino. Because there was also a failure in the fire alarm system, the first Norman and Clare knew of it was when the flames were licking at the door of their dressing room.'

'But surely there must have been a fire exit?' Joseph asked.

'Yes, but it was blocked with boxes,' Lewis said. 'Aura Holdings, the company that owned the casino, was obviously fined for that, and not properly maintaining the fire alarm. A sizeable settlement was handed over to their son, Liam Robinson. I did my best to press for a prosecution against Aura Holdings, but the CPS didn't think there was enough evidence to convict them of manslaughter. Unbelievably, the insurance company even paid out, and if you ask me, off the record, that's what I think this was all about—insurance fraud.'

'But if you believed that, surely you didn't just let the case drop?' Joseph asked.

Janette answered for her husband. 'Lewis tried everything, but no one was prepared to listen to him.'

The retired officer shrugged. 'I really did, Joseph. But with such a distinct lack of evidence, nobody was prepared to pursue the case any further. Also, the insurance company didn't find any evidence of fraud either and paid out in full, so that didn't help my cause. But even after all these years, none of this has sat well with me.

'I'm certain that Harper and Forbes were the frontmen of the business, even though they had their mothers listed as directors. I'm certain they were as guilty as hell for the casino fire. And it seems now, based on recent events, that someone else was too.'

Joseph slowly nodded. 'So if this happened sixteen years ago, their son, Liam, would be around twenty-nine by now?'

'Yes, I suppose he would be.'

Janette sipped her tea with a sad look on her face. 'Liam was obviously devastated by the loss of his parents.'

Lewis nodded. 'He certainly blamed Harper and Forbes for not maintaining the casino properly. Then when they walked free without a charge in sight, I'm afraid to say he also ended up blaming the police for not bringing those two men to justice. His aunt tried to bring Liam up, but he was too broken after the loss of his parents. The last I heard of him, he'd been taken on by foster parents.'

Janette nodded. 'Meanwhile, Jimmy and Matthew were able to get on with their lives as though nothing had happened. What sort of justice is that?' Her gaze tightened on the detectives. 'You think Liam could have been behind these killings, then?'

'After everything you've just told us, he certainly had a clear motive for wanting those two men dead,' Joseph said.

'And the use of a double-sided coin as a possible homage to his parents is the clincher, in my opinion,' Megan said.

Lewis sighed. 'I'm afraid it does sound like you may have found your chief suspect.'

He opened the box folder and took out a smiling photo of a young, dark-haired lad with a wide grin. The lad was wearing cricket whites and holding a bat in one hand, a trophy in the other. A man and woman stood on either side of him, their arms draped around the boy, all of them beaming at the camera.

'As you can see for yourself, the Robinson family was very happy before their lives were ripped apart by tragedy.'

The photo was of a family who clearly loved each other. This had been Liam's world before his parents had been so cruelly stolen away from him. Then he stared harder at the cricket bat.

He turned to Megan. 'You know in Doctor Jacobs's post-mortem report it said something about a blunt-edged weapon like a crowbar being used to knock Harper and Forbes out, what if?'

'Bloody hell, the side of a cricket bat would certainly fit the bill.'

'Oh good grief, that makes more sense than you probably realise,' Lewis said. 'Liam's dad was a keen cricketer and encouraged him to take it up. His dad even gave him his first bat.'

Joseph slowly nodded. 'How better to avenge your parents' death than by using your father's old bat to brain the people you thought were responsible for their deaths?'

Janette put her hands to her mouth. 'How awful.'

They nodded. 'Do you mind if I hang onto this photo?'

'Of course,' Lewis replied, handing it over.

'We'd better get straight back to Oxford to see what we can dig up about Liam and his whereabouts,' Joseph said. He stood, gently dislodging Tux, who gave him a disgusted look before stalking off back to his hedgerow. 'We can't thank the two of you enough. This could be the breakthrough that we've been looking for.'

Lewis and Janette both shook the detectives' hands as they got ready to go.

'I'm glad your visit might have been some help,' Lewis said. 'But just one last thing. Take it easy with Liam when you do eventually find him. I realise there's no excuse for murder, but if it really was Liam who was responsible, he's almost certainly been on a long, dark road to push him to that point. In some ways, even if he wasn't there at the casino fire, he was just as much a victim as both his parents were.'

Joseph looked at the photo, taking in the fresh-faced lad's smile, and nodded. 'We'll certainly try our best.'

With a nod to the couple's went back, they headed back to the Volvo, ready to pursue this new lead wherever it might take them.

CHAPTER TWENTY-THREE

'What are you two doing here, when I specifically told you to take the weekend off?' Chris asked the moment Joseph and Megan walked into the incident room.

'This couldn't wait,' Joseph said, as he headed over to his screen and powered up his computer.

Megan nodded. 'We've just got back from interviewing a DCI Sanders about a casino fire sixteen years ago. Thanks to that, it looks like we have a new suspect for our case.'

Chris looked between them, confused. 'What casino fire?'

'Harper and Forbes ran a casino together sixteen years ago called Excalibur,' Joseph said. 'More significantly, it also just happened to burn down, leaving two people dead.'

Every set of ears in the room perked up at that, and all other conversations fell away.

'In that case, the floor is yours,' Chris said.

Joseph turned to address the other detectives, and went over everything they'd found out and how.

'So you're saying Liam, who is an adult now, might have killed Harper and Forbes out of revenge?' Chris asked.

'It's certainly an avenue of enquiry worth pursuing. There

are a couple of other things DCI Sanders told us that line up. Liam's parents ran a magic act at the casino, and his father used a double-sided coin in one of their tricks. Also, the post-mortems for both Harper and Forbes indicated they'd each been struck across the head with an object with a long, flat edge. Guess whose father gave him a cricket bat that fits the bill?'

'Holy crap,' Ian said. 'So, are you saying our mystery motor-cyclist and this Liam Robinson are the same person?'

'That's certainly my hunch.'

'Then we better dig up all the information that we can find about Liam and pull him in for questioning as quickly as possible,' Chris said.

'Already ahead of you there, boss,' Megan said. She had powered her computer up, and was already scanning the screen. 'Apparently, Liam disappeared ran away from his foster parents within a few months of being placed with them. After that, there's no trace, and he was eventually listed as a missing person. However, there is a link here to his old Facebook page which might be worth a look.'

'Go for it, and share it with the class,' Chris said.

A Facebook page appeared on her monitor. With a couple of clicks, Megan had put it up on the large screen on the wall so everybody in the room could see it.

Joseph took in the number of comments under Liam's last Facebook post. It was a picture of Norman standing next to his son, his hand on Liam's shoulder. Then he realised what the lad was sitting on—a Yamaha motorbike.

'Is that the same bike the arsonist has been seen using?' Sue asked.

'Damned right it is,' Chris said.

'Then I'd bet good money on it belonging to his dad as well. Check if Norman Robinson had a motorbike registered in his name.'

'On it,' Ian said, as a palpable surge of energy swept through the room.

Joseph went through the comments beneath the photo as Ian got to work.

'*Where are you, Liam?*' That was followed by, '*Just let us know you're safe,*' and similar posts after that. But it was the last entry that really twisted the DI's heart. '*Wherever you are now, we hope you're thriving, Liam. We know how much you miss your parents, but we will be here for you in any way we can. There will always be a bed for you here. Just know that we love you with our whole hearts. Gillian and Glen xxx.*'

'That last entry was posted only a year ago by Liam's foster parents,' Megan said.

'In that case, can someone contact them to see if they have even the faintest idea where Liam might be now?' Chris asked. 'There's always a chance he might have contacted them since they posted that comment.'

'Leave it to me,' Sue said, turning to her own screen.

'What if Liam assumed a new identity?' Megan asked.

Chris scratched his chin. 'That's certainly something we're going to have to keep in mind.'

Joseph took the photo of Liam that Lewis had given him and handed it to Chris. 'You might want to ask Amy to get a forensic imaging specialist to see if they can age this photo of Liam. It would be great to see what he looks like today as a twenty-nine-year-old. They'll also probably want to look at the other photos of Liam from his Facebook page to help them with that task as well.'

Chris nodded. 'Okay, everyone, this feels like a major break-through. Let's pick up these threads where we can and get going.'

As everyone in the room returned to their work, the DCI looked at Joseph and Megan. 'Great work, you two.'

'Let's just hope we can locate Liam, or whatever it is that he calls himself now,' Joseph said. 'We're obviously dealing with a very damaged individual, who, apart from anything else, needs serious psychological help.'

Megan and Chris both gave him a sombre look and nodded.

'Now will you both please get out of here and recharge your batteries like I ordered you to?' Chris said. 'Leave the rest to us for now. We'll see you two tomorrow.'

'Understood, boss,' Joseph said, with a wry smile. 'Besides, I could do with checking in with John and Paul at the hospital to see how they're doing.'

'Of course, and pass on my best wishes to John if he's awake. Anyway, I'll see you both fresh-faced first thing tomorrow,' the DCI said, pointing towards the door.

Joseph headed into the ward, clutching a basket of fruit.

He had always been stoic when he was the one in a hospital bed. However, when it came to someone else being injured, the DI had an overriding sense of powerlessness—dread even. But there was something new thrown into the mix on this occasion— the feeling of guilt and the wish that he could trade places with either of the young officers.

Then there was the whole business of him deliberately giving John a wide berth before the shooting, which only added to the sense of weight lurking inside his gut.

On the way over to the hospital on his bike, Joseph had been mulling over his behaviour towards John. The more he'd thought about it, the more he realised he really had fallen into the classic overprotective dad trap, where no one would ever be good enough for his daughter. Upon reflection, he'd certainly had some form of it with her previous boyfriends as well.

When Ellie had been sixteen and had got serious about a lad at school, Joseph had given him the third degree in the same way he might have interviewed a suspect. The lad had been so traumatised he'd quickly broken things off with Ellie.

His daughter had never forgiven him completely for that episode. Until now, Joseph had thought he'd learned something from it. So why had he behaved that way towards John, who was about as decent a man as he could ever hope for his daughter to date?

He walked down the corridor and made a silent vow that his passive-aggressive attitude was going to be a thing of the past. If someone was good enough for Ellie, then he was going to have to respect that. After all, Ellie had a good instinct about people.

After checking in with the nurse's station about which room John was in, he headed towards it. The first thing Joseph saw as he entered was Ellie curled up on the bed with John, who appeared to be asleep, her head resting on his good shoulder.

Joseph took a mental breath. *You've got this.*

Ellie looked up at him and smiled as her dad approached and she saw the basket of fruit he was carrying. Then, Joseph noticed at least six other similar baskets, along with twice as many bouquets, placed around the room in vases.

'Ah, the phrase "bringing coals to Newcastle" springs to mind,' Joseph said, as he placed his own offering among the other gifts already crowding every available surface.

'Well, all this fruit is certainly going to keep John regular for weeks,' Ellie whispered. She swung her legs off the bed and gave her dad a hug.

'How's he doing?' Joseph said, also keeping his voice down in an attempt to not wake the patient.

'Just a bit knocked out with all the painkillers they have him on.'

Joseph looked down at John and the bandages enclosing his left shoulder. 'I'm just so sorry, Ellie.'

'Don't be. Like the doctor said, he's going to make a full recovery. It's just going to be a while before he plays five-a-side with his mates again.'

'Right... Anyway, I just wanted to say I'm really pleased that you two have found each other.'

Ellie looked into her father's eyes, as though she was waiting for the *but*. 'You really mean that, don't you?'

'Absolutely, and the moment John is up and about again, we're going to go and have that dinner you talked about.'

'Then I look forward to it,' John's voice said.

They both looked around to see the PC had his eyes open and was looking at them.

'Oh, for feck's sake, how much of that did you hear?' Joseph asked.

'Enough,' John said with a slow smile.

But as he started to struggle into a sitting position, he winced. Ellie rushed to his side, repositioning his pillows and helping him up.

Joseph gave the man a slightly hopeless look. 'So...'

'Yeah,' John said, equally embarrassed.

'Surely, the two most important men in my life can manage more than a monosyllabic conversation?' Ellie said, exasperated.

'That tells us,' Joseph said, as he felt a smile forming.

'God, yes,' John replied. 'I would rather take on an armed criminal any day than risk upsetting your daughter.'

Ellie stared at him. 'Talk about in bad taste!'

'Hey, if anyone can make a joke about getting shot, it's me. Besides, as I'm the one lying in a hospital bed, you're duty-bound to be nice to me, Ellie.'

Joseph chuckled. 'He has a point, oh precious daughter of mine.'

'Bloody hell, you two are as bad as each other,' Ellie said.

Joseph nodded towards John. 'Maybe you and I should grab a drink sometime at the Scholar's Retreat?'

'I'd like that, sir.'

'If you've got big enough nads to date my daughter, it's Joseph when I'm not on duty, or else.'

John laughed, then his face became serious again. 'Any update on how Paul is doing?'

The DI grimaced. 'I popped in to check with his wife before I came over here. His condition has stabilised. The doctors are saying it's just down to Paul now to pull through this.'

John nodded. 'In that case, I'd like to head over to his room to see him. Maybe the offer of a pint will help to rouse him...' But then any hint of a smile flitted away. 'When those men jumped out of that ambulance and shot us...' His eyes became haunted.

'I know...' the DI said. 'Has anyone offered you trauma counselling yet?'

'They have and I'm going to begin it as soon as I feel able to.'

'Well, some advice from an older copper to a much younger one—take them up on it. It might feel like a waste of time to start with, but just talking these things through helps. Besides, you are welcome to pop round anytime to see me on my boat for a chat, if you need to.'

'I'd like that,' John replied.

Ellie looked between them. 'So all it takes is for one of you to get shot for you two to hold a proper conversation?'

'So it would seem,' Joseph said, smiling with a far greater sense of lightness than when he'd first entered the room.

CHAPTER TWENTY-FOUR

LATER THAT NIGHT, Joseph was fast asleep on board *Tús Nua*, when his mobile started buzzing and vibrating like a very pissed-off wasp. With a quagmire of tiredness wrapped around his brain and threatening to pull him straight back to sleep, the DI reached out in the darkness, fumbling for his mobile. When he saw that it was only three in the morning, he resisted the urge to turn the bloody thing straight off, at least until he saw who was daring to disrupt his sleep.

The DI took the call. 'Megan, why on Earth are you ringing me at this godforsaken hour?'

'Because there's been a major development. Lewis and Janette's house has just been torched.'

Any vestiges of sleep were instantly swept away as the DI sat bolt upright in his bed. 'Jesus H. Christ. Please tell me they're both okay?'

'They are, but badly shaken.'

'Okay, okay...' Joseph took a breath, remembering what Lewis had said about Liam blaming the police for not solving the case. 'We need to get over there immediately.'

'Already on my way. I'll pick you up in five.'

'And I'll be ready in three,' Joseph replied, as he leapt out of bed and began pulling on his clothes.

It wasn't long before the two detectives were speeding back toward Stow-on-the-Wold, a full moon hanging directly over the country road like a giant guiding star.

When they finally reached the town, the fire wasn't hard to spot. A column of amber smoke was rising into the night sky, flames flickering at its base. The strobing lights of emergency vehicles around it turned the scene into a surreal frozen tableau.

'Oh, bloody hell, that poor couple,' Megan said, looking up at the column of smoke.

'I know, but maybe it's not as bad as it looks,' Joseph replied with no conviction whatsoever.

When the detectives finally arrived at the house, having negotiated their way past the local police cordon, the situation was far worse than either of them could have imagined.

Despite the efforts of at least a dozen firefighters in attendance, the whole cottage was ablaze, flames billowing from the roof. The crews were directing their hoses onto the flames, sending enormous clouds of steam roiling up into the sky.

Megan parked up next to an ambulance, its doors wide open, but with no one inside.

Joseph's heart clenched. Did that mean the couple were still inside the cottage? But then relief surged through him when he caught sight of Lewis and Janette sitting together on a stone bench in a neighbour's garden, clutching each other's hands as they watched their family home burn to the ground. Two paramedics were crouched on either side of them.

Lewis had an oxygen mask clamped onto his soot-covered face, and a pile of what looked like partly burned photo albums on his lap. Janette had a cat carrier next to her, with Tux peering out of it at the fire and mewing mournfully. That really twisted the knife in Joseph's heart. Most people would try to save their pets and photos before anything else. The rest of the things people thought mattered, didn't when it came down to brutal moments like this.

'Look, we really need to get you for a proper checkup, Lewis,' the female paramedic was saying to him, her hand resting lightly on his arm as the detectives approached.

Lewis waved her off. 'Not just yet, please give me a moment.'

Janette clutched his hand tighter, tears in her eyes. When she looked up and saw Joseph and Megan standing there, a sob escaped.

In three strides, Joseph was with her and, despite barely knowing her, he drew the woman into a hug, just like he would with his mam had she been watching her own cottage burn down.

'I'm so sorry,' was all he could think to say.

Janette took a shuddering breath and pulled away from him, wiping the tears from her eyes, her hands trembling.

'We really need to get them both to the hospital as soon as possible,' the female paramedic said to the detectives. 'If you could help persuade them, it would be a great help.'

Lewis shot the woman a furious look. 'How many more bloody times…' he said, his voice muffled by the mask. 'Just give us a minute.' Then his face crumpled. 'Sorry…'

Megan turned to the paramedics. 'Leave this with us and we'll see what we can do.'

They nodded, then withdrew a short distance away to wait.

Megan kneeled before Lewis. 'What happened?'

'We were nearly killed in our beds because some psychopath took it upon himself to burn our house down. If it hadn't been for Tux, who woke us when the smoke began, we would have died in there—' He started coughing and gestured with a hand towards the crackling flames coming from an upstairs window where the glass had shattered.

Janette looked at her husband with glistening eyes. 'And my brave fool of a husband, once he got me and Tux out, insisted on heading back in there to fetch our photo albums.'

Lewis managed a shrug. 'Memories are so important when you're about to lose everything else.'

With his whole being, Joseph felt for this couple, but he also needed to ask them some urgent questions. 'Can you tell us anything about the person who set the fire?'

Janette nodded. 'A neighbour, who's a doctor at the hospital over in Gloucester, was just arriving home after a long shift when he spotted smoke coming out of our kitchen window. When he headed to the front door to check whether we were still inside, a man wearing a crash helmet burst from the hallway and charged past him.'

Joseph's eyes widened. 'And then what happened?'

'He leapt onto a Yamaha motorbike and screamed off into the night before our neighbour could stop him,' Janette continued, confirming what the DI already suspected. 'But of course, our neighbour was far more focused on getting us out than chasing the intruder and didn't have time to get a number plate.'

'So, without putting words in your mouths, who do you think might have done this?' Megan asked, looking at the couple.

Lewis pulled off his oxygen mask. 'Oh, come on, we're all thinking of the same person—Liam Robinson, obviously. The timing seems to be strange though. Only yesterday, I was telling you both that he held a grudge against the police and the next thing we know our house is torched—' Lewis started coughing again, and Janette patted his back.

'My guess is that Liam has been keeping your house under surveillance, planning his attack,' Joseph said. 'But when he spotted us, he decided to act sooner rather than later.'

'But how could Liam track us down?' Janette asked. 'We're ex-directory and opted to keep our names off the electoral register. And we're certainly not on any sort of social media.'

'There are still ways of finding out,' Megan said.

Joseph nodded. 'Absolutely. For example, Liam could have contacted an old colleague of yours, saying he'd lost contact with you and was trying to track you down. That sort of thing. You know how it works when someone is really determined.'

Lewis opened his mouth to say something, but started coughing again. Janette quickly slipped the mask back over his mouth.

'Right, time to get yourself properly checked out at the hospital,' Joseph said. 'I promise you we'll be in touch if we find anything out.'

Lewis nodded and then waved the paramedics back over. 'I'm ready to go with you to hospital now.'

Janette gave her husband a relieved look as the paramedics helped him towards the ambulance. Then she turned to Joseph and Megan as she picked up the cat carrier.

'I don't suppose I could ask a huge favour of the two of you, could I?' she said.

'Just name it,' Joseph replied.

'It's Tux here. I won't be able to keep him with me, as my sister, who's already agreed to take us in, is allergic to cats. Unfortunately, Tux absolutely loathes catteries and I'm at my wits' end about who I can trust enough to look after him. So I was wondering...'

Megan was already pulling a face. 'I would if I could, but my landlord doesn't allow any pets.'

Joseph was about to follow his colleague's lead and explain

how living on a narrowboat would make that all but impossible, when Janette gave him a beseeching look that melted his heart.

'No problem. I can look after the little fella until you're both back on your feet,' he found himself saying.

Megan stared at the DI as though she couldn't quite believe her ears. That was pretty much how Joseph was feeling as he took the cat carrier from Janette, with his best attempt at an *I-will-absolutely-look-after-him* smile.

Janette gave the DI a peck on the cheek. 'I can't tell you how grateful I am. At least it's one less thing for us to worry about after this catastrophe. I promise you won't find Tux any sort of bother at all.'

'I'm sure I won't,' Joseph said, not at all convinced.

Janette squeezed his and Megan's hands, before following her husband towards the ambulance.

'God, you've got a soft heart,' Megan said to the DI.

'Guilty as charged.' He brought the carrier up to his face and Tux immediately hissed at him. 'Yes, I can already see this is going to go just swimmingly.'

Megan grinned. But as she returned her attention to the fire, finally starting to be dampened down by the firefighters, her expression became drawn again. 'They both could have been killed here tonight.'

'If the arsonist hadn't been interrupted, I'm pretty sure we would have probably found Lewis's body with a coin in his mouth.'

'So assuming this was Liam's handiwork, and there is every reason to think it is, I wonder how he started it? Maybe a Molotov cocktail like back at the garage?'

Joseph pointed towards one of the fire crew he recognised just getting into his pickup truck.

'Isn't that the fire investigator, Thomas Reid? By the looks of it, he's already finished his work here.'

'It certainly looks like it, so let's go and see what the expert thinks,' Megan replied.

As the detectives headed towards the pickup truck, Thomas, who'd just started the vehicle, spotted them approaching and lowered his window.

'This is a bit outside your jurisdiction, isn't it?' he said, as the detectives reached him.

'We were just following up on a lead. Anyway, I could say the same of you. I thought you covered the Oxford area?'

'No, I'm called in to investigate fires right across the Cotswolds. So based on the fact that you're already here, am I safe to assume you think this attack is linked to the other Burning Man arson?'

'There's certainly more than a passing possibility,' Joseph said. 'I was just wondering if you had discovered anything that might confirm our suspect's MO?'

Thomas gestured towards the remains of the front door he'd just exited from. 'The fire was started in the hallway with nothing more sophisticated than a fuel can filled with petrol. But I also discovered the exploded remains of a second can at the bottom of the stairs. It appears to have detonated when the flames reached it, creating a fireball that torched the rest of the house.'

'Maybe the arsonist was forced to abandon that one when the neighbour disturbed him,' Megan suggested.

'If so, that was probably the one the intruder intended to pour over Lewis before doing his coin trick,' Joseph replied.

The DC gawped at him. 'Bloody hell, but what about Janette?'

'Thankfully, whatever he'd planned there, wasn't allowed to play out as he intended.'

Thomas looked between them, shaking his head. 'What sort of sick mind would do something like that?'

'We may have some idea,' Megan said.

'Really?'

'Yes, but that's not something we can discuss,' Joseph added.

'Of course,' Thomas replied, his heavy-lidded eyes looking between them.

Just for a moment, Joseph had the strangest feeling he knew this man from somewhere other than just the fire scenes where he'd run into him. But if so, he couldn't quite place it.

'Anyway, I must shoot back and get my report written up,' Thomas continued.

'Bloody paperwork, hey?' Joseph said with a smile.

'Tell me about it,' Thomas replied, and with a wave, the fire investigator drove away.

'Talking about paperwork, we'd better head back to the station to do the same,' Joseph said, as the first hint of dawn lightened the sky. 'Chris is going to want to be briefed fully about this as soon as possible.'

'And what about our latest recruit?' Megan said, gesturing towards Tux, who gave her a pitiful mew.

'Oh, I already have a cunning plan. Dylan is as good with cats as he is with dogs. So I thought I'd ask him to help me look after Tux when I get back to my boat. But there's another matter we urgently need to attend to.

'I didn't want to say anything in front of Lewis, but if he's been targeted once, there's no reason the murderer won't try again. We need to contact the Gloucester Constabulary and get them to arrange an armed guard for Lewis while he's in the hospital. Then we'll move him and Janette to a safe house until we have Liam in custody.'

'I know the guy wants vengeance for his parents, but how sick do you have to be to try something like this?' Megan said.

Joseph's expression became drawn. 'Trauma, in an extreme

case, especially at a young age, can permanently damage a person. Our job now is to make sure we catch Liam before he can do this ever again.'

CHAPTER TWENTY-FIVE

JOSEPH AND MEGAN headed into the incident room with Tux mewing in his carrier.

'Who have you got there?' Ian asked, looking up from his computer.

'The latest addition to our team,' Joseph said. Then, without missing a beat, added, 'He's been trained to take over from our sniffer dogs.'

'Really?' Ian asked.

Sue looked over at him as she headed over for a closer inspection of the cat. 'Sometimes you really are the most gullible person on the planet, Ian.'

'Oh right, of course. I knew Joseph was pulling my leg,' the DI said, his face flaming.

By the time Joseph deposited the cat on his desk, Sue was already kneeling before Tux, making cooing noises to him inside the carrier. She looked up at Joseph. 'I didn't have you pegged as a cat guy.'

The DI shook his head. 'I'm not. I'm just doing a favour for a retired DCI and his wife. Their house was burned down this morning, and it looks like it was linked to the Burning Man arsonist. They just needed someone to look after Tux here until they get themselves sorted out.'

'Flipping heck, those poor people,' Sue said. She stuck her fingers through the bars and started scratching Tux behind the ears. Sue was rewarded by an incredibly loud purr. 'You poor little fellow, but I'm sure Uncle Joseph will do a great job of looking after you.'

The DI rolled his eyes at her, but when he saw the way Tux immediately warmed to the DS, a thought struck him. 'I don't suppose you'd consider taking him on for a short while?'

Sue shook her head. 'I would if I could, but my two cats wouldn't take kindly to an interloper. It's much easier to bring a new cat in when they're a kitten for that sort of thing, rather than when they're fully grown.'

'Right...' Joseph cast a hopeful look around the rest of the incident room. 'Would anyone else be up for looking after a cat for a couple of weeks?'

Everyone became totally engaged in whatever work they were pretending to do.

'Tsk, tsk, are you trying to offload your parental responsibilities already?' Megan said, as she powered up her computer.

'It's just now that I've had a chance to think about it, trying to keep a cat on *Tús Nua* could prove to be something of a challenge.'

'Hang on, I've seen plenty of narrowboats with cats living on them,' Ian said. 'But if you really don't want him, you could always book him into a cattery.'

Tux gave him a straight look, almost as though it was the cat equivalent of saying *what the actual feck?*

'Sorry, his owner told me Tux absolutely hates catteries,' Joseph said, quickly capitulating under the cat's gimlet-eyed stare.

'Oh, that's going to be tricky in that case, but let's get you sorted out with some water,' Sue said, returning her attention to the cat. 'When did he last eat, Joseph?'

The DI shrugged as his screen lit up. 'I've absolutely no idea.'

'And what about the last time he's been to the loo?'

'Jesus, do I look like a vet?'

Sue exchanged a headshake with Ian.

'Okay, leave it to me. I'll pop over to that pet place on Botley Road to get some things for him until you can sort something out,' she said. 'You can pay me back later.'

'Thanks for that. You're a superstar.'

'You'd better believe it,' Sue said, as Chris walked in.

The DCI took a long look at the cat carrier, then the black-and-white cat within it, and finally at Joseph.

'Don't ask, I'll only end up repeating myself,' the DI said. 'The short version is he won't be here long, boss.'

'Glad to hear it. Anyway, you'd better give us an update about the fire at Stow-on-the-Wold.'

'Of course. According to the fire investigator, Thomas Reid, it's another clear case of arson. A man was spotted by a neighbour, fleeing the scene on a Yamaha motorbike. Also, it goes without saying that DCI Sanders's home being targeted is highly likely to be linked to our current investigation. If a neighbour hadn't raised the alarm in time, we might have been looking at two more victims.'

'Sounds like the Burning Man has struck again,' Ian said.

'It certainly looks that way,' Joseph replied. 'Talking of him, any luck here digging up leads on Liam Robinson's current whereabouts?'

Chris shook his head. 'We've looked at everything, but I'm afraid the trail really does go stone-cold after he turned sixteen and ran away from his foster parents. However, we do have confirmation that the Yamaha motorbike in the photo belonged to Norman Robinson. Apparently, he was really into them and had a couple. After his death, his sister stored them in her garage. But they were stolen about five years ago. She didn't want to report it at the time because she suspected Liam might be involved and didn't want to get him into trouble.'

'That explains why they didn't come up as stolen during our search,' Megan said.

'Exactly. We also have another thing that could prove useful. I had a psychological profile put together on what we know about the arsonist. It makes very interesting reading. Here, you and Megan will want to see this for yourself.' The DCI handed a document over to Joseph.

Megan went over to read it over the DI's shoulder.

'*Psychological Profile: The arsonist is likely to have a history of pyromania or fascination with fire. They are also likely to have a deep-seated anger towards society and may feel powerless in their own life. The individual likely experienced a traumatic event in their past, triggering their obsession with fire.*'

'Well, that absolutely describes Liam to a T,' Megan said.

'It really does,' Joseph replied. 'Having your parents burned to death could certainly have triggered his love of burning things down, but it also seems to have sent him down a dark path of vengeance towards the people he held accountable.'

'Exactly. I think the profiler has basically confirmed what we already know anyway, that Liam is very much our man,' Chris said. 'But carry on reading because the next part is where it gets really interesting.'

Joseph and Megan both nodded as they went back to reading.

'*Modus Operandi: The arsonist typically operates under the cover of darkness and uses accelerants to start fires. They may observe their targets before setting the fire to ensure maximum damage. The arsonist is highly skilled and knowledgeable about fire behaviour and may have experience working with fire or in a related field.'*

'Hang on, that sounds like we're talking about a firefighter, or someone similar,' Joseph said.

Megan stared at him. 'You're not seriously suggesting that someone who dedicates their lives to putting out fires, could also be an arsonist?'

'It wouldn't be the first time,' Chris said. 'There are plenty of cases where people joined the fire service because they were obsessed with fire.'

Joseph nodded as he read the final paragraph of the report.

'Signature: The arsonist often leaves behind a distinct signature at the scene of the fire, in the form of a coin. That suggests that this act is symbolic and of some significance to the arsonist. They may also return to the scene of the crime to observe the aftermath.'

'I have to say I've always been a bit sceptical about profilers, but this guy seems to have hit the nail on the head,' Chris said, as Joseph and Megan finished reading.

But the DI ignored him as an idea had taken over all other thoughts. *Return to the scene of the crime...* He'd already pulled out his phone and was dialling Amy. Within three rings, she had picked up.

'I have a favour to ask. I don't suppose you've had a chance to get the aged photo version of Liam Robinson put together yet?'

'Actually, it just landed in my inbox about a minute ago from the Digital Forensic Unit. I was literally just about to open it.'

'Can you send it over right now? I'm following up on a hunch.'

'Of course, just give me a moment...' There was a whooshing sound at the other end of the line as she shifted in her chair, then the sound of a mouse being clicked. 'It's on its way.'

'You're an angel. Talk soon.' He ended the call and headed over to his computer.

'By the look on your face, you're onto something,' Megan said.

'Yes, but think about it. If we're talking about a firefighter, who have we run into at every single scene, Megan? I thought I recognised him from somewhere and now I know why.'

Her eyes widened. 'Hang on, you're not talking about Thomas Reid, are you?'

'If you look closely, there's a definite likeness to Liam in those photos of him as a kid. Also, everything fits. A person who made a career out of fires and is always around to revisit the scene of the crime under the guise of his job as an investigator. It's the perfect cover.'

Chris rubbed his neck. 'But this is still conjecture, and quite a stretch. Just because the profiler says it's likely to be someone like a firefighter, doesn't mean that Reid is our man. There are lots of firefighters in the service and just because the report said they might return to the scene of the crime, doesn't mean they actually did. Apart from anything else, Reid is going grey, so at the very least, that puts him in his late thirties rather than someone who's in their twenties.'

Megan shook her head. 'If Thomas Reid is really Liam, and was set on hiding his old identity, a bit of hair dye and a beard wouldn't exactly be a high price to ask.'

'Absolutely, so let's find out for sure,' Joseph said. He clicked on the attached image in Amy's forwarded message and any lingering doubts he might have had were instantly swept away.

At a casual glance, it wasn't a perfect fit for Thomas, not least because of the lack of greying hair and full beard. But the resemblance to the fire investigator was definitely there if you looked for it. The same set jaw and those heavy-lidded eyes.

Chris stared over Joseph's shoulder at the photo, his expression widening. 'I take it all back. Good grief, talk about a hunch panning out.' The DCI clapped his hands. 'Okay, heads up, everyone. We've a new chief suspect for the murders of Jimmy Harper and Matthew Forbes, as well as the attempted murders of retired DCI Lewis Sanders and his wife, Janette. I want everyone to dig up as much information as possible about Fire Investigator Thomas Reid. I want a full background check, including his current home and work addresses. As soon as we have those, Ian and Alice, you'll head to his work. Joseph and Megan, you'll be with me to raid his home.'

'I'm certain Reid is our man, boss,' Joseph said.

'After seeing that photo, so am I, but let's play this by the book. Having said that, I'm not prepared to take any chances. Reid is a flight risk. That's why we're going to go in with the cavalry to make sure there's no danger of him slipping through our fingers again. If he is our mystery motorcyclist, he's already proved rather too good at doing exactly that.'

'Not this bloody time, if I've got anything to do with it,' Joseph muttered, loud enough for everyone in the room to hear.

Chris raised his eyebrows at him, but nodded.

CHAPTER TWENTY-SIX

THE HOUSE WHICH JOSEPH, Chris, and Megan were standing in front of was nothing extraordinary. It was a standard three-bedroom semi in Abingdon, complete with an attached garage—a cookie-cutter version of all the other estate homes around it.

The DCI had been serious about leaving no escape route open for their new chief suspect. Patrol cars had been positioned, creating a circle of roadblocks across the entire area around the house. If Reid managed to slip past them again, he wouldn't get far. A police van was already parked up around the corner from the house, with the Tactical Unit who'd just disembarked from it, getting ready for the raid.

For a suspect like Reid, it was better to assume he might have a gun, especially given that he hadn't hesitated to kill two people and attempted to murder two others.

Joseph adjusted the straps of Megan's stab vest, ensuring it was secure. 'You don't want that slipping off you at the wrong moment.'

'You're worse than my mum, always making sure I was wearing my coat properly before I headed off to school.'

'Well, this is potentially a bit more dangerous than that.'

Megan raised her eyebrows at him. 'You don't know the school I went to. Even the mice carried flick knives.'

The DI gave her an amused look as he finished adjusting the straps.

Chris, who'd been briefing the TU, walked back over to the detectives.

'I just heard from one of the team back at the station. We've now had confirmation that Thomas Reid has a motorbike license, just in case anyone wasn't already certain we have the right man.'

'There was little doubt in my mind,' Joseph said, as the TU Incident Commander Erol Kentli joined them.

'I have officers positioned around the rear,' Erol said. 'We're ready to enter the property.'

'Then proceed,' Chris replied.

The Commander nodded and returned to his colleagues.

Joseph felt the hum of anticipation as the tactical officers positioned themselves alongside a hedgerow, hidden from view of the windows. As the DI watched the house for any flicker of movement, his thoughts drifted back to everything they had learned about Thomas Reid's background during the team's intensive research.

It had surprised no one that Thomas Reid was an alias. At sixteen, he had assumed the identity of someone who had been killed and then he'd simply vanished.

The team had uncovered the usual mix of items for a man intent on creating a new identity for himself—a false passport and birth certificate that made him twelve years older than he actually was, no doubt in order to try and confuse anyone trying to track him down.

There was also a raft of fake qualifications. They had been just the right mix to secure him a position in the fire service, where he quickly climbed the ranks until he became a fire investigator three years prior. The irony of the fire service employing a pyromaniac in that role, akin to putting a fox in charge of the henhouse, wasn't lost on Joseph.

According to the records, Reid was the only person registered living at this address, and apparently, he'd never been married. There was no record of any partner, either. That could have been by choice, but Joseph had a hunch it was connected to the trauma the man still likely carried inside him from his childhood.

Megan cast Joseph a look as they waited. 'Nervous?'

'Always at a time like this. You?'

'God, yes. I just want to get this started, already.' Megan didn't have long to wait for her wish.

A second later, Erol barked into the mic on his helmet. 'Go, go, go!'

Like a well-oiled machine kicking into action, the three detectives watched the tactical team rush towards the house, among them, a man carrying a battering ram. The armed officers took up positions on either side of the door.

Joseph noticed Chris's knuckles turning white as he clenched his fists. This was what responsibility for a raid looked like. If any officer was injured in the line of duty, the DCI would bear the burden of that, as the senior officer who had got this raid authorised. Just like Joseph felt he bore the burden for the shooting of John and Paul in the prisoner transfer ambush.

The DI's pulse quickened as the man with the battering ram aimed it at the lock, swung it back, and sent it crashing into the door.

But rather than opening, the frame splintered and held.

'Shit, a bloody Euro lock—so much for the element of surprise,' Chris said.

However, it obviously wasn't the tactical officer's first encounter with this type of lock. He calmly repositioned the ram at the bottom and, with a second swing, destroyed the bolt built into the door frame.

It still held.

'Bloody hell, just how tough is that thing?' Megan asked.

'A Euro lock has catches built into multiple points around the doorframe,' Chris explained.

'Yes, they not only make it a nightmare for thieves, but as you can see, for us as well when we need to get through one in a hurry,' Joseph added.

Megan nodded. 'Every day is a school day on this job.'

'I still feel like that, and I've been doing this job for years,' Joseph replied.

The man with the battering ram swung it back and hit the top of the door frame with the third blow. With a groaning sound, the demolished door finally gave way and flew inwards.

'About bloody time. Talk about giving Reid a huge heads up we're all out here trying to get into his house,' Chris muttered, as Erol and his armed officers darted in.

Shouts of *'Armed police!'* echoed from inside the house.

'Okay, we're up,' Chris said.

The three detectives extended their batons as they headed towards the house after the others. As they neared, Joseph heard a beeping sound coming from the hallway. That was quickly drowned out by a much louder banging sound. The source of that became obvious the moment the detectives stepped into the hallway. The officer with the battering ram had already set to work on a locked door into the garage.

A warning beep from a number pad mounted on the wall suddenly became a deafening internal alarm, echoed by one outside the house.

'Can someone turn that bloody thing off?' Chris asked, casting a malevolent look towards the keypad.

Joseph was getting ready to smack it one with his baton,

when the rumble of a powerful motorbike came from the other side of the door to the garage.

'Crap, he's trying to make a break for it!' Chris shouted.

The officer with the battering ram swung it harder. With a resounding crash, the door flew open, and the grinding sound of a garage door opening in the room beyond reached them.

Not waiting for the armed officer to go in first, which would have been the sensible thing, Joseph pushed past him. He entered the garage to see the motorcyclist with the familiar black helmet, revving a Yamaha YZF-R, waiting for the garage door to finish opening. Parked next to it was the trail bike the DI had last seen fleeing Forbes's garage.

'Stop right there, Liam, it's over!' Joseph bellowed.

'Not until I've finished what I started,' Thomas replied, confirming that he and Liam were one and the same.

Even as Joseph rushed towards the suspect, Robinson revved the bike and roared out through the garage door. Megan and Chris, who'd just appeared outside, had to dive aside as the motorcyclist hurtled straight towards them.

Joseph sprinted outside just in time to see the motorcycle speeding away down the road towards the police roadblock set up at the end of the street.

One officer, who deserved a medal for quick thinking in the DI's opinion, had already deployed a Stinger Spike System across the road. But without even pausing, Robinson mounted the pavement and raced safely past it and the police car.

Chris had already grabbed his radio. 'Don't let that bastard get away!'

The police officers at the roadblock dived into their vehicles. Seconds later, sirens blazing, they were racing off after the rider streaking away from them down the suburban road.

The DCI clasped his hands on top of his head. 'Fuck!'

Joseph was about to join in with his best Irish expletives when Megan pointed back towards the garage.

'Is that some sort of bomb?' she asked, gesturing towards a series of gas canisters with some sort of device stuck to them.

Joseph took one look at it and his blood iced. The countdown had less than thirty seconds to go.

'Feck. Get everyone out of the house, now!'

Chris was already on his radio. 'Abort, abort, abort, there's a bomb in the garage!' The DCI pulled Megan with him to the other side of the street.

Joseph had other ideas. He needed to make sure Erol and his officers got outside in time. He hadn't been able to do anything about John and Paul, but this time, he could try to make a difference.

Before the DI had a chance to think about what he was doing, he was already racing back through the door and into the hallway.

'Move your fecking arses!' he bellowed at the men who appeared at the top of the stairs.

They rushed down them, and headed for the front door as Erol appeared from the back of the house.

Joseph glanced back through the garage door to see the timer had reached the final three seconds.

'Go!' he bellowed at the commander.

Feet pounding, hands clawing the air, the DI sprinted through the front door after Erol.

Outside, he spotted Megan frantically beckoning them from behind the unmarked police Volvo where she and Chris had taken cover. Joseph and the Commander half ran, half dived towards them. A flash of light and a loud *whump* came from behind them.

Joseph felt a wave of heat on his back, throwing him and Erol forward. Then, Chris and Megan were grabbing hold of them, hauling them into cover behind the car as a wave of roaring fire boiled over the bonnet of the Volvo, and the garage door crashed into the other side of the vehicle.

The DI's heart thumped in his chest as the explosion died away. With the others, he slowly raised his head to peer over the bonnet of the Volvo at the house.

The garage was a burning cauldron of flames, the windows of the house blown out, smoke billowing from every single one of them. Even the hedge in front of the house was on fire.

As the three detectives and Erol stood, the other tactical officers emerged from behind the other vehicles where they'd taken cover.

'Bollocks!' Chris shouted. Then his shoulders dropped as he turned towards Joseph and Megan. 'That frigging psychopath tried to kill all of us!'

Joseph bit back his immediate retort that his senior officer was stating the bleeding obvious. 'Yes, it's not good, boss,' he settled for instead, as Chris's radio crackled into life.

'I'm afraid we've lost Robinson,' a woman's voice announced. 'We had to break off because of the danger to the public. He must have been easily doing over a hundred through the estate.'

'Understood, and it was the right call,' Chris said, trading a frown with Joseph as he lowered the radio. 'It seems Robinson has got away clean yet again. We'll send a general alert out straight away and will also make an immediate press statement. Wherever that bastard has gone, we'll find him.'

Joseph raked his hand through his hair. 'We're going to have to make sure that happens sooner rather than later.'

The DCI narrowed his gaze at him. 'Why's that?'

'Because Robinson said one thing to me before he escaped, something about not being finished yet.'

'What's that meant to mean?' Megan asked.

'Considering he's already killed Jimmy and Matthew, not to mention attempting to murder DCI Sanders, who has he got left to kill?' Chris said.

Megan's face paled. 'Maybe he's going to try and finish what he started with Lewis and his wife?'

Chris gave her a sharp nod. 'I'll double the armed guard for them at the hospital.'

'Good idea,' Joseph said. 'We should also put a heavy surveillance operation in place, with a helicopter on standby. That way, if Robinson is stupid enough to show his face there, we'll catch him.'

'I can almost hear DSU Walker weeping over the costs on his spreadsheet from here,' Chris replied.

'What an absolute tragedy,' Joseph said, giving his senior officer the barest smile.

CHAPTER TWENTY-SEVEN

'WHAT DO you mean there's no bloody sign of Liam Robinson?' Derrick bellowed at Joseph and Chris in his glass office a day later. 'The bastard almost barbecued a tactical unit, not to mention yourselves. I want him brought to justice like fucking yesterday.'

Chris looked distinctly uncomfortable in the hotter of the two seats, as Derrick focused his wrath on him. Once again, it reminded Joseph why he didn't want Chris's job. But it wasn't lost on him that when the SIO was dragged in, the superintendent also viewed it as an opportunity to have a go at Joseph. Two for the price of one and all that.

'We've had hundreds of false leads from the public appeal, and there's been no sign of Robinson anywhere,' Chris replied.

Derrick peered at him, several veins standing out on his forehead. 'Not fucking good enough. Am I surrounded by incompetents? And you, Joseph, almost had him in your hands and you literally let him waltz out of his garage.'

'I would hardly call it waltzing, sir, more like speeding like a bat out of hell on his motorbike,' Joseph replied.

He caught Chris trying to suppress a grin.

Derrick's look went from pissed off to one of incandescent rage. Joseph leapt in before the big man attempted to rip him a second arsehole.

'Oh, before I forget, I've been meaning to ask you, how's the NCA's investigation into the ambush of Daryl Manning's transfer going?' the DI asked. 'Have they managed to discover how the Night Watchmen knew about the prisoner transfer yet?'

Derrick blinked and sat back in his chair. 'They've found out nothing at all, so they're working on the assumption that the solicitor probably tipped the syndicate off, even if they can't prove it,' he said in a much meeker tone.

'It's good to hear we don't have a bent copper on the team,' Joseph said with his most agreeable expression.

'Of course,' Derrick said, before narrowing his eyes at Joseph. 'Anyway, I haven't got you both here to discuss that. We need to work out what the hell you're going to do about this huge balls-up with the Liam Robinson case.'

'We have some lines of investigation we're actively pursuing,' Joseph replied, and clocked the surprised side-eye Chris gave him.

'Which are?' Derrick asked.

Joseph raised his hands. 'Let's just say that, although it's early days, it's already looking promising. We'll get back to you once we have something more concrete.'

'Then that sounds more like it. Why didn't you say that at the start?'

'You didn't really give us a chance to,' Joseph replied.

'Okay, maybe I didn't.' Derrick took a deep breath. 'I suppose now's as good a time as any to inform you, and I doubt this is going to come as any sort of surprise, but the NCA have finally informed me they're going be taking over the Burning

Man investigation first thing tomorrow. They believe it and the Night Watchmen case may be interlinked.'

'Oh hell,' Chris responded. 'I guess it was only a matter of time.'

'My thoughts exactly, and it doesn't reflect well on any of us. So whatever rabbit you're intending to pull out of a hat before tomorrow's deadline, you'd better flipping get to it,' Derrick said. 'And keep me updated.'

Both detectives nodded as they headed for the door.

'What promising leads?' the DCI asked the moment they were both safely out of the superintendent's office.

'Just buying us some time,' Joseph replied. 'I have this itch of a feeling we've overlooked something significant. I'm going to grab Megan and trawl through everything we can find about the casino fire to see if we can turn anything else up.'

'Then let's hope that itch of yours turns into a breakthrough, and isn't just a case of eczema breaking out. If you don't, the NCA will swoop in and take this investigation away from us faster than we can blink.'

'Don't worry, I'm going to leave no stone unturned,' Joseph replied as they headed back to the incident room.

A sound of scratching reached Joseph's ears as he boarded *Tús Nua* later that evening. After a fruitless day trawling through all the information they had about the casino fire, he was already in a bad enough mood. Muttering to himself, he opened the door a fraction to see Tux nonchalantly stretching on his small sofa and giving it a good going-over with his claws.

'For feck's sake, will you bloody stop that!' he bellowed.

The cat turned and gave him a nonplussed look before he

miaowed at the DI, jumped down, and started rubbing against his legs.

'Oh, you think you can win me over with your catty ways, do you?' Joseph said, smiling despite himself. He bent down, scratched Tux's head, and was rewarded with a loud purr.

A knock came from the cabin door. 'Joseph, I have something here that you're going to want to see,' Dylan said.

The DI opened the door to see the professor standing there, minus his dogs, a folder clutched under his arm. 'You'd better get in here then, before Tux makes a break for it.'

Dylan did as instructed, shutting the door quickly behind him. The professor's attention was drawn to Tux, who was already making figure-of-eight patterns around his legs.

'Yes, I'm pleased to see you, too,' Dylan said. He stroked the cat's head, which resulted in a far louder purr than Joseph had been given for his efforts.

'How's the little fella been getting on in my absence?' Joseph asked, gesturing towards Tux as they both sat down.

'Actually, really well. He's taken to your home like the proverbial duck to water. Also, he's got a good appetite, which means he can't be too upset about being uprooted and brought here.'

Joseph looked at the cat with a sense of relief. 'That's grand, although I could do without his litter tray in my loo.'

Dylan shrugged. 'I don't imagine it's a bed of roses having to share his toilet facilities with you, either.'

Joseph laughed. 'No, it probably isn't.' He pointed to the folder under his friend's arm. 'What is it you have there? Something for me?'

'Indeed, it is. It's information that may prove your prime suspect, Liam Robinson, has another victim he hasn't got around to yet.'

Joseph gawped at him. 'Bloody hell, who?'

Dylan opened his folder to reveal a photocopy of a page from a newspaper with the headline, 'Fire Inspector Killed Whilst Investigating Business Inferno.' The article appeared to be dated three years previously.

'Sorry, as tragic as that is, I'm not getting the connection here,' Joseph said.

'The man who was killed was called Adam Kelly. He was Thomas Reid's, or maybe I should say, Liam Robinson's, predecessor. He was killed when a gas storage cylinder no one knew was present in a business unit exploded in a fire. That cleared the way for Robinson to be promoted and take on his role.'

'You're suggesting Robinson deliberately set him up to be killed and made it look like an accident, just to get his job?'

'I think that's a reasonable assumption, and not just for the reason of climbing the career ladder. You see, when I looked up the old records to see who owned the business unit that had been burned down, it turned out to be none other than Aura Holdings.'

'Jesus, the NCA will certainly want to know about that, if they don't know already.'

'But surely they would have shared that information with you if they did?'

'Normally they would do, but the breaking news is they are taking over the Burning Man investigation tomorrow. So they probably thought there wasn't any point.'

'I see. That must be incredibly galling for you after all the legwork you've put into trying to solve this case.'

'That's one way of putting it, although "very pissed off" would be a more accurate description.'

'Then I'm here to inform you not to lose hope just yet.'

Joseph felt that hope stirring inside him. 'What exactly is it you've found, Dylan?'

The professor drew his fingertips together and looked over

his glasses at the DI. 'Guess who the investigating fire officer was for the Excalibur casino fire that killed Robinson's parents? It was in an investigation report of the casino fire that a retired firefighter friend of mine dug up for me.'

Joseph stared at him. 'Hang on, you're not saying it was this Adam Kelly you mentioned a moment ago, the same officer Liam may have also murdered?'

'Bingo!' Dylan said, grinning from ear to ear. 'And Kelly's official report about the casino fire stated it was an accident. No wonder Liam had him down as a marked man. He was obviously in on the plan with Harper and Forbes to defraud the insurance company. No doubt, in Liam's mind, that made Kelly complicit with what he saw as his parents' murder.'

'Bloody hell, you really are a golden man when it comes to this sort of thing,' Joseph said, looking at his friend with sheer admiration. 'So that suggests Adam Kelly was probably on the payroll of the Night Watchmen as well. I bet they paid him to look the other way when the casino was torched for the insurance payout.'

Dylan nodded. 'But don't you find it strange that, despite all of that, the insurance company paid out?'

A thought surfaced from the back of Joseph's mind and came into sharp focus. 'Hang on, that's a very good point. Surely, the loss adjuster at the time would have spotted something amiss, unless...'

The professor beamed at him. 'I knew you'd work it out before I got to it.'

'Jesus, the only reason would be if they were also on the Night Watchmen's payroll. Talk about a den of vipers. Right, I need to find out who the insurance officer was ASAP.'

Dylan held up his hand. 'One of my missions in life is to make your life easier. That's why I already reached out to yet another friend of mine who's the head at Saïd Business School.

He has connections everywhere, and after a bit of digging on my behalf, he managed to discover the man's name.'

'Blimey, talk about being well connected. I don't know why St Aldates doesn't just shut up shop, and hand this entire investigating lark over to you. Go on then, please put me out of my misery. Who is it and where can we find them?'

'John Winters.'

Joseph shook his head. 'That name doesn't ring any bells.'

'It won't, because it turns out Liam wasn't the only person who changed his name.'

Dylan dug into his folder and took out a printout of a webpage of the British Insurance Awards. The article beneath it was titled, 'John Winters Wins the Claims Excellence Award for Second Year Running.' Below that was a photo of a bald man accepting an award—a person Joseph recognised from his incident board photo.

The DI threw his hands up in the air. 'For feck's sake, it's Ralph Richards.'

'Exactly. He must have changed his name. No wonder no one realised that Ralph was the insurance investigator for the Excalibur casino fire. Maybe his work for the Night Watchmen came to light during an internal audit, or somebody may have started asking too many difficult questions about why he kept signing off on suspicious insurance claims. So Winters, as he was known then, just melted away to start his new life running his gastropub.'

'Not forgetting he was also an old school friend of Jimmy and Matthew, and he also helped fix races with them. That must have been why Liam was at Branton, to track down Winters. No prizes for who Robinson is going to target next then.'

'Which was my thought exactly.'

'Right, I'm heading to Winters's gastropub right now. Even

if he doesn't realise it yet, his life's in danger. Robinson said he wasn't finished, and I thought he was talking about Sanders. But no, he means to finally avenge his parents' death by killing the only other man still standing. And Robinson, who's now on the run, won't want to hang around before striking again.'

'Then you'd better get to it, whilst you're still officially assigned to the case,' Dylan said.

Joseph quickly gestured to Tux, who was now sitting on the professor's lap. 'Can you do the honours with him again tonight?'

'It would be an absolute pleasure. Although, I'll give it a bit longer before I introduce him to Max and White Fang. Now go and save a man's life, if only so you can arrest him and hand him over to the NCA.'

There wasn't any time to waste. The DI rushed outside, phone already in his hand, dialling Megan. Then he'd call Chris, who could call in the troops, and let Ian and Sue know what was happening as they were on stakeout duty at Richards's gastropub tonight.

CHAPTER TWENTY-EIGHT

WITH MEGAN at the wheel of the Peugeot, the detectives were speeding towards the village of Thistlewick. After what seemed like forever, they finally caught sight of The Feasting Fox in the distance.

Joseph was no stranger to a good inn. However, the one John Winters, AKA Ralph Richards, owned, looked like it had been taken to the next level. If there was a poster child for what you might imagine as an award-winning gastropub, this would be it.

The thatched-roofed pub sat in a perfect spot on a hill overlooking a wooded valley, where a river snaked through the bottom. Rare-breed cows with long horns grazed in the fields as the last remnants of sunlight faded away. It was like a pastoral scene John Constable might have painted back in the day.

As for the pub itself, several stepped terraces bordered by old railway sleepers and planted with beds of lavender had been built at the back of the pub. The shaded gazebo's extensive patio area filled with tables was just visible, and flaming garden lanterns framed the idyllic view of the rolling hills for the diners sitting there.

'Nice isn't it?' Megan said.

'You could say that,' Joseph replied, scanning for any sign of Ian and Sue, who, worryingly, he hadn't been able to reach so far on his mobile. Then he felt some of the tension he'd been carrying let go when he spotted the nondescript black BMW 3 Series parked up in a layby.

Megan had spotted it too and slowed the car to a stop next to the other vehicle. The driver's window was already descending. A heavy scent of fish and chips wafted out of it, hitting Joseph in the face.

'To what do we owe the honour of your esteemed company during our stakeout?' Ian asked, his mouth full of chips, as he and Sue looked across at them.

'Bloody hell, man. I've been trying to ring you for the last thirty minutes, but it kept going straight to voicemail,' Joseph said.

'You can blame the local opposition for removing any cellular masts that spoiled their view. We've been lucky to get even a single bar. We've actually had to use an old phone box in the village to report in. Anyway, you look like two people on a mission.'

'Damned right we are. We're bringing Winters in for his own protection before Robinson targets him with another arson attack.'

'Winters?' Sue said, putting down the piece of fish she'd been about to tuck into.

'That's Richards's real name,' Megan explained. 'It turns out he was the insurance loss adjuster for the casino fire. Liam almost certainly has him in his sights and we think there is every chance he will target Winters and his gastropub tonight. We've been in contact with Chris, and the cavalry is already on its way. The boss even managed to get Derrick to sign off on a helicopter.'

'Bloody hell,' Ian replied. 'Then we'll follow you in.'

'Okay, but you hold the fort outside while we go in, in case Robinson decides to make an appearance on his motorbike.'

'Then we'd better get going,' Ian said, tossing his bag of chips onto the back seat. The next person to use the pool vehicle wasn't going to thank him for that.

Joseph put his foot down, and they sped off towards the pub, followed closely by the other detectives.

In less than a minute, both vehicles had screeched to a stop in the car park outside The Feasting Fox. Joseph nodded to Ian and Sue, as he and Megan hurried towards the pub.

The DI scanned the car park, but apart from a number of cars the car park was almost empty. There was certainly no sign of a motorbike.

It was fast approaching closing time, and several patrons were filing out as the two detectives headed into the bar area. A track Joseph recognised as Ella Fitzgerald's *'Ev'ry Time We Say Goodbye'* was playing softly in the background. On one side of the room was a bar made from rippled glass, glowing with a soft blue backlight that made it resemble a block of ice.

'Okay, I'm going to revise my opinion of this place from nice to *very nice*,' Megan said.

'Steady there with that high praise, or you'll get giddy,' Joseph said.

The DC just gave him the look.

One of the two bartenders turned to them as they approached the bar. 'I'm sorry, but we've already served last orders.'

'We'd actually like to see the owner, Ralph Richards,' Joseph said, as he and Megan discreetly flashed their warrant cards.

'I'm afraid he's rather busy out on the terrace checking that our diners enjoyed their meals.'

'Don't worry, he'll want to talk to us,' Joseph said, as he gestured to Megan to follow him.

'But Detectives...' the barman called after them, which they studiously ignored.

The DC spied the blackboard above the fireplace. 'What on Earth is a Carpaccio of Venison served on a bed of mixed grains with a mulberry coulis?' she asked, pointing towards the first item listed under *Specials Today*.

'You know, Bambi, or didn't your generation watch the Disney classics?'

She pulled a face at him. 'I know what flipping venison is, I meant the carpaccio part.'

'That just means it's raw marinated meat, although there's also the famous Peruvian dish made with fish marinated in lime juice.' With air quotes, he added, 'To cook it.'

'Raw meat, no thanks, although I do like a bit of sushi.'

'Don't knock it until you've tried it,' Joseph said, as they made their way outside to the patio area.

Another group of guests were just standing to leave and shaking hands with a bald man with a chiselled face. The DI recognised the man from his photo on the evidence board— Winters. He was wearing a dark blue silk suit, a perfectly folded handkerchief poking out of his top pocket. Whatever else he was, he certainly had great sartorial style.

There was also an ease in the way Winters handled himself, his smile warm and broad to match those of his customers. Joseph could tell just by looking at him, he was someone who felt on top of the world. But not for much longer. When they broke the news to him that Robinson was likely already on his trail, that would probably change.

As Winters shook the hands of his departing guests, the detectives intercepted him before he could head away to another table. The patio area emptied of its last diners.

'Mr Richards, can we have a quiet word?' Joseph said.

'Sorry, was there a problem with your meal?' he asked with a voice that dripped honey, as he turned towards them.

'Nothing like that as we didn't eat here tonight. Although your menu certainly looked appetising to me, DC Anderson here is less sure.'

Winters's expression tightened. 'You're detectives?'

In answer, they both showed him their warrant cards.

'Maybe you have somewhere we can speak to you out of earshot of your guests,' Joseph said, raising his eyebrows at the man.

Winters glanced at the last table of remaining diners and nodded. 'If you'd like to follow me.'

They all headed through a side door into an empty lounge with comfortable-looking armchairs and sofas, arranged around a large unlit fireplace. It was flanked by crystal flower sculptures placed in glass vases, glowing with hidden internal lighting like the bar had been.

Winters gestured to the seats. 'We shouldn't be disturbed here. Now, what can I help you with, officers?'

Megan already had her notebook open as they sat down.

'First of all, do you happen to know a man called Liam Robinson?' Joseph asked.

Winters gave them a blank look. 'I've never heard of him.'

'Are you sure about that? Cast your mind back sixteen years or so. Starting to ring any bells yet?'

A puzzled look filled Winters's face. 'I think I know the surname, but I can't quite place it.'

'Then maybe Liam's parents' names will prompt your memory, Norman and Clare Robinson?'

Winters's eyes widened. 'Oh Christ, you're talking about that poor man and woman who were killed in that awful casino fire. I think I remember reading about it in the papers. And Liam was their son, wasn't he?'

'That's the one,' Joseph replied in a measured tone.

'But I don't understand. Why would you want to talk to me about someone I've never met?'

'Because Liam has something of a vendetta, determined to avenge what happened to his parents, and you're in his crosshairs.'

'I still don't understand. Why would he have a problem with me?' the man asked, looking the very picture of innocence.

'Weren't you an insurance loss adjuster in your former life, when you were known as John Winters?' Megan asked.

His eyes widened. 'Sorry, you've mistaken me for someone else.'

'Are you sure about that?' Joseph asked, taking the printout from the website for the British Insurance Awards, and specifically, the photo of the man accepting a trophy.

Winters's eyes flicked between the photo and the detectives. He opened his mouth to say something, but then closed it again.

'Are you going to waste our time by trying to deny that the man in that photo is actually you?' Joseph asked in his most genial voice.

Winters looked between them and shook his head. 'I expect there would be little point, as you've already done your homework. Yes, I used to be known as John Winters, but for reasons I don't want to go into now, I decided to change my name.'

I bet you don't without your solicitor present, Joseph thought.

'And you used to be an insurance loss adjuster, is that right?' Megan asked.

'Yes, but that was my old life.'

'Maybe it was, but you must remember the Excalibur casino fire?' Joseph asked.

Winters looked at him warily and slowly nodded. 'Yes, and I made a full investigation of the fire. If I remember correctly, it was caused by one of the extinguished gas cooker burners in the kitchen that was accidentally left on. The leaking gas was ignited by a faulty light switch. It was a tragic accident. No one knew the Robinsons were still in their dressing room when the fire broke out.'

'An accident?' Joseph said. 'Are you sure about that? Liam certainly doesn't seem to think so.'

For the first time, Winters's expression hardened. 'I don't know what you're driving at, Detective Stone.'

'Surely you must be worried about your safety after both Jimmy Harper and Matthew Forbes, the owners of Excalibur, lost their lives in recent arson attacks. Not to mention Adam Kelly, who investigated the same casino fire and who was also killed in a fire a few months ago. Liam even targeted the investigating DCI at his home, but he and his wife were able to escape the fire just in time.'

Winters's eyes slitted, calculating. 'You mean Liam Robinson is targeting anyone involved with the casino fire case? That's why he targeted Jimmy and Matthew?'

'It would appear so, and I'm afraid it appears you're almost certainly next on his to-do list.'

'But why? It was a tragic accident.'

'You keep using that word *accident*,' Megan said, raising her eyebrows at him.

Before Winters could reply, one of the bar staff walked in. 'The last of the diners have left, Ralph, and we're cashing out now.'

'You can go home when you've finished that. I'll lock up,' Winters replied, gesturing dismissively.

The barman's eyes flicked to the detectives. Then he nodded and headed back out.

Winters returned his attention to Joseph and Megan. 'Obviously, this Liam character has some serious problems if he's trying to blame me for what happened.'

Joseph exchanged a look with Megan. The time had come to press their man harder.

'It sounds as though you have a totally guilt-free conscience, although I'm sure our colleagues at the National Crime Agency may take a different view when they interview you,' Joseph said.

Winters dragged his upper lip over his teeth. 'The NCA wants to talk to me?'

'They will do, and for many reasons. But to be honest, your past indiscretions aren't actually of any concern to us right now. However, your life is very much in danger and we're going to need to bring you in for your own protection.'

Winters sat back in his chair. 'Don't be so melodramatic, Detective. If there really is a threat to my life, then I can make arrangements to head off to my other home in Edinburgh until things blow over if I need to.'

'I'm afraid our colleagues at the NCA will take a rather dim view of that, as you are now a person of significant interest to them. Besides, before we hand you over, we need to formally interview you back at the station regarding our murder investigation.'

The pub owner glared at them. 'You really don't want to go down this path, Detectives,' Winters said almost casually.

Megan peered at him. 'Sorry, was that some sort of threat?'

'No, just a promise that there will be consequences,' he replied, his voice of iron, as they heard the bar staff head off with a chatter of voices.

The man before the detectives had completely transformed from the amiable man they'd first met, to someone who looked like he was used to being in control and getting exactly what he wanted.

But not on this occasion, you little fecker...

The DI was tempted to drag Winters over the coals about what was increasingly looking like a case of insurance fraud, but that would step on the toes of the guys and gals over at the NCA. However, once he had this little bollox in an interview room, then maybe they would soften up the gobshite for the agency.

Megan was frowning as she wrote Winters's not-very-subtle threat down in her notebook, when all the lights went out, dropping the pub into sudden darkness.

Joseph took his phone out and turned its torch on.

'Not another bloody power cut,' Winters muttered. 'This village is plagued by the bloody things.'

But Joseph's instinct had kicked in. He glanced at the window where he could see the neighbouring properties' lights.

'No, it must have just been your main breaker circuit tripped,' he said. He couldn't stop himself from adding, 'Probably a faulty light switch in the kitchen. You need to be careful of that sort of thing.'

Winters shot him a frown. 'I'll need to reset the tripped switch so the freezers don't defrost overnight.'

'No, we need to get you out of here pronto,' Joseph said.

'You think this power cut is something to do with Liam?' Winters asked, looking between them incredulously.

'Unlikely, as there are two other detectives outside, but to be on the safe side, you should shift your arse and let's get out of here.'

For the first time, Winters looked rattled. He got up and led them through a staff door into a corridor. Joseph and Megan both had their batons out, ready to use them if they heard so much as a mouse fart.

CHAPTER TWENTY-NINE

JOSEPH AND MEGAN followed Winters past a door with a small round window set into it. The DI glanced through it as they passed to see a spotless kitchen beyond.

The pub owner headed towards a cupboard at the end of the corridor. He opened it to reveal the poshest cupboard Joseph had ever seen. It was lined with oak panels and totally devoid of the usual clutter you might expect to find somewhere like that, mops, brooms and the rest.

Winters flipped down a panel to reveal a series of trip switches, two of which, including the main power supply, showed green dots indicating the circuits had faults. He reset the smaller switch, but when he flipped the main one, it tripped again.

Joseph directed his phone's torch towards the panel as Winters leaned in to read the hand-written label beneath the switch.

'It looks like some sort of power fault in the kitchen. It seems to be tripping the whole supply,' Winters said. 'I need to check it out, otherwise, as I said, we'll lose everything in the freezers.'

The DI resisted the urge to grind his teeth. His gut was

telling him it was too much of a coincidence. 'No, we need to go; feck your frozen food,' Joseph replied. 'Besides, we have an interview room with your name on it back at St Aldates Police Station.'

In way of an answer, Winters shoved past Joseph. However, rather than head back down the corridor, the man ducked through the kitchen door before either of the detectives could stop him. The moment he stepped through, Winters came to a stop.

'What the hell?' he growled.

The DI didn't need to ask what, because the smell of gas had hit him squarely in the nostrils as he joined him.

Winters rushed over to the cookers, checking all the gas rings. 'They're not on, so where the hell is it coming from?'

'It doesn't matter. We need to get out of here—' The words died in Joseph's throat as he heard a buzzing noise. He turned, trying to locate the source of the sound, and spotted a light switch hanging off where a screwdriver had been stuck into it. Of much more immediate concern was the source of the buzzing sound. A spark was arcing between the tips of two exposed wires.

'Feck, run!' Joseph shouted.

But Winters, who had just spotted the light switch as well, had frozen.

'Move your fecking arse!' Joseph bellowed, pushing him out through the door.

Megan turned towards them as both men erupted from the kitchen. Before Joseph even had a chance to shout a warning, a deafening boom came from the kitchen, numbing his ears. The whole building shook as a massive gout of flame surged out of the kitchen. Without even thinking of the danger to himself, Joseph hurled himself at the door, using all his strength to shove it shut against the blast wave.

His body thrumming with adrenaline, the DI glanced through the round window into the kitchen to see utter devastation. Stoves and refrigerators had been thrown aside like a tornado had just ripped through the kitchen, fire already licking every surface. Two deep fat friers ignited with a whoosh and more flames roared out from them like twin volcanoes, charring the ceiling and spreading quickly outwards.

'What the hell just happened?' Megan asked, as Joseph herded her and Winters back down the corridor.

'A gas explosion, which has Robinson's bloody fingerprints all over it,' Joseph replied, as they all rushed out into the bar area and headed straight for the main door.

The DI reached it first, but when he tried the door, it didn't budge. Someone had locked it. He saw the tiny, typical Cotswold pub windows that were about big enough for a small child to escape through.

He whirled around to stare at Winters. 'Get this bloody thing unlocked now, before that fecking fire spreads and barbecues us all!'

'But it shouldn't be locked. You heard me tell the staff I'd shut up for the night,' Winters said, dazed. But then he shook himself out of it and dashed back to the bar. He began hunting behind it. 'Where the hell are the keys?'

'Shite on a stick,' Joseph said, as Megan shot him a desperate look.

He heard the door rattle as someone on the outside tried to get in, and then a muffled thud as someone kicked it from the outside, but the solid oak door was too sturdy and barely moved in its frame.

Then he spotted Sue peering in at them through the window.

'What happened?' she shouted through the thick glass.

'Liam's handiwork—it has to be. He set the gas to explode in the kitchen and probably locked this fecking door, too.'

'But we've seen no sign of him or his motorbike,' Sue replied.

'That little scrote either slipped past you, or was here already,' Joseph replied.

There came another thud on the front door. Then Ian's face appeared with Sue's in the window, nursing his shoulder. 'It's not bloody shifting.'

Winters, ashen-faced, pointed towards another door on the far side of the bar area. 'We should try the fire exit.'

'Why the feck didn't you mention that before?' Joseph bellowed at the man, making him shrink away from him.

'You'd better get a move on, guys, there's smoke billowing out of a vent on the side of the building,' Ian called through the window. 'It won't be long until the entire pub is on fire.'

'We're not about to hang around long enough to start toasting marshmallows in here,' Megan replied.

Despite the grimness of their situation, that elicited a grin from Joseph.

Ian and Sue disappeared, and Megan and the DI followed Winters to the fire door. He tried to open it, but the door thudded into something on the outside.

'Someone's bloody chained the thing up,' Ian said from the other side of the door a split second later.

'Can you bust it open?' Joseph asked.

'No. The lock looks big enough to moor the bloody Titanic.'

Joseph fought down the desire to punch something. Liam Robinson really wasn't messing around this time.

'We can still escape through the patio area,' Megan said.

Joseph gave her a sharp nod. But before any of them could move, a flash of light came from the lounge area between them and the patio. A loud boom shook the entire building again, and a ball of flame snarled through the lounge.

'What the hell is happening?' Winters asked, staring in disbelief at the swirling flames beyond the shattered glass door.

'Liam is toying with you before he finally burns you to death, and we're going to get caught in the crossfire. That's fecking what,' the DI said.

Megan pointed at the bar.

Joseph looked at where she was indicating, and his heart stuttered. Partly hidden behind a potted plant was a familiar timer and a small box tied to a gas canister. It was almost identical to the device Robinson had set up in his garage. A bloody bomb.

Four seconds ticked down to three on the display. Joseph spun around, but there was only one way to go to take shelter. The same way they'd just come.

'Back into that corridor now!' he shouted.

Just as they entered the corridor again, a *whump* sounded behind them. A boiling, churning cloud of fire roared through the bar area. Joseph just had time to register the bar shattering, glass splinters flying everywhere to slam into the walls and furniture, and expensive bottles of spirits detonating like hand grenades.

Once again, he found himself slamming another door to try and shut out the flames. He just prayed that Sue and Ian had already called the fire brigade. The problem was, he knew their chances of surviving this were growing slimmer by the moment. Robinson had prepared the groundwork for Winters's death far too well.

Joseph started to feel light-headed as the door's varnish began to blister.

Megan was sucking in deep lungfuls of air, and Winters's

breathing had become ragged. The DI put a hand on the wall to support himself.

'The fire is sucking the oxygen out of the air,' the DC explained between breaths.

Joseph nodded, battling down the fear threatening to swamp his thoughts. He took in the door to the kitchen as charred holes appeared in its surface. It wouldn't be able to hold back the flames for much longer, let alone the other door to the bar area.

The DI put his hands on his head. 'There's no way out of this bloody death trap.'

Winters closed his eyes for a moment. 'You're not going to be so lucky this time, Liam...' he whispered, almost to himself. Then he opened his eyes again. 'If you want to live, follow me.' The pub owner walked away, past the kitchen door as flames started to roar through the holes in it like Bunsen burner jets, heading back to the fuse cupboard.

'I don't understand,' Megan said, staring at the man, who obviously had a screw or three loose if he thought a cupboard would give them any sort of protection from the inferno.

But then Winters pressed one of the square cross sections in the wooden panelled wall. Try like a magician's disappearing trick the whole rear wall swung back to reveal a hidden door.

Winters stepped through and glanced back at them. 'What are you bloody waiting for? There's another exit in the basement; we can escape that way.'

Joseph exchanged a look with Megan. With a bellow, the kitchen door finally disintegrated and fire roared into the corridor behind them.

CHAPTER THIRTY

JOSEPH FOLLOWED Megan down the steps after Winters into the basement. Before he reached the bottom, the pub owner let out a muffled cry, followed by a thud.

'Stay right there!' Megan shouted.

Joseph rushed down the remaining steps and raced into a large, plush room with its own bar. He came to a skidding stop as he took in the scene before him.

A figure stood looming over Winters, lying unconscious at his feet. Megan held her baton in one hand, making a downward motion in a placatory manner.

Liam Robinson looked up from the pub owner with grim determination, a cricket bat in his hand.

In the next second, Joseph noticed the stench of petrol filling the space. A lighter was already in Robinson's hand. So this had been the fire officer's plan all along, to herd Winters here so he could end his life in this room.

In the millisecond after that, the DI took in the card tables with discarded hands on them and the roulette wheel with drinks left next to it. This hidden basement had all the fingerprints of an illegal casino.

For now, Joseph ignored all of that and concentrated instead on the immediate concern—stopping Robinson from doing anything stupid. There was another door at the far end, but it had been locked with another length of chain wrapped around the handle.

Megan tried to hold Robinson's gaze, as though she was dealing with a skittish animal. 'Whoa there, Liam. You don't need to do this.'

'Oh, but I do,' he replied. 'This bastard is the last one who needs to pay for murdering my parents.' He bent and snatched up a petrol can at his feet, pouring it over Winters, who moaned as he came around.

Joseph took a step towards the arsonist, but in response, Robinson held up the lighter and shook his head.

'Please, no heroics. I haven't got much time to tell you what you need to know,' Robinson said. He reached down again and grabbed a canvas bag, throwing it over to the DI.

'What's this?' Joseph asked, looking inside to see a leather-bound A4 notebook.

'The ledger from Jimmy Harper's safe. It lists a whole range of dodgy companies that Aura Holdings has a stake in, including the one you're now standing in, an illegal gambling club. I've been digging for years, trying to work out who was really behind the fire that killed my parents, pulling the strings. Harper, Forbes, and Winters here, all work for the Night Watchmen, an illegal crime syndicate who needed a way to launder their dirty money.'

'Yes, we know all about them now,' Joseph replied.

'Good, so you've been doing your homework too. Mind you, that nearly cost you your life when you were driven off the track by one of Forbes's scum during that race at Branton. Anyway, you'll find evidence all about that particular gambling ring and so much more in that ledger.'

'That will be a great help to the investigation,' Joseph said, as he noticed Megan discreetly inching towards Liam to get the man within baton range. He tried to keep Liam's eyes on him. 'But why are you giving this to us now?'

'So you can go after the scum behind all of this and bring their whole bloody edifice crashing down around their ears. I'm one man, I can only do so much. That's why I needed that ledger, to confirm what I suspected—that the Night Watchmen had been the ones pulling the strings. This bastard at my feet, had taken backhanders to look the other way, as had the fire investigator, Adam Kelly. But it was Forbes and Jimmy who actually torched the casino. They were the ones who didn't take the time to check that everyone had left. They murdered my parents.'

'Okay, let's slow down. Although they were certainly guilty as hell, at best, a jury would convict them for manslaughter.'

'Exactly. Why do you think I took things into my own hands?' Robinson replied. 'I knew I couldn't rely on the original investigation team to get any sort of conviction because they were incompetent. That's why DCI Sanders had to die. He allowed Harper and Forbes to walk away from their crimes. Admittedly, I screwed that up when I was interrupted, but...' He shrugged.

Rattling came from the exit as someone on the outside tried to open it. It had to be Ian and Sue. They must have found this other exit.

Robinson glanced behind him, distracted just long enough for Megan to take another small step towards him like a high-stakes game of Grandmother's Footsteps.

Above them, the bellow of crackling flames was growing louder. Already the ceiling was starting to smoke. Regardless of Liam using his lighter on Winters, Joseph realised it was only a matter of time before the blaze reached the basement anyway and killed them all.

'But Sanders could only work with the evidence they had,' Joseph said, trying to keep Robinson's attention focused entirely on him rather than Megan. 'You targeted an innocent man.'

Liam let out a hollow laugh. 'Only in your mind. In mine, he's as guilty as the rest of them.'

The DI could tell that it was pointless trying to argue with somebody so deranged, let alone point out the fact that he'd almost killed Lewis's wife as well, someone who was just as blameless as Robinson's parents had been. But rationality wasn't what any of this was about. Blind vengeance was driving Liam forward now. He'd been scarred for life as a boy and had grown into the bitter man standing before them.

'But it was an accident,' Winters said, his voice weak as he tried to push himself up onto his elbows.

Robinson stamped his boot onto the man's back, forcing him back to the floor. 'The hell it was, and you know that better than anyone, Winters. You know Harper and Forbes doused the whole casino in petrol, yet strangely, there wasn't one bloody mention of that in your report—just like there wasn't in that fire officer's. Just because you weren't there, doesn't mean you're not as fucking guilty as the rest of them.' He flicked the lighter, and a flame appeared. His focus was off the detectives just long enough for Megan to take another small step towards him.

A loud *bang* made Joseph jump. Ian and Sue must have been attempting to use something heavy to smash into the fire door, but the chain held.

Robinson hadn't reacted at all. His focus was locked on Winters, hatred burning in his eyes.

'Steady there, Liam,' Joseph said. 'There's no need for any of this.' But even as he spoke, he was scanning the room, looking for something he could use to stop this. Then the DI spotted a fire extinguisher near the door.

'Oh, don't worry, I have no intention of killing you or DC Anderson. You've been far more tenacious in your investigation and were well on your way to revealing the truth. It's only Winters I want, and I'm going to die with him. I'm broken, Joseph... I can call you that, can't I?'

'You can call me whatever you want as long as you don't set light to that gobshite.'

Liam chuckled as ash began to drift down from the ceiling. 'Good to know. But like I was saying, you should both go while you still can. Besides, I need you to make sure the Night Watchmen pay for what they've done.'

'And they will, you have my word,' Joseph replied. 'But we can't leave without you and Winters. You've made your point, Liam. I will personally make sure this man pays for what he's done.'

'Listen to him,' Winters said, his voice wheedling.

'Bloody shut up, you piece of shit,' Robinson said, grinding his foot into the other man's back and making him groan.

Gaps were gradually appearing in the ceiling, ringed with glowing embers, as the temperature soared.

The whole door shuddered in its frame as it was struck again and again, their colleagues outside becoming increasingly frantic in their efforts to free them. But Joseph knew time was running out. The time for talking was done. He gave Megan the barest nod.

The DC didn't hesitate and leapt forward at the same moment Joseph did.

Her baton struck Robinson's arm, sending the lighter flying.

Joseph followed up by lowering his head and crashing into the man like a bull, throwing him backwards into the edge of the roulette table. Without pausing, Megan had grabbed hold of Winters and hauled him to his feet.

The DI staggered, regaining his balance. 'Get out of here now, Megan!'

'But Robinson—'

The DI dismissed her protest with a shake of his head. 'Leave him to me. Go—that's an order!'

Megan opened her mouth to protest, but Joseph gave her a sharp look. With a nod, she half dragged, half supported Winters as she staggered with him towards the exit where the doors was still thudding into the chain stretched across it.

'No!' Liam bellowed, watching them go. He grabbed hold of the roulette table and hauled himself back to his feet.

But Joseph had already placed himself between Robinson and the others, as Megan frantically tried to undo the chain.

'It's over, Liam. Just come with me and have your day in court, have your say, and we'll make sure Winters really does pay,' he said.

Robinson shook his head violently. 'The only sentence that man deserves is death, and you've deprived me of that! There's nothing left for me to live for.'

Liam grabbed a fuel can from beneath the roulette table, and poured its contents over himself.

Joseph's gaze flicked to the lighter on the floor, still well out of Robinson's reach. 'If I have to, I'll knock you out and drag you out with me. Now move!'

A slow smile crept across Liam's face as he took a box of matches out of his pocket.

'Always have a backup plan.'

The DI's eyes widened. He whirled around and grabbed the fire extinguisher from the wall, yanking the safety catch from it. He spun back, aiming it at the other man. Of all the things he might have expected to see, it certainly wasn't the wide grin that filled Robinson's face. That didn't make any sense. If he tried to set himself on fire, Joseph would be able to extinguish him in seconds.

Robinson struck the match, and it burst into life, his grin reaching his ears. 'You think you can stop me?'

Joseph shrugged. 'Have it your way.' He squeezed the extinguisher's trigger, but nothing happened. He shook the canister and tried again. Same result.

'Oh, I made sure I swapped out all the fire extinguishers for duds before setting up my fire bombs,' Robinson said. 'After all, I couldn't have anyone stopping my fun.'

Before the DI could react, Robinson dropped the match onto the floor. Blue flames rushed up his petrol-soaked clothes. In less than a second, he was a raging inferno. As his screams ratcheted up, he thrashed about.

Joseph desperately looked around for a blanket, anything to smother the fire with, but there was nothing.

Robinson stumbled back into the roulette wheel and fell, his body fully engulfed, skin blistering and hair crackling.

Joseph took a step forward, but with a *bang* a beam and part of the ceiling collapsed, straight on top of Robinson, crushing him and smothering the man in a blazing funeral pyre. There was a muffled scream from Robinson, then silence except for the raging inferno that filled the basement with its mighty roar.

The man didn't stand a chance.

Megan finally freed the chain and threw open the fire door. Relief surged through Joseph as he watched her drag Winters outside. Sue was there to help. Ian, spotting Joseph, took a half step towards him. But then a curtain of flames roared up between them as everything in the room seemed to ignite at once.

Joseph couldn't see anything through the fire, and his lungs filled with sooty smoke. Sparks danced around him as a furnace-level of heat built rapidly.

Like he'd done once before back in the garage, the DI dropped to the floor, beneath the choking cloud, and crawled on his belly towards where he knew the door to be.

Tendrils of flames crawled over everything like a living thing that boiled and flowed, consuming whatever it touched.

There was almost a macabre beauty to it, and in a moment of clarity, Joseph understood why Robinson had become so fascinated with fire. Unleashed like this, it was a strangely beautiful, living thing, an untamed force of nature.

The DI kept crawling, hanging on with everything he had. He knew he had to be close to the exit, but he wasn't sure he was going to make it.

Suddenly, heavily booted feet appeared next to him and strong hands grabbed hold of him and hauled him to his feet. A firefighter, his eyes locking onto the DI's through his mask, nodded to him and Joseph managed a vague one in response. Then, together, they staggered out through the door and up some steps to where Ian was waiting, jigging from one foot to the other. Looping his arm under Joseph's shoulders, he nodded to the firefighter, and bore his friend's weight.

As Ian helped Joseph towards a waiting ambulance, his stinging eyes took in the scene.

Three fire engines were parked outside the pub, their crews desperately trying to douse the fire with hoses. But Robinson's plan had been executed too well. The Feasting Fox was a roaring inferno. Flames surged out of the windows, transforming the pub into a scene straight out of hell. The thatched roof was engulfed, a raging bonfire under the dark night sky. Swarms of sparks pirouetted and twirled, climbing into the smoke-filled sky in a mesmerising display of destruction.

Joseph took all this in as he began to hack his lungs out.

A patrol car pulled up and Chris erupted from it, racing towards them.

'Are you okay?' the DCI asked, joining Ian to help manoeuvre Joseph towards an ambulance. Megan and Winters were already inside, breathing masks strapped to their faces, as Sue looked on anxiously.

'I'll live,' Joseph replied, as he fought and lost an attempt to try and suppress a rib-rattling cough.

Chris glanced at the basement door to see it was completely roaring with flames. One of the fire crew was directing a blast of water into it that was vaporising instantly into a roiling cloud of steam.

'And Liam?' the DCI asked.

Rather than risk another coughing fit, Joseph just shook his head.

Chris's brows furrowed deeply, but then he nodded. 'He lived for fire and now he's died for it. Despite everything, I hope he found some peace at the end.'

Joseph looked at his boss. 'I strongly doubt that,' he said, before another coughing fit stole away the rest of his words.

CHAPTER THIRTY-ONE

SEVERAL WEEKS LATER, Joseph was relaxing in the University Parks in Oxford with Ellie and his friends.

The collection of picnic blankets they'd managed to assemble between them, to the DI's eye at least, looked like the beginnings of a giant patchwork quilt laid out on the parched grass.

The spot Ellie had chosen for the party was under the much-needed shade of one of the larger trees. His daughter had already told him she'd faced some stiff competition from other students trying to stay cool.

'I would almost welcome some classic dreary British weather after all this sun,' Joseph said.

Ellie nodded as she helped herself to her third strawberry. However, these were anything but your regular variety. Dylan had marinated them in balsamic vinegar and sugar, and served them with mascarpone rather than regular cream.

'God, these are so good,' she said, licking the mascarpone off her fingers.

'I'm glad you approve,' Dylan said. 'I hand-picked the strawberries first thing this morning at Binsey Farm. They're infinitely superior to the supermarket's offerings.'

'They certainly are,' Amy said, offering one to Joseph, who looked at it with scepticism.

'I've got a pretty open mind when it comes to food, but the idea of strawberries with vinegar would have my grandma spinning in her grave,' he said.

'Trust me, the sweetness of the balsamic is an education on the palette,' Amy said, holding it closer to him.

He sighed. 'You're not going to give up until I try one, are you?'

Amy just smiled at him and ran her tongue over her lips.

'Oh my God, will you two get a room already?' Ellie said, raising her eyebrows at them.

Amy grinned, then smacked her lips together like she was feeding a recalcitrant baby. Joseph gave her *the look* which had absolutely no effect whatsoever. Then, reluctantly, he opened his mouth. Amy popped the whole strawberry in before he could change his mind, with what could only be described as a look of glee.

Joseph mentally sighed as he chewed. The first taste was the tang of balsamic, but that was quickly overtaken by the sweetness of the strawberry and finished off by the silky smoothness of the mascarpone.

The others were looking at him like some sort of primate in a zoo at feeding time, an expectant look on their faces waiting for his verdict.

He sighed. 'Okay, it's fecking delicious. Are you all happy now?'

'Deliriously so,' Amy said.

This felt like the first time in ages that he'd seen Amy, and he always enjoyed her company, however, it remained to be seen if there was any real future for their relationship. For now, he'd decided he would just try to enjoy the moment and leave the future to sort itself out. *Carpe diem* and all that.

Joseph spotted Megan and John heading towards them, with yet more picnic blankets.

Despite his reticence of only a moment ago, the DI helped himself to another strawberry as he stood to greet the new arrivals.

Megan waved a bottle of Mumm champagne at the DI.

He gave it an approving look. 'You brought the good stuff.'

'I thought we should celebrate the closure of the Burning Man case.'

'You'll get no argument from me.' Joseph turned to John and for a moment both men stood awkwardly, looking at each other. He was painfully aware of his daughter giving him the beady eye. All that the DI could come up with was, 'So, John...'

'Indeed.' John replied.

Dylan arched an eyebrow. 'Shakespeare has nothing on you two with your erudite conversations.'

Ellie stood and looped her arm through John's, before turning to her father, widening her eyes the barest fraction.

Then Joseph felt his foot being nudged. He glanced down to see that Amy was gently pushing it with her own foot. She was also giving the DI a pointed look. Meanwhile, Megan and Dylan watched on with considerable interest. No doubt this moment was going to go down in the annals of family history and be spoken about in hushed tones of awe by future generations.

Joseph sighed inwardly, feeling their expectations weighing down his shoulders. He reached out and John did the same, giving each other a firm handshake like Doctor Livingstone and Stanley coming across each other on the shores of Lake Tanganyika.

'Fancy a drink?' Joseph asked.

'I thought you'd never ask, sir—' The words died in his throat as Ellie gave him a sharp jab in his ribs with her elbow. 'I mean, Joseph,' he corrected himself.

The DI caught Amy giving him a silent hand clap. He rewarded that with a suitable eye roll as Megan added her blankets to the quilt collection, John doing the same with a little tartan number.

'Interesting choice of picnic blanket there,' Dylan said. 'Is there a Scottish connection in your family history somewhere?'

'No, it's my parents' old National Trust one,' John replied. 'They're threatening to leave it to me in their will because I'm their eldest born.'

And just like that, Joseph was chuckling and patting the man on the back. 'Oh, I hear you. The things my ma has been threatening to bequeath me, including her set of Wedgwood figurines. I ask you... I mean, what am I meant to do with those on my boat?'

'They'd look great on your desk at work,' Amy said.

'That would certainly be one way of personalising it,' Megan added, grinning.

The ice well and truly broken between the men, Joseph raised his eyebrows at John as he filled his champagne glass.

'It sounds like you and Megan had a close call in that blazing pub,' John said to the two detectives.

'It was certainly closer than we would have liked, but that's just the nature of the job sometimes,' Joseph replied.

'Says the man who has a knack for always being in the eye of a storm,' Amy observed.

'It certainly seems to be my gift,' the DI replied with a shrug.

Dylan looked at Joseph. 'Do you mind if we talk shop for a moment? I'd love to get an update on the case.'

John's eyes darted between the professor and the DI.

'Surely, we shouldn't be discussing something this sensitive in front of a member of the public?'

'You'd think that, wouldn't you?' Ellie said. 'But Dad shares pretty much all the details about a case with the professor so he can pick his brain.'

John looked really confused. 'But—'

Amy held up her hand to cut him off. 'I advise you to just roll with it. After all, don't you share details with Ellie about what you've been up to at work?'

Ellie nodded. 'Our SOCO here makes a good point. Apart from anything else, Dylan is as much a part of the police family as I am.'

John sucked the air over his teeth. 'Right...'

'So with that sorted, I wanted to ask about the ongoing investigation into the Night Watchmen case,' the professor said.

If possible, John looked even more surprised that Dylan knew anything about the crime syndicate, but this time chose to keep his mouth shut.

'Well, the NCA was very interested in that ledger Robinson handed over before he died,' Joseph replied. 'Apparently, it details at least a hundred businesses they run across the country. Coordinated raids are being organised to shut them down. But according to Kate, she strongly suspects it's still just the tip of the iceberg.'

'Your mum knows about this as well?' John said, looking even more confused.

'Well, she is married to the DSU, as well as being an investigative journalist,' Ellie said.

'I see... Sorry, carry on, don't mind me.'

Joseph felt a pang of sympathy for the young PC. Right then, John was probably wondering what he'd let himself in for by dating the DI's daughter.

He gave Dylan a thoughtful look. 'Unfortunately, John

Winters is keeping his mouth shut, despite being offered a plea bargain by the NCA for a reduced sentence.'

'Probably because of what happened to Daryl Manning,' Amy said. Then, without ducking the issue, she looked at John. 'Talking of which, how's your shoulder doing?'

Although the others were taken aback by her German directness, Joseph smiled to himself. He'd always admired Amy for not pussyfooting around, something the British were particularly prone to do.

'Much better, as you can probably tell, and besides, now I have a great scar to impress the ladies.'

Ellie shot daggers at him.

'I mean you, dearest.'

Joseph snorted. Even though he'd known John for several years at work, the last few minutes had made him like the young man all the more. The PC was even starting to remind the DI of himself at that age.

'So what's the latest news about Paul Burford?' Amy asked, without missing a beat.

'I come bearing good news about Paul,' John said with a smile. 'The swelling in his brain finally went down, and they've been able to wake him up. I left him an hour ago, literally sitting up in his hospital bed and chatting to his wife and daughter like nothing happened.'

'God, that's such a relief to hear,' Joseph said.

'I think that definitely calls for a toast,' Amy said, refreshing everyone's glasses with champagne.

'Talking of our resident investigative journalist, where's Kate anyway?' Dylan asked after he broke out the blinis with smoked salmon and horseradish. 'She should be here to join in the celebrations.'

'I was expecting her to be here, but she said she might be a bit late with something at work,' Joseph said.

'Hang on, surely it can't be anything to do with the Night Watchmen case?' Amy asked. 'I thought the NCA just got her to sign an NDA until they finish their investigation, which could easily take years.'

'That's right, and Kate's promised me she'll finally let it drop,' Joseph replied. 'At least until the NCA eventually gives her the nod to write an exclusive story about it for the paper one day.'

The DI's phone pinged, and he looked at his screen to see a picture of a burnt-out shell of an Aston Martin. It had been sent by Chris. Beneath it was the caption, *Welcome to our new project!*

Then his phone rang, and the DI headed off a short distance to take the call. 'What do you mean, *our* new project?' Joseph asked.

'I mean, I need a man with your mechanical skills,' Chris replied. 'So, I have a proposal for you. I need your help to fix up the TR4, but also that Aston Martin I managed to get my hands on.'

'Jesus, don't tell me it's Jimmy Harper's old car?'

'No, this one crashed during a race and the owner hasn't the time to put into restoring it. So, what do you think? Fancy being my grease monkey? I can pay you with homemade beer.'

'You brew? Seriously?'

'I'm a man of many talents,' Chris replied. 'Anyway, what do you say? I might even let you take the wheel of the DB5 one day, at least if you promise not to total her.'

'With my driving record?' But the more Joseph thought about it, much to his own surprise, the more he found himself warming to the idea. Now that the prospect of driving no longer broke him out in a cold sweat, he rather fancied being behind the wheel of an Aston Martin. 'Okay, you're on. Every man needs a hobby and it will be good to put my old skills to use.'

'Great news. Anyway, must dash. The DB5 is due to be delivered any moment now. Speak soon.' The line clicked off.

Ellie wandered over to Joseph with a salmon blini and champagne glass in hand. 'You look like you're in a good mood.'

'That's because I am, oh darling daughter of mine.' He scooped his arm around her shoulders and gestured towards John, who was chatting with Dylan. A conversation they could just hear was about the best gins. 'I think you've chosen well, Ellie.'

His daughter turned to look at him. 'I can't tell you what it means to hear you say that, Dad.'

'Then I'm glad, but you don't need your old man's opinion about anything. You're a free spirit in this world, able to make your own choices, and certainly don't need my approval.'

Ellie narrowed her eyes at him. 'Can I have that in writing, please?'

Joseph laughed. 'Steady there.'

She mock-punched him in the arm, then headed back to save John from Dylan, who had dived into an extended lecture about the right botanicals to have with a craft gin.

Joseph stood apart from the others for a moment, thinking just how lucky he was. These people were all part of his real family. If only Kate had been there, it would have been complete. Then he headed back over to join them and to make the most of this evening of summer, laughter, and some of the people he cared most about in the world.

Later that evening, Joseph was back on board *Tús Nua* with Tux. Amy had been called into work at short notice, which had put their romantic plans on hold for the evening. So nothing new there then. Instead, for companionship, he was stroking the cat, who was purring like a steam train. The DI wouldn't admit it to anyone else, but he was going to miss this little guy once his owners sorted out suitable accommodation for him.

The DI's attention was currently on his secret incident board he had hidden behind a picture on the wall. The last time he'd used it had been for the Midwinter Butcher case, but there was an itch in his brain again that wouldn't go away, and it had everything to do with the Night Watchmen.

Joseph had barely got going with it, but he already had Harper, Forbes, and Winters's photos near the top of the board. The three men were linked by red string to another photo of the burned-down Excalibur. Above that, he had more lines leading from all of them to a pink Post-it with, *'Who are the Night Watchmen?'* written on it.

Although the crime syndicate investigation was now under the control of the NCA, that wouldn't stop the DI from mulling this question over. Fuelling that, was something Kate had said to him about the crime syndicate having people in positions of power.

The DI's gaze travelled across to another green Post-it with, *'An inside man on the police force?'* written on it. He bounced the pen against his lips. That was the specific itch that wouldn't go away.

Despite the NCA's conclusions about the prisoner transfer of Daryl Manning not being a result of a tip-off from inside the police department, Joseph wasn't so sure. Instinct had been shouting at him that it was someone far closer to home; someone who had become increasingly erratic in their performance at work; someone who had everything to lose. There had been too many things that had felt increasingly off with the man, and Joseph's suspicion had finally grown too large to ignore. The thing was, if his hunch played out, the fallout would be enormous. However, he still felt duty-bound to pursue the truth, whatever the cost.

Joseph gently nudged Tux, who gave him a disgruntled look, off his lap as he stood and crossed to his evidence board. He paused, and then with a heavy heart took down the inside man Post-it and replaced it with a blank one.

He wrote a single name on it.

'Derrick?'

A lead weight grew in the DI's heart as he connected a length of red string, linking the big man to the Night Watchmen Post-it.

The DI prayed with every fibre of his being that he was wrong, but seeing the DSU's name written up there felt right.

The question now was, what the hell was he going to do about it?

JOIN THE J.R. SINCLAIR VIP CLUB

To get instant access to exclusive photos of locations used from the series, and the latest news from J.R. Sinclair, just subscribe here to start receiving your free content: https://www.subscribepage.com/n4zom8

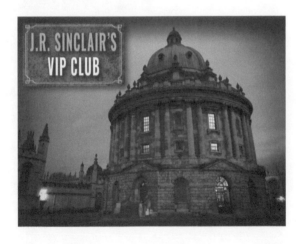

PRE-ORDER THE GAMES PEOPLE PLAY

DI Joseph Stone will return in
The Games People Play

Pre-order now: https://geni.us/TheGamesPeoplePlay

Made in United States
Troutdale, OR
01/02/2025

27510773R00181